CRY YOUR WAY HOME

DAMIEN ANGELICA WALTERS

ISBN 978-1937009-61-8 (TPB)

Also available as a DRM-free eBook.

Apex Publications, PO Box 24323, Lexington, KY 40524

Visit us at www.apexbookcompany.com.

For
Dedad
and
Tristan

Of our hurts we make monuments of survival. If we survive.

— JOYCE CAROL OATES

CONTENTS

Tooth, Tongue, and Claw   1

Deep Within the Marrow, Hidden in My Smile   14

On the Other Side of the Door, Everything Changes   31

This Is the Way I Die   43

The Hands That Hold, the Lies That Bind   56

Not My Circus, Not My Monkeys: The Elephant's Tale   77

The Judas Child   88

S Is for Soliloquy   96

The Floating Girls: A Documentary   102

Take a Walk in the Night, My Love   115

Falling Under, Through the Dark   128

The Serial Killer's Astronaut Daughter   138

Umbilicus   155

A Lie You Give, and Thus I Take   172

Little Girl Blue, Come Cry Your Way Home   182

Sugar and Spice and Everything Nice   196

In the Spaces Where You Once Lived   209

Publication History   225

Acknowledgments   227

About the Author   229

Also by Damien Angelica Walters   231

TOOTH, TONGUE, AND CLAW

Once upon a time there was a monster. This is how they tell you the story starts. This is a lie.

He isn't cruel, and he didn't eat her.

She isn't sure if that's a kindness or not. She isn't sure of anything but the locks and the keys and the secret scream hiding in her throat. And the last is suspect; sometimes it tastes like laughter.

But she's still alive. She tells herself this means something.

He tugs on the tether attached to the chain around her neck. A gentle tug, but it's enough. His claws click on the stones of the rocky path leading away from the cave, toward the town, a sound like chattering teeth, and although the bottoms of his feet are thick and leathery, she feels every jagged edge, every sharp point, beneath the soles of her satin slippers. He moves lightly for his size; beneath his steps, the ground merely quivers. She takes a few steps until he stops again.

People stand on either side of the path. A few wear smiles, but most carry only relief on their faces, for they all know what she did.

The gazes touch, linger, penetrate. She wants to scream that they have no idea what it's like—how can they?—but she won't. Even if she could, they wouldn't care. All the faces here belong to strangers, but even if they were her people, they would extend neither hand nor choice.

She's on display so they know she's still among them. So they know they're still safe. Does he want them to know he didn't tear her head from her shoulders, rip her limbs from her torso and toss the pieces aside? He has that right. He's had that right since the day she was given to him.

They don't do that anymore, her mother said time and time again, but her eyes said otherwise.

Or does he want to merely assure them that she didn't succeed, that his power is still nothing to be trifled with, to be challenged? Yes, it's apparent in the set of his jaw, the carriage of his spine.

She keeps her chin raised, too, so they don't forget she was strong enough to try.

$\approx$

L ies *are like bits of straw. When there's only one, it would be easy to pick it up, break it in two, bring the pieces out into the light. But then you add a second, and you can't find a way to dislodge one without the other. A third, a fourth, a fifth, and soon the weight of the pile is impossible. It becomes a maze with no solution.*

Best to pretend it's truth, not a tangle of fiction.

$\approx$

W hen they return inside, he closes the iron gate set deep into the stone. Locks it. Closes the outer door. Locks it, too. Then the inner door. When the final tumblers clunk into place, he slips the key ring onto a chain around his neck, the same sort of chain that circles hers, yet she doesn't fool herself into believing he's a prisoner too.

∼

L ie #1: *This is a great honor.*

∼

H e doesn't touch her once they're in bed. He has before and he was as gentle as possible; she knows he wants to again and in time, he will. No one told her about that part. That was a kindness.

On her side, she stares at the bed curtains, heavy and embroidered in gold and silver like everything else in his home. (She refuses to call it hers. She never will.) Strange that monsters would adore such finery, or perhaps it's only her monster that cares for such things.

No curtains surrounded her bed at home, no tapestries covered the walls, yet she would trade all the gilt in the world for the chance to return. She presses her face into the pillow, willing away the impossible dream.

One hand sneaks to the chain around her neck. The links are small and delicate, but a chain is still a chain; it marks her as a possession, a *thing*, not a person.

∼

T *here is neither spell nor curse to break. This is not a love story. He will always be a monster. She will always be chained.*

∼

I n the morning, he traces the side of her face with one of his claws, not hard enough to break the skin but firm enough to leave behind a sting. She doesn't lean into his touch, nor does she pull away.

His eyes are the color of leaves beneath an early twilight sky, his teeth slivers of moon reflecting on water, and his pelt a shade of night. He speaks mainly in his native tongue—all grunts and hisses, rolling growls and throaty sounds that remind her of a cat when its head is scratched. When he speaks the language of humans, the words sound as if they're formed by a mouth full of pebbles.

Though many have tried, no human has ever deciphered the language of monsters. Who can say if things would be different if they had.

He leaves the bed chamber without touching her again, though he seems to pause briefly in the arched doorway.

She wishes she could be content, because it would be so much easier for her, for him, for everyone. This is the way it's supposed to be. This is the way it's been ever since the monsters awoke from their deep slumber and claimed their place as leaders of men and beasts alike. This is the possibility for every secondborn daughter, something she was taught from the moment she was capable of learning.

Why she isn't content, she doesn't know.

(Maybe the others aren't content either.)

~

After the drawing, while the councilmen waited outside, her mother brushed her hair for a long time without speaking, without meeting her eyes. She thought she heard a faint whisper, a muffled *I'm sorry*, though it might've been only what she wished to hear.

He brushes her hair now, the silvered handle awkward in his grip. She closes her eyes, pretends she is still a child, pretends it's her mother's hand holding the brush. But the breath touching her neck and the musky smell of him tells her the truth.

~

Lie #2: *In time, you will forget your old life and come to embrace the new.*

~

His muzzle, forelegs, and belly are heavily scarred from the fight with his siblings and sire for the right to rule. Eventually, he, too, will sire young with one of his own kind and when his male offspring reach full maturity, they will challenge him for the right to rule. The last left alive will rule until it becomes time again to sire and fight. (She will be long gone before then; the monsters live a lifetime equivalent to that of five humans.)

A barbaric practice, to be sure. Yet is it any more barbaric than humans tossing an etched stone into a pot to select a random girl to become a monster's consort, all in the name of peace?

~

There is a story she and her friends (and how she misses them most of all) told each other, of someone like her and something like him and love, love enough to break the chains, to not care of the consequences. They would sigh and fall back with a hand pressed to budding breasts, gazing flutter-lashed at ceiling or sky, daydreaming of a great romance so powerful and beautiful that stories would be told and remembered forever and always.

But they were young and knew nothing of monsters.

~

When he isn't there, she walks the cave, a series of circular rooms and curving passageways. Soft carpets cover the stone, even in the passageways, and turn her steps to mere whispers. One passage, wide enough for two monsters to walk side by side, leads to a library, but secondborn daughters are no longer taught to read until they pass the age of the drawing. Still, she likes to open the books, breathe in the pages, pretend she understands the words. She thinks of her friends learning letters and words and stories, and her hands fist tight enough to hurt.

Be brave is the last thing she remembers her mother saying.

But she isn't brave. Stealing keys and trying to creep out in the middle of the night is foolish, not brave. Everyone knows monsters have exceptional hearing; she knew she wouldn't get away. And she doesn't want to be brave. She wants to be free. She will never learn to be content, she will never stop dreaming of life outside the cave, and she shouldn't have to. She refuses.

She puts her face in her hands, not to hide her tears, but to hold in her rage.

~

L ie #3: As a second daughter, your natural born duty is the safety and security of others.

~

I n the morning, he reaches for her face. She pulls away. He stares, considering her, for a long time, his eyes inscrutable, but he doesn't try to touch her again.

When he leaves, she hides her smile behind a palm. A small victory, but a victory nonetheless.

~

T he council kept her drugged, something she only realized when she woke alone on a dais, mouth throbbing with pain, the entrance of the cave a great maw waiting to swallow her whole. She was nude save for a modest cascade of flowers of a type she'd never seen, their petals white, but limned in the deepest red. She wondered who'd bound her wrists and ankles, who'd undressed her and placed her on display. Did they look at her breasts, her sex? Did they dare a forbidden touch of velvet skin? Or did they not even see her at all?

When he approached, she refused to cower, refused to close her eyes. He was not as bad as she'd imagined. He was also worse.

The center of the cave holds a pool lined by rocks worn smooth by the passage of many monstrous steps. The cerulean water is deep and always warm, and she spends many afternoons floating, staring at a circular hole in the stone high overhead—the only break in the outer cave walls not locked and barred.

Today, though, she doesn't disrobe. Instead, she runs her hands over the pitted walls and curls her fingers into a gap in the stone. She finds a toehold, then another. Not quite like climbing trees as she did when a child, but near enough. Reach, pull. Reach, pull. Until she meets nothing but smooth surface, no nook or cranny for even one finger. With a sigh, she eases down and moves to the other side of the water.

Although she climbs higher this time, she reaches a spot where she can't grasp the next handhold, no matter how hard she strains, willing her spine to lengthen, her arms to stretch. She tries again and again until her palms are scraped and raw. Back on solid ground, she rubs her hands together, relishing the burn as she scans the rest of the walls.

Tomorrow, she'll try again. She isn't sure how she'll traverse the top, where it begins to curve toward the hole. Maybe she'll simply tumble into the water below or perhaps to her death on the rocky path.

He touches her palms gingerly. His eyes ask questions that his mouth does not, questions he knows will go unanswered save for clumsy pantomime, and she's in no mood for games of any kind. When he pushes her down on the bed, she presses against his massive chest, and shakes her head hard enough to make her ears ring.

Again, he pushes. Again, she shakes her head. He growls, but he storms from the room, his every step leaving behind a heavy thump.

She doesn't bother to hide her smile.

L ie #4: *They cut out your tongue so your voice, your words, will
not anger him.*

~

F or several days, he ignores her. She spends hers climbing, each
time ascending higher and higher. She paces the cave and its
passageways, inspects the bars in every window and every doorway,
testing for loose stone, crumbling mortar, any weakness at all. The
discontent grows inside her like an unborn babe.

Do any of the others feel this way? And what of those who came
before? The stories, the histories, say no. They say all the girls handed
over to the beasts were honored and treasured, but who can say for
sure. Who knows who truly wrote the stories.

Was Livia of Northingate gifted with furs and rubies and opals?
Did Rebecca of Southton have the most magnificent library ever built,
with spiraling staircases and secret cushioned nooks? (This was before
it was decided secondborn daughters should not know how to read
and write.) Yet in spite of the finery, they were all prisoners still. The
stories didn't say that. They didn't have to.

Her mother said she would grow to be happy. (Barring the other
option of ending up between teeth and jaws, of course.) But her
mother was a firstborn daughter. She never had to worry. She was
never to be given to a monster.

Is *he* content? Why wouldn't he be? He doesn't sacrifice, he
doesn't pay with silence and disfigurement, he doesn't pay at all.

So why should she?

~

H e takes her shoulders, lowers his muzzle until it's nearly
touching her nose, pushes her toward the bed. Holding out her
hands, she makes a sound that isn't a word but wants to be. He halts,
his eyes wary, unsure, ghosted by a touch of anger.

She bites her lower lip, but doesn't look away. Will he kill her? One slash of his claws could split the skin of her neck, sever her head from her shoulders; one snap of his jaw could tear apart her body from nape to tailbone.

He exhales a carnivorous breath, gives her his back, and, after a long moment, leaves the room, trailing the echo of a growl. She sinks to her knees, heart racing. Although she doesn't want to live this way, she doesn't wish to die either.

What happened to the others who shared this cave with him? Did they dash themselves to pieces on rocks while climbing to an illusion of escape? Did their lives end in his gullet and gut? Did they grow old and aged and infirm? The stories never tell of such things, for no one knows. No one ever returns. They're never allowed to. To do so would break the agreements—ancient ones written in old languages no one can speak anymore.

The words may very well be lies themselves.

∼

She touches her mouth, feels the weight of forced silence. *Her* people did this. *Her* people allowed this to happen. No, encouraged it. Her silence and captivity ensured their safety so they were more than willing to do whatever was necessary. It was never for the monsters' sakes, but for theirs.

When they delivered her to the council, did they weep or simply erase her name from their lips and her face from their memories as though she were dead, not imprisoned? Did it help them sleep the sleep of the just and dreamless at night? Would that she could haunt their nightmares, turn their own voices to silent screams.

∼

Lie #5: *He is the monster.*

∼

Her shoulders no longer ache as much as they did when she made her first attempt at climbing. Hand over hand, she rises, so intent on her progress that she only becomes aware of his presence when he grabs her around the waist, plucking her from the wall as a child plucks a blossom from its stem.

Instead of dashing her against the rock, he lets her drop. She lands on her side with a jolt, and her teeth clamp together, the sound like a snapping twig. Bending close, he bares his own and roars. She recoils from the noise, from the heat and stink of his breath, and then he's gone.

Hands shaking, she wills herself not to cry and fails, miserably so.

~

That night, she pushes him away with all her might, fights as long and as hard as she can, but he's stronger. Damn him, damn them all.

A day later, the hole in the cave above the pool bears a set of bars.

Emphatic messages that speak louder than any voice could project —she belongs to him, and the only way out is death.

~

Every night, she fights. Every day, she ignores him and pretends the bars don't exist. She climbs, bloodying her palms, tearing her clothes. In the passageways, she paces and wills herself to stop thinking of the outside, to stop thinking of choices and hope, to be content. But all the will she can muster can't make a thing so. Would that he would do her the kindness of killing her, of ending it all.

Sometimes she dreams of his teeth tearing her flesh, ripping her into tiny pieces. Other nights, she dreams of someone breaking through the bars, rushing in to sweep her away, but in the morning, the lie fades. No one will save her from the monster. No one will take that risk.

They never have and never will.

~

Finally, she reaches the top of the wall where it begins to curve. With one hand firmly grasping the edge of a small cleft and her toes tucked into two more, she extends her free hand, fingers dancing across the rock in a gentle waltz. Here and there, she finds gaps, spaces she's sure she could grip to swing herself across to the window.

She flexes her hand and a sound darts through the air. Tightening her hold, she peers over one shoulder to see him there, his massive body reclining against the wall. The sound comes again, and it takes her a moment to place it—laughter. The largest insult of them all. Her face blooms with heat; her mouth twists.

No more, she vows. No more.

~

In a narrow passage, she finds a loose chunk of stone twice the length of her hand, one end wide, the other narrowing to a jagged point, and tests it against her palm. As pearls of red bubble to the surface, she smiles, but there are tears in her eyes.

She waits until the middle of the night, until the cave fills with the sound of his slumber. On her knees with heels resting against the backs of her thighs, she lifts her arms high, palms protected by knotted silken scarves.

The stone pierces pelt and sinew, and blood gushes crimson and warm from his neck. He roars as his eyes open, lashing out with claws extended. Pain flares bright and hot in her upper arm, but she doesn't stop. She can't. There's so much blood. Rivers—oceans—of it. Fingers slick, mouth filled with the taste of wet metal, she stabs again and again and again until her breath is ragged, until his is no more.

Sobbing, she drops the stone and draws her knees to her chest. Will they flay the flesh from her bones? Pummel her with rocks? Merely give her to another monster?

No. She won't allow the latter. She'll *never* allow it. She strips off her sodden nightgown and uses another to scrub the tears from her cheeks and the blood from her skin.

His body is heavy, but she manages to drag it to the floor and she works through the rest of the night, cutting away the furred skin, carefully scraping the fat and meat free. Using strands of her hair braided with strips of the beast's viscera, she sews the rents from the stone. She rips the heart from the carcass and smears the clotted blood on her skin, then she curls her body into the hide, pulls it close, and slips her hands into the paws.

Her flesh warms, melts into the pelt until there's no way to know where one ends and the other begins. Her muscles flex and expand, growing to fit a new shape, a new purpose. Her bones break and knit back together in a stronger construction. There's no pain, but she isn't surprised. She's already paid a thousand times over.

She opens her reshaped mouth and what emerges is neither the mewl of a tongueless girl nor the roar of a monster, but the triumph of a great and terribly beauty. All around her, the colors are more intense, the edges sharper. She gets to her feet and heads toward the entrance of the cave, trailing her claws along the walls, cutting gouges in the stone. Her new form isn't ponderous, but graceful. Powerful.

And she remembers.

She remembers the council handing her over without a second thought. She remembers everyone standing outside, watching her led with tether and chain. She remembers their gazes upon her and their silence. Peace, they called it. She has a different word for what they've done.

Emerging into the sunlight, she throws back her head, cries out to the sky. The ground trembles fury beneath her feet, and she bares her new teeth.

The people want a monster. She'll give them one.

∽

O nce upon a time there was a girl ...

DEEP WITHIN THE MARROW, HIDDEN IN MY SMILE

I wear you in my bones.

No one else can see you, but I know you're there. I feel the weight of you within the shape of me like a tumor, a disease. If I look too long in the mirror I'm afraid I'll see you staring back.

Sometimes late at night, when the house is quiet, I whisper your name, but you never answer.

~

My mom talked the whole way to your house, which was weird because she never liked talking while she was driving, and when I tried to turn on the radio, she swatted my hand away. I watched the houses and trees blur past and tuned her out. I'd already heard everything she was saying: *Alyssa can't wait to meet you. And her birthday is only three weeks after yours. Almost like twins. Isn't that neat? Thom is so excited for you to see the house.*

Our parents had been dating for over a year, and they already had a wedding date set. I don't know why they waited so long for us to meet, unless they had a feeling it wouldn't go so well. Or maybe they just wanted to make really sure it was serious.

I didn't want a sister or a stepfather. Didn't want to move from the only house I'd ever lived in, didn't want to leave behind the gouge in the kitchen doorframe which I'd made with a field hockey stick or the marks on the wall in the kitchen measuring my changing height or the spare bedroom that was my dad's old office, that still smelled of his aftershave, even after three years. Your mom was dead, too, something mine told me a thousand times, and she met your dad in a support group for grieving spouses. I guess they weren't grieving *that* much. I knew better than to say that to my mom, though.

"We're here, honey," my mom said as she pulled into a driveway.

The house, more than twice the size of our townhouse, was brick with dark green shutters and a big front yard, and, gauging by the trees towering over the dark-shingled roof, an ever bigger back yard. My mom's face was all smiles, but I bit the inside of my cheek until I tasted blood.

At least it was big enough so we wouldn't have to share a bedroom —that would've been awful—and I wouldn't have to change schools either. My mom asked if I wanted to switch to the private school you went to, but I said no. I didn't care that I'd have to wake up way early to catch the bus. She was making me leave everything; I wasn't going to leave my friends, too. She asked me a couple times, but once she realized I wasn't going to change my mind she stopped.

You dad met us at the door and that wasn't a big deal. We'd met before. You were in the living room, slouched on one end of an uncomfortable-looking sofa. We said hello, but your gaze said *Invader*.

You were a lot smaller than me and your cheeks were still chubby, like a little kid's. You looked ten, not thirteen. But your eyes were dark and serious, and you stared at me so long and hard that I cleared my throat and shuffled my feet and eventually looked away.

Your dad said, "Why don't you show Courtney the rest of the house while Grace and I work on some wedding stuff?"

"That would be wonderful, wouldn't it?" my mom said to me.

It wasn't like I could say what I really wanted to, so I followed you around the first floor while you pointed out the rooms in a low, flat voice. The staircase off the front foyer was a wide curve leading to the second floor. I thought it would be fun to slide down the banister, but when I asked you if you'd ever done it, you said, "Of course not."

All the furniture in the living room looked formal and unused; the dining room was dark wood and heavy curtains; the study held leather chairs, a desk with clawed feet, and lots of bookcases. You didn't say the rooms were off-limits, but they were all museum silence and sharp edges.

Kind of like you, honestly.

Everything smelled weird. Not bad, just the way other people's houses always do, and I wondered if me and my mom would start to smell like this, or if everything would start to smell like us. And worse, would we even notice?

The kitchen was big, but there were no pictures or school notes tacked on the refrigerator, no crumbs on the counter, no dishes in the sink. The breakfast nook was the first room that looked lived in—there was an open book face-down on a placemat and a cup with traces of orange juice. Two steps led down into a family room with a huge television and a wrap-around sofa with throw blankets and pillows. There were two more books on the coffee table, and one of the pillows had a dent in it from someone's arm or elbow.

At our house, we always had magazines or my homework or unopened mail on the coffee table and half the time, I shoved the pillows on the floor because they mostly got in the way. It drove my mom nuts. Our sofa was a lot smaller than the one here, but I didn't see anyplace where it could fit. I bet my mom was going to donate it like she did with the old clothes that didn't fit or I didn't want anymore, and my chest got tight. Someone else would sit in my spot. My spot that used to be my dad's spot. I really wanted to run over and cut open the cushions of *your* sofa so we'd have to bring ours. Same with the pillows and the blankets. But I was too old for temper tantrums. And a sofa wouldn't change anything.

"We use this one most of the time," you said, pointing to a narrow staircase off the kitchen.

Carpet the color of instant oatmeal before water's added swallowed the sounds of our feet. Your dad's bathroom was almost the size of my room at home and the bedroom had room for a sofa, coffee table, and another television nearly as big as the one downstairs along with all the regular bedroom furniture.

You pushed open the door to an empty room across the hallway. "This is yours," you said, sneering as you spoke the words.

The room was big with pale blue walls almost the same color as my bedroom at home. The paint wasn't wet, but it smelled new. Two wide windows looked out into the back yard, which was even bigger than I thought it would be, and there was a hot tub off the deck and a pool with an enclosure so it could be used all year long.

"Your bathroom's there," you said, nodding toward another door.

I was secretly relieved when one quick look inside revealed that I wouldn't have to share.

"Where's your room?"

You pointed at the end of the hallway. I caught a glimpse of bookcases and pale grey walls through the half-open door, and I thought you'd show me the whole room, but you didn't, just stared at me again the way you did downstairs, like you could see through—inside—me. My arms broke out in goosebumps.

"I have a soccer ball in the car," I said, rubbing my arms. "Want to kick it around?"

You shook your head. "I don't play sports."

"Do you swim?"

Another shake of your head. "The pool was my mom's."

I traced a circle in the carpet with the tip of my shoe. "Can anyone else use it?"

"I didn't say they couldn't," you said, each word bitten off and spat at my feet.

I didn't know what to say to that, so we stood there in the hallway —I kept my face turned away so I wouldn't have to see your eyes— until I wanted to scream to break the quiet.

"We can go back downstairs," you finally said.

In the car on the way home, my mom asked, "What did you think?"

"It's big and it's way too quiet," I said. "But I like the pool and the back yard, and it'll be neat having my own bathroom."

"Not the house, kiddo, but Alyssa?"

"She's quiet too," I said. And weird, I didn't say.

~

A few weeks after the wedding, after my mom and I moved in—I was wrong about my sofa being donated; it fit in my bedroom—I took a soccer ball into the back yard. You were in your room, reading, which was pretty much all you did. My mom kept telling me to ask you to do stuff, but you weren't interested in anything I was, so most of the time I lied and told her I'd already asked and you said no.

Your dad came out of the kitchen with a bag of recycling and waved as he went around the side of the house. On his way back, the ball traveled into his path and I called out, "Sorry!" He kicked it my way and I returned it without a thought, the way I used to do with my dad.

I held my breath, thinking he'd get mad, but he didn't. He grinned and said, "Now you're on." He grabbed two lawn chairs, setting them on their sides for makeshift nets, and the two of us ran back and forth across the lawn, kicking the ball and laughing. Not sure how long we played, but it was a lot longer than I expected. I won, but it was close; he was pretty good and played hard.

After he went back inside, I saw you through your bedroom window, half-hidden by the curtain. I started to wave, but you stepped out of sight. I waited to see if you'd peek again, but you didn't.

I guess it made you jealous, but it wasn't my fault that your dad liked soccer. You could've come out to play too. No one was stopping you.

~

E ven when it was just the two of us, my mom was big on family dinner. She said it was too easy to get into a routine of not eating together. So every night we'd sit at the table, and I'd tell her about school and she'd tell me about work. Then we'd talk about things happening in the world, silly stuff from social media like viral videos or ridiculous memes, everything and anything.

We did the same thing at your house, too, and your dad joined in the conversation. My mom tried to get you to talk, but you answered with "Fine" every time she asked how school was and shrugged and forked another bite into your mouth when she asked what you did in class.

That lasted for about a month and then one night, my mom called everyone to the table and from the top of the stairs you called down, "I'm not hungry."

Your dad said it wasn't really a big deal, but my mom's eyebrows were halfway up her forehead. "I want us to eat as a family," she said.

"You can't force her to eat if she isn't hungry," your dad said.

"She doesn't have to eat if she doesn't want to, but I'd like her to sit with us at least. She shouldn't hide away in her room all the time."

"She's not hiding, she's probably reading. We never really made a big deal about dinner before."

"I understand that, but things are different now."

"Grace, honey, she's still getting used to all the changes. Every kid deals with things at their own pace," your dad said. "Don't worry about it tonight, okay?"

I knew my mom didn't want to let it go, but she did. I was surprised. The next night, you did the same thing, and although my mom narrowed her eyes, she held her tongue.

Later, I saw you in the kitchen, making a sandwich.

I said, "I thought you weren't hungry."

"I wasn't," you tossed over your shoulder.

"My mom's trying," I said. "You don't have to be mean to her."

Your eyes were laser beams, boring into mine. "I didn't ask her to try. I didn't ask her to come here at all."

I flopped on the sectional in the family room, grabbed the remote, and started flipping through channels before I saw you curled up in the corner of the sofa with a book in your hand. You glared at me from atop the cover. I wanted to leave the room, but I didn't want you to know how I felt so I stayed put.

"I was sitting here reading," you said.

"Okay, sorry." I turned off the television. Crossed my arms over my chest and swallowed hard. "Want to play checkers or Uno or something?"

You let out a long sigh and, from behind your book, said, in a singsong voice, "Why don't you go play soccer with my dad?"

I didn't, but I did go swim in the pool. I didn't understand what your problem was. We were supposed to be a family, right? I didn't like it a whole lot either but I was trying. After a while, my mom and your dad came outside and got in the pool with me. When we finished, you weren't in the family room anymore and your bedroom door was shut. I made a face as I walked by, but paused because I heard your voice, your words low and growly. It definitely sounded like you were talking to someone—you kept pausing like you were waiting for an answer—except I knew you were the only one in your room. Your footsteps moved close to the door and I took off, heart pounding. You talking to yourself was nothing to be scared of, but I was.

My mom opened my bedroom door and stuck her head in. "Courtney, are you going to get up sometime this morning?"

I groaned and smacked the snooze button on my blaring alarm clock, fighting to keep my eyelids from fluttering shut again. Wondering why my sheets felt gritty, I pushed back the covers, scrubbed the sleep from my eyes, and struggled to a sitting position. Both my sheets and the soles of my feet were flecked with dirt, and smudged footprints tracked across the floor, leading in from the door.

I sat motionless. I'd showered the night before—my towel discarded in a pile on the floor was proof, not that I needed any. And I didn't sleepwalk. I never had.

My hands started to shake. It had to be you, but why would you even do something like that? I left you alone, and I *never* went in your room.

I heard footsteps in the hall and caught a blur of motion, too short to be my mom. She called out again for me to get a move on and I did, wiping my feet on the towel and cleaning away the footprints on the floor as fast as I could.

While I was rinsing out my juice glass in the kitchen, I stared out the window over the sink and saw my favorite soccer ball in the middle of the yard. I never left it outside. Ever. It was the last thing my dad ever gave to me. When you came in the room a few minutes later, you had a tight-lipped, secretive smile. I wanted to shove your cereal bowl off the counter. I also wanted to run out of the room. Behind my mom's back, I mouthed the word *why*. You kept on smiling. I wanted to tell my mom what you did, but I didn't.

I should have. I guess I was afraid she wouldn't believe me, and, although I didn't want to admit it, I was afraid of *you*.

~

In the formal living room, gilt-framed photographs sat on the side tables and the fireplace mantel. There were a couple of pictures of you as a baby and one with you, your dad, and your mom at the beach. The three of you were squinting into the sun, but I could tell you looked a lot like her; you had the same hair color and the same round face. She looked normal, though, not creepy.

A picture from our parents' wedding hung over the fireplace. In it, they were smiling so big it made *my* cheeks hurt. I was standing beside my mom; you beside your dad. All four of us had our arms linked—the photographer's idea. You were smiling, too, but it was more like the weird smile from the kitchen than a real one. I'd never noticed before but once I did, I couldn't *not* notice. I heard a snort behind me and you were there, book tucked under your arm, mouth crooked into a sneer. "O happy family," you said.

"At least some of us are trying," I shot back.

"She'll never be my mom," you said.

"She isn't trying to be."

"You'll never be my family. You'll never be my *sister*."

You made the word the ugliest thing in the world, and I wished my mom had never met your dad.

"Why do you hate me so much?" I asked.

"Who said I hated you?"

"You put dirt. In. My. Bed."

You smirked. "Did I?"

"Stay out of my room," I said, squaring my shoulders and fighting to make my voice strong.

"It's *my* house."

"It's your *dad's* house, not yours."

You leaned close enough so I could smell your peanut butter breath. "You and your mother should leave," you said, and left the room without a look back. I didn't go upstairs for a long time and when I did, I ran past your room, even though your door was closed.

∾

I padded downstairs to get a drink and paused on the bottom step when I heard our parents talking with hushed voices.

"Thom, I really think you should talk to her, try to bring her out of her shell."

"She's a quiet kid. She's always been that way."

"I know, but sometimes I feel like there are only three people who live in this house, not four, and that isn't right. Even when she's with us, it's like she isn't. Have you considered that she might need to talk to someone else, someone professional?"

"She doesn't need that, Grace. She needs time, that's all. She'll come around, I know she will."

"But—"

"She's fine. Look, I know you're concerned, but I know my kid. It takes her a long time to get used to change."

"I just feel like—"

"Just give her time. Trust me, it's the best thing we can do."

I snuck back to my room before I got caught eavesdropping. So my mom, too, knew something wasn't right, but I was still afraid to talk to her. It's not like she was going to pack up and leave. She sold our house; we had no place else to go.

~

I woke in a room still swathed in shadows. I blinked in the darkness, saw movement beside my bed, and there you were, bending forward.

"What are you doing?" I said.

You froze in place, one finger held to your lips. I must've fallen back to sleep because the next thing I knew it was morning. I stormed down the hallway, my hands curled into fists to keep them from shaking, and knocked on your bedroom door.

"I told you to stay out of my room," I said, when you peeked through a four-inch gap.

"I wasn't in your room."

"Yes, you were. I saw you last night."

"Maybe you were dreaming," you said as you shut the door.

"Stay out or I'm telling your dad," I called out, my voice a little kid whine, but what else was I supposed to say? I didn't know what you were doing, but I knew it wasn't a dream.

My soccer ball was exactly where I'd left it; my sheets were clean. Nothing was missing, at least not that I could tell. My legs were sore, the way they were after I went swimming, and my bathing suit, draped over the arm of my sofa, felt damp, too. I ran my fingers over the straps with my lower lip pinched between my teeth. I hadn't been in the pool in days, and I would never ever put wet clothes on the sofa.

That night, I locked my door and propped my desk chair beneath the doorknob and breathed a sigh of relief to find it still locked and barred in the morning.

∾

Every night my mom set the table for four, but you only joined us half the time. I guess my mom had given up trying to convince your dad because she never seemed surprised either way. When you weren't there, she made a plate for you, wrapped it in plastic, and left it in the fridge, but the plates always went untouched and she eventually stopped.

I liked it better when you weren't there. When you *were*, I tried to pretend that everything was fine, but I swear you watched me the whole time. I didn't understand how your dad couldn't see that there was something wrong with you. I guess parents never want to think that way about their kids.

One night, your dad had to work late and when my mom and I sat down at the table, I toyed with my fork and took a deep breath.

"Mom? Something weird has been—"

"Are those stuffed shells? I love stuffed shells," you said from behind me.

"It is," my mom said, and her face lit up Christmas tree bright. She got up to fix a plate for you and you slid in your seat and blinked slowly, your eyes all innocent and sweet. Your smile might have looked real, but I knew it wasn't. My mom bought it, though, and I knew then that I couldn't say anything. You wouldn't let me.

∾

I guess I forgot to lock my bedroom door, because I woke up with you in my room again, halfway to my bed. I sat up, the sheets pooled around my waist. "Get out of my room," I said.

You inched closer. "Do you think they'd like me more if I was like you?" you said.

"What?"

"You're the ash-girl turned princess and I'm the ugly one who cut off her toes and still can't fit the shoes," you said.

"What are you talking about? You're not making any sense."

You laughed, but the sound wasn't happy and it prickled the hairs on the back of my neck. Once you were gone, I turned the lock, but I couldn't fall back to sleep, not for a long time.

∾

Me, your dad, and my mom were watching *Star Wars* in the family room, and my mom sat in the middle with a huge bowl of popcorn on her lap. Halfway through the movie, your dad grabbed the remote, hit pause, and said, "We should go camping next weekend."

My mom laughed. "Where did that come from?"

"I have no idea, but doesn't it sound like a good idea? What do you think, Courtney?"

"Sure," I said. "I haven't been camping in a long time, not since I was little."

"We can go to Cunningham Falls State Park. Sleep in tents, roast marshmallows, hike the trails," your dad said. "Not sure if any of my old gear is any good, but we can buy new stuff if we need to."

"I think that sounds awesome," I said. I meant it, too. "Want me to tell Alyssa?" I didn't want to, not really, but it seemed like the kind of thing I *should* say.

Your dad blinked and my mom shook her head a little, not in a yes or a no but in the way people did when they were surprised. Then your dad said, "I will. I'll ask her."

When he came back downstairs, his face was drawn. "She doesn't want to go."

I tipped my chin down to hide my disappointment. Of course you didn't want to. You weren't happy and you didn't want us to be happy either.

"But you know," he said, "she's old enough to stay home by herself, so we can still go."

"Really?" I said.

He looked at my mom and after she nodded, he said, "Yes, really."

∾

In the months that followed, the three of us went camping a bunch of times. We also went to the movies, to play miniature golf, and bowling. Sometimes when I forgot to lock my bedroom door, I woke up in the morning tired, my hair smelling of chlorine or my feet dirty, but I never said anything. If I did, then you'd know your tricks were working. You were just mad because we were out having fun while you stayed home.

The picture of you and your mom and dad at the beach disappeared from the living room. I found broken glass and part of the frame in the kitchen trash can and waited for your dad to notice, but he never did.

∾

In the middle of the night, I woke with you atop me, your body fitted against mine, limb to limb. I was too startled to say anything, to shout, and then you pressed down, impossibly heavy. I inhaled your exhalation, tasted your breath, felt the fine hairs on your skin brush against mine, felt your heat in the delicate cleft between my thighs, absorbed the dampness of your sweat through my pores. As I drew in a breath to scream, you said, "Mine." I choked on the word and everything went hazy. I felt you fall inside me, through my skin and into my bones. I sat up, running my hands over my arms and legs, breathing hard, my body strangely heavy, though unchanged on the outside. I could still taste you in my mouth—meat and anticipation and need and rage—and my thighs quivered with an unresolved ache.

A dream, it had to be a dream, I told myself. You were in your room, sleeping. All I had to do was creep down the hall and check, but I didn't. I couldn't.

I stared at the ceiling until sunlight crept into my room and when I got out of bed, I fell to my knees. I used the edge of my mattress to pull myself up and hobbled across the room, my back bent, every step quicksand slow. My mouth was dry, my hands trembling. It was Sunday and I didn't have to worry about school, so I paced in my room until I grew accustomed to the new weight in my spine, refusing to think about what had happened, refusing to think it was anything other than a dream and that I must've slept wrong or tossed and turned so much.

When I heard our parents go downstairs, I slipped down the hallway and stood outside your closed door. I lifted my hand to knock, but let it drop instead. I didn't know what I was more afraid of—seeing you there or not seeing you at all.

The smell of bacon wafted up the stairs and I waited by your door, leaning as close as I dared and hearing nothing, but you never came out and in the kitchen, there were only three place settings on the table. I sat with my shoulders hunched and didn't say anything to our parents about my dream or the plates or you.

After breakfast, I tucked my soccer ball under my arm and went out back. My kicks were awkward and half the time, my foot missed the ball. My arms didn't want to move the right way when I ran, either. Your dad came outside and when I waved, he said, "Are you okay? You seem a little off your game today."

"I know. I don't feel so hot." I patted my stomach so he'd assume it was a period thing and not the flu.

Cheeks flushed, he said, "Maybe you should come inside and rest, instead of playing."

"Yeah, I'll come in in a little while."

But I stayed outside, kicking and re-kicking the ball, getting angrier and angrier with each fumbling arc of my foot, each miss.

∿

Now there were only three of us in the wedding photo over the fireplace. Our arms were still linked, but in the space where you should have been was only background. I touched the picture with one trembling finger, half-expecting it to disintegrate or burst into flame or change back to right. My mom's footfalls clicked in the foyer and I called her in.

"What, honey?"

"Look at this."

She smiled, steepling her fingers to her chin. "That was such a wonderful day."

"Right, but don't you see something wrong with the picture?"

"No." She stepped a little closer. "Should I?"

"Don't we look ... off center to you?"

"Now that you mention it, yes, we do. Funny how I never noticed it before." Her brow creased and for a moment I thought for sure she knew exactly what was wrong. Your name danced across my lips and I held my breath.

Then she smiled. "I'll have to take it and get it reframed at some point. Come on, want to help me get dinner ready? I'm making your favorite—stuffed shells."

I froze, unable to blink or breathe. "Sure," I finally said, my mouth sandpaper rough, and glanced over my shoulder as I followed her out of the room.

Without thinking, I pulled four dinner plates from the cabinet, but before my mom could notice, I put one back.

~

Your dad rapped on my doorframe with his knuckles. "Want to watch a movie with us?"

"No, that's okay. I have to finish this." I lifted my notebook, hoping he wouldn't look too closely at the blank page.

"You sure? It has that actor you like, the one who played Loki."

"Yeah, I'm sure."

"Are you okay, kiddo? You've seemed distracted lately."

"I'm fine," I said, putting a smile on my face. "Just busy with school. It's like all the teachers have decided to give us extra work to do right now."

He ran his thumb along the hinge. "You know, you can tell me if something's bothering you. You can talk to me about anything at all."

"I know. Thank you." I swallowed hard against the lump in my throat.

When he stepped out of view, I tiptoed across the room and peered into the hallway. He paused by your door and cocked his head with his hands in his pockets, but after a moment, he headed for the stairs. I sat on my bed with my arms wrapped around myself and whispered your name, but you didn't answer.

~

I waited until our parents went out to dinner one night and took the front stairs to the second floor. My mouth was dry and a cold snake slithered from between my shoulder blades down to my tailbone, but I opened your bedroom door without knocking. The bookcases and pale grey walls were still there, but the shelves were empty and the only thing hanging from the bar in the closet was a square of cedar.

I checked beneath the bed, underneath the pillows, behind the curtains, in every drawer of the desk, but there was no indication you'd ever been here at all. I stood with my back against the wall, breathing hard. "This isn't right," I said, one hand to my chest. "This isn't possible."

I dragged the desk chair over to the closet and in the back corner of the top shelf, I found a folded photograph—you and your mom and your dad at the beach. The missing picture from the living room. I hissed in a breath. Here, then, proof that you were real. I stood on the chair for a long time, turning the picture over and over in my hand.

~

Every morning, I check my feet for unexplained dirt and flex my muscles for unexpected stiffness. I tell myself I'm okay—I want to be okay—but I still can't hit the soccer ball well and when I swim, my arms and legs can't find the proper rhythm. I'm mostly afraid of the changes I don't know about yet.

And what if never know until it's too late? Maybe you're changing me a little more every day, and I'll wake up one morning and feel your shape beneath my clothing, taste your words on my tongue, and hear your voice in my ears. You wouldn't do that to me, would you?

I don't know how you did it or why or what you thought would happen. Maybe you figured you could take my place and somehow got stuck. Maybe you wanted to disappear and be forgotten. Maybe you were angry and wanted to scare me.

Well that part worked so you can come back now, okay? You can come out.

Our parents remember that they've forgotten something. Now and then, your dad stands in the doorway of your bedroom, hands in pockets, eyes serious, shoulders slumped. My mom never got the wedding portrait reframed and sometimes she stands in front of it, her forehead creased and her mouth pursed. I can almost understand her forgetting —she wasn't used to two kids around and you were always in your room—but your own dad? I think you made them forget you. I wish you'd made me forget you, too.

At night I take out the photograph I have hidden under my mattress and tell you I'm going to show it our parents and tell them what you did. I'll make them remember you, and then you won't be able to hide inside me anymore. Then you'll have to come back out.

But I'm scared they won't believe me. I'm scared you're never going to leave. And I know you know it, too. I feel it in my bones.

ON THE OTHER SIDE OF THE DOOR, EVERYTHING CHANGES

*H*annah opens her bedroom window, wincing at the low creak, and pauses with one leg over the sill. A pile of dirty laundry sits on the floor by the foot of her bed, One Direction posters hang on the walls, and her laptop is open, but turned off, on her desk. She hasn't dared turn it on for days; the messages coming in on her phone are more than enough.

Dark smudges, the shadows of her mom's feet, creep along the floor beneath the door. They linger, and Hannah pulls her leg back inside, careful not to make a sound, worrying an already ragged cuticle between her teeth. Part of her wants to open the door and let her mom in, wants to let the truth spill from her lips like vomit, wants to tell her everything, no matter what she says, no matter what happens after, but she can't make her feet or mouth move because the other part of her knows it's too late.

Her phone vibrates and tears burn in her eyes. The monsters are relentless. No need to look at the message; she knows what it says. She deleted them when it started, but now she doesn't even bother. Her phone vibrates again and she pinches the inside of her cheek between her teeth. It's Friday night, almost ten o'clock. Weekends are the worst.

The shadow feet beneath her door move, pause, and move again,

---

this time moving away. Hannah takes a deep breath, shoves her phone in the pocket of her hoodie, and gives her room one last look.

~

Leanne paces in the living room in the open space between the television and the coffee table, fingertips to temple, as though she can hold back the ache nestling there. Hannah's upstairs in her bedroom, and while Leanne wants to go and apologize, she knows her daughter well enough to know it would go over as well as a fart in church. They both need time to cool down. To breathe.

This isn't the first time they've argued—life with a thirteen-year-old is anything but idyllic—but it's the worst thus far. And prompted by such a silly thing, too. Leanne squeezes her hands into fists, releases, squeezes again. Walks another series of footprints into the nap of the carpet.

Would you please empty the dishwasher? A simple request that tornadoed into tears, stomping feet, and the slinging of silverware into the drawer so fast and hard the clatter rattled Leanne's teeth.

"What is wrong with you?" Leanne asked, knowing her tone of voice was too sharp, but unable to catch it quick enough.

Hannah turned with a fistful of spoons, eyes pinched. "Nothing's wrong with me."

Leanne kept her tone gentle. "You've been quiet for days. You haven't been hanging out with your friends or doing much of anything other than staying in your room. Is everything okay? Did something happen?"

Hannah shrugged one shoulder.

"You know you can talk to me if you want, right? About anything at all."

Another shrug, then Hannah crossed her arms over her chest and said, "I'm not hanging out with my friends because they've been calling me names."

And Leanne laughed. It wasn't that she found it funny—and it was more a snicker than an actual laugh—but Hannah's response was unexpected and petulant, the words something out of grade school. Leanne bit back the sound a moment too late, and Hannah exploded. F5. She threw the spoons across the counter, her mouth twisted, her face blotched bright red, and she yelled, "I knew you wouldn't understand. You're too old."

Silence hovered in the air, thick as molasses, bitter as bile. As Leanne opened her mouth to say *I'm sorry*, a spoon balanced on the edge of the counter fell to the floor. Before the echo of the clink faded, Hannah's words rushed out, too fast for Leanne to follow, drowning her apology in chaos. She heard *everyone hates me* and *I hate it here* and *I want to go home*, the pitch escalating with each declaration.

Leanne stood immobile, her weight on her heels, desperately wishing David were home and hating herself a bit for it. But he'd be able to turn things around. With Hannah, he was always been able to. When she was small and afraid of monsters hiding in her closet, he'd open the closet with one hand while brandishing a toy lightsaber in the other. He'd stab and swing the lightsaber at the shoes and hanging clothes—while making a reasonable facsimile of the distinctive lightsaber sound—until the hangers were dancing on the bar and Hannah's fear gave way to laughter.

At a lull in Hannah's tirade, Leanne said, "Please stop being so dramatic. Whatever happened will all blow over and they'll stop. Act like it doesn't matter and it will stop even faster. In a few years, you'll barely remember it. It isn't the end of the world."

Hannah burst into tears and ran from the kitchen, stomping her feet up the staircase and slamming her bedroom door. Leanne sagged against the counter and counted to ten. A few times.

Now, she pours a glass of wine but leaves it untasted on the coffee table. She regrets what she said to Hannah, regretted it as soon as the words were in the air, but everything will be okay once they've both calmed down. Everything will be fine.

∾

Hannah climbs onto the back porch roof, closes her bedroom window behind her, and shimmies down a support column until her feet touch the top of the railing. From there, it's a quick crouch-and-drop to the porch. Luckily, the light isn't on—it burned out a few nights ago and no one's replaced it yet—and the side of the porch she used isn't visible from the kitchen window, not unless you open it and stick your head out. Plus, it's late enough that none of the neighbors, all old people, are outside. With light steps, she moves around the side of the house, dipping low beneath the windows. Once across the lawn, she doesn't look back.

Invisible hands in her chest squeeze tight as she reaches the end of the street, and she wipes tears from her cheeks with the cuff of a sleeve. Bawling like a baby is pointless. All the tears in the world won't change things, and anyway, the monsters like it when she cries. They feed off the salt and the sorrow.

She shoves her hands in her pockets and hunches her shoulders. It's early March and still chilly, colder than she thought it would be.

The neighborhood is a series of culs-de-sac jutting off a main road like tumors. When she passes the cul-de-sac where Larissa lives, she pulls up her hood and turtles into the fabric. Even though Larissa lives at the top of the circle and the chance of her looking or coming outside at the exact same time Hannah passes is small, she doesn't want to risk it. Her phone vibrates and she walks faster, a bitter taste in the back of her throat.

She follows the road to another and makes a left, pausing to glance over her shoulder. From here, she can't see her house, only the curve in the road right before the turn off. Larissa's house, with the big flagpole in the middle of the front yard, is clear as day. Larissa, the first person she met when they moved here right before Thanksgiving five months ago. Larissa, who she thought was her friend. Larissa, one of the monsters, never mind that the human mask she wears isn't nearly tight enough to hold in the darkness it tries to conceal.

But it fooled Hannah.

"I didn't know," she says, the thump of her soles on the pavement swallowing the sound.

Her phone vibrates yet again.

"Fuck you," she says, but the words are deflated balloons.

She isn't sure how far away the interstate is. A mile? Two? It never seems that far in the car, but it's still walking distance, and even if it really isn't, it will be tonight.

An SUV drives by, going too fast, the way everyone seems to drive around here. Too many cars, too many people, and all of them rude, nasty, or dismissive. The air always reeks of exhaust, cat piss, and charred meat, the latter from a nearby diner open twenty-four-seven.

She hates it here, hates everything about it. This place will never be home. It's a bad dream and when she wakes up, it's a nightmare. She misses her old house, misses her room and her friends, but most of all, she misses the water. Their house, on the South River in Edgewater, had a dock and a small beach. In the summer she liked to run the length of the dock and jump into the water, savoring that moment of weightlessness, hovering over the water and waiting to fall. That was always the best part. That moment that always felt longer than it truly was, that moment when you weren't part of the world at all, but floating above it.

Even when it was cold, she would sit on the sand and run her fingers through the coarse grains. Her dad always said you could never be sad or angry sitting by the water. If she were home by the water, maybe she'd feel better. Then again, if she were home, none of this would've happened. No Larissa, no Jeremy, no pictures.

She traces the outline of the phone in her pocket, thinks for the hundredth time of calling Mira, her best friend back home, but she doesn't want her to know. Besides, Mira is sort of pissed at her for making new friends so fast and spending time with them.

She was so stupid. She should've known better.

At the first major street, she waits for the light to change, scuffing the toe of one shoe against the pavement. Her phone vibrates again. She doesn't need to look but she does.

Dirty little whore.

She doesn't cry. Doesn't delete the message.

When Hannah told Larissa what Jeremy had asked for, Larissa said it was no big deal, said they all did it, said Hannah was special because Jeremy never asked anyone. A lie, but one Hannah couldn't see at the time because she still thought they were friends.

Hannah didn't even want to take the picture, but Larissa kept talking about it and talking about it. A dog with a bone, she wouldn't let it go. Funny how after Jeremy sent her picture to *everyone*, Larissa was the first person to send an email. *Slut*, it read. Hannah thought she was joking, until the other emails and text messages started coming in.

She was such an idiot.

And the absolute worst part? The part she doesn't even like to think about? She *liked* taking the picture, liked the way it made her feel, liked the way she looked—older, different. It made her feel pretty and powerful. Did that make her a terrible person? Did it make her a slut? She almost didn't hit *send*, wanting to keep that sense of awe to herself, and the moment she did, the power fizzled away, leaving an empty hollow in its place.

All weekend long the messages came in, a barrage of ugliness and mockery and hate, and on Monday, she walked into school with a dry mouth and shaking hands. At first she thought everything would be okay. They had their fun, they made her weekend miserable, time to pick on someone else. Then she saw their faces, their true faces, with their masks off. Everyone had vampire smiles and glitter-dark eyes, fingers hooked into cruel talons. Hateful and predatory. Monstrous. So sharp and clear, she wondered how she didn't see it before.

Every time tears burned in her eyes, their faces brightened, drool ran from the corners of their mouths, and their cheeks plumped. They hid laughter and the names behind palms, smothering them in coughs that served only to amplify.

Slut was scratched into the paint on her locker in uneven block letters; *Hannah is a whore* penned on a bathroom stall in rounded, girlish script with bright pink lipstick; *Show us your tits* scrawled in black marker on a torn piece of notebook paper left on her desk. When she found the note, Mrs. Langan asked if everything was okay, and

Hannah's cheeks grew warm, then hot, and the truth pressed against her lips, but she said instead that yes, everything was okay, even though a small voice was screaming. Long after Mrs. Langan nodded and walked away, that small voice continued to scream and she picked the rough edge of the paper until the words were gone and she had a shredded pile in her lap.

If she could talk to her mom, she'd tell her that she's tried to ignore it all, hoping they'd stop—she's tried so hard—but inside she's all broken glass and she can't put her pieces back together. There's no way anyone can. And real monsters don't hide under the bed or in the closet; they aren't afraid of sunlight. They stand out in the open and smile and smile and smile.

If her parents knew, they'd hate her. They'd be ashamed and would never look at her the same way. She'd never be able to explain it. To explain why. Mostly, though, she doesn't know how to try anymore. She's tired, and all she wants is the water, the weightlessness before the cold.

Just past a gas station and a half-constructed fast food restaurant, she drops her phone into the gutter. Rocks her foot back and forth until the screen cracks and then grinds her heel into the pulverized screen, exposing the metal guts. The light changes and she moves on.

∼

Leanne tiptoes upstairs and perches on the top step, the way she did when Hannah was a baby asleep in her crib, resting her elbows on her knees and chin atop linked fingers.

Girls can be cruel. It's always been that way, even when she was in school. The surge of hormones brought something dark and primal to the surface, a savage sort of competition that, sadly, never went away for some. Even when the cruelties were relatively minor, the hormones also brought sensitivity that affected perception. Maybe it wasn't the end of the world, but it felt that way to Hannah, and Leanne belittled her feelings.

She wants to go in Hannah's room, sit at the foot of her bed, and read her a story or sing a song. Would that such devices would work for a teenager. At best, she'll get a roll of the eyes and an impassioned *Mo-ther*; at worst, she'll make it two steps into the room before Hannah yells *Leave me alone!*

Silly, maybe, sitting here, stressing about a fight that in a few days will fade into memory, and in a few years to nothing at all. She allows herself a smile. All the angst and chaos. All the drama. Her memories of her own early teen years are threaded with band names, pining for cute boys in the neighborhood, and yes, volatile fights with her own mother, for reasons now unremembered.

Leanne heads downstairs, makes it to the bottom, and turns around, wincing when one of the steps creaks, the sound a snapping bone in the hush. If her mother were still alive, she'd call and ask for advice. God, how many times had she done that when Hannah was an infant? Far too many to count. *Should she be sleeping so much? Should she be sleeping so little? How do I know she's getting enough milk? Am I a terrible mother because she has diaper rash?* But non-Hodgkin's lymphoma took her when Hannah was three, and Leanne doesn't have that sort of relationship with her mother-in-law.

She passes Hannah's room on the way into hers, making enough noise so it's clear she's there. Maybe Hannah will come out and decide she wants to talk. Humming one of Hannah's favorite songs, a syrupy pop number about a girl who is unaware she's beautiful, Leanne fetches the half-full hamper from the walk-in closet. In their old house, they'd moved the washer and dryer upstairs; here, though, she has to go down to the basement. As she walks by Hannah's room again, she clears her throat and says, "I'm doing laundry if you have something you want me to run through."

There's no answer, not that she truly expected one, but at least now Hannah knows Leanne isn't angry with her. A subtle olive branch, of which she thinks her own mother would approve.

She adjusts the laundry basket balancing on her hip. Once this blows over, she'll explain that her reaction had nothing to do with Hannah and had everything to do with the move, with her dad's job, and the hours he's spending at the office.

That's partly true, but most of all, what she's upset about and can't mention to Hannah yet, is what David told her last night. He said he regretted taking the job, that he didn't think the money was worth it, that his old boss had already indicated—and strongly so—that they'd love for him to come back, and that he's seriously considering it.

Leanne said nothing, too shocked to speak. They'd uprooted their entire lives to move here. A good career step, David said. Unlimited potential. No more worrying about their credit card debt or money for vacations or Hannah's college fund. Over and over again, and now she wonders if he was trying to convince himself as much as he was trying to convince her.

They spent weeks hashing out the options, the downsides, the changes, and, once they decided the benefits outweighed the risks, several more weeks setting everything in motion. And now he wants to undo everything and move them back? Without even considering how this will affect Hannah or Leanne? Not to mention the logistical hassle. They signed a year's lease for this house and rented out their old—thankfully they hadn't sold it, though it was a near thing. Breaking the lease will cost them money, and then they'll have to find somewhere else to live in Edgewater until the tenants' lease is up, unless they're willing to move out before then.

Leanne's been doing remote paralegal work for the firm she worked for in Edgewater, so in theory that won't present a problem, but once they move back her boss will expect her to come into the office and she likes working remotely, likes knowing she's there when Hannah gets home from school.

She can't even imagine how Hannah will react to the news. She took the move harder than any of them, and it was a huge relief when she made friends so quickly. Nice girls, all of them, especially Larissa. If they do decide to move back, will that only make things doubly hard for Hannah or will she be too happy to see Mira again to care?

Leanne pinches the bridge of her nose between finger and thumb. Readjusts the laundry basket. Maybe she should mention the possibility to Hannah and feel her out. Then again, it might only upset her even more.

❧

Beneath the overpass, through Hannah's tears, trucks rush past in a blur. She wonders if her mom's already figured out that she isn't home. If so, she probably thinks she's with one of the monsters. She touches a hand to her chest. In a way, she'd be right. If she peeled back the skin of her chest, she thinks there'd be claw marks in the chambers of her heart.

It isn't the end of the world, that's what her mother said. Hannah lets out a sharp sound halfway between laugh and sob. Her mom has no idea.

Her dad probably isn't even home yet. He never worked so much at his old job. She told him that in the beginning, told him she missed him, and he said he missed her too and he wouldn't have to work like that forever. She thinks maybe he lied and wishes he'd liked his old job a little more.

At least they won't ever find out what she did.

She peeks over her shoulder, half-expecting to see the monsters, smiling and waiting. No one's there, of course, but she feels their presence, their hot breath on the back of her neck, their claws tracing the length of her spine.

For a brief moment, she wonders what it would've been like to talk to her mom. Then she shakes off the thought and checks over her shoulder again, this time to make sure no cars are driving past.

She climbs over the railing and stares down at the trucks, listening to the rumble of their tires on the asphalt. Inside, she's cold and still and unafraid, but she hopes it's fast. She hopes it doesn't hurt.

❧

Leanne stands outside Hannah's room, arms crossed and elbows cupped in her palms. She fidgets in place, lifts a hand to knock, lets it fall. It's almost ten o'clock; Hannah might be getting ready for bed.

At the low creak of Hannah's window, she gives a wry smile.

Hannah is so like her father that way, always wanting a window open at night, even when it's chilly. Leanne prefers a downy pile of blankets, regardless of the weather.

She reaches for the door again and again hesitates. Take a deep breath before making a decision—a bit of advice from her mom, one Leanne's passed down to Hannah. Silly, perhaps, to think a lungful of air caught then expelled could help so much, but it always does. Leanne knows it from years of practice.

If she goes in now, will they be able to talk without it turning into another argument? Maybe it's better to wait until the morning. Everything looks better after a good night's sleep, and tomorrow *is* Saturday. No rushing in the morning, no watching the clock. She can make waffles with raspberries and powdered sugar—Hannah's favorite—and help her work through whatever's upset her. She'll listen, no matter how silly everything seems. She'll let Hannah cry or yell, whatever she needs.

Leanne stares down at the shadows her feet have made on the floor and takes a deep breath. With a shake of her head, she heads back downstairs and texts David: *Hannah and I had a big fight tonight.* His reply, a few minutes later: *On my way home. I'll talk to her when I get there. Everything will be OK. Love you.*

She scrubs her face with her hands and takes to the stairs. Maybe letting David swoop in and take care of everything isn't the best decision. Maybe this time it's on her to fix things. Standing outside Hannah's room, she says, "I'd like us to talk now, babygirl. Or I can talk and you can just listen, but if you tell me to go away, I will."

There's no answer and Leanne sighs in relief, picturing Hannah lying in bed with one hand under her cheek, listening. She sits with her back against the wall next to Hannah's door, pulls her knees to her chest, and rests her chin atop folded arms. "Okay, then, here goes."

She closes her eyes, scrunches her toes inside her socks.

"When you were little, I told your dad I wanted to roll you in bubble wrap. He thought it was because you were clumsy, but it wasn't. I just wanted to protect you from everything, from the world. Sounds so silly, doesn't it?"

Hannah doesn't answer, but she doesn't need to because it *does* sound silly. You can baby-proof a house, but you can't life-proof a child. A tiny breathless laugh slips from Leanne's lips. "You know, the last time I did this, sitting outside your door like this, you were six, almost seven. We got home from your cousin Felicity's birthday party, and it was late and you were tired and said you wanted ice cream.

"We said no. For one thing, it was way past your bedtime and for another, we didn't have any ice cream. We didn't remind you that at the party, you said you didn't like it, even though we knew you did. You shrieked at the top of your lungs that we were the meanest parents ever, and you stomped into your room and threw yourself down on your bed, crying like nobody's business. I sat outside your room talking for a long time until you calmed down.

"The funniest part was that we offered you ice cream the next day and you said no, you didn't like it anymore. That lasted about a week, I think. Such a goofball you were."

Leanne shakes her head. Blinks away tears.

"I'm so sorry for tonight, babygirl. I'm sorry I didn't listen better and let you talk. I'm sorry if I made you feel like I was making light of what you said. I didn't mean to. The last thing in the world I want to do is to hurt your feelings or make you feel like they're not important, because they are, and I want you to be able to talk to me about anything. Like the way you can talk to your dad.

"It was hard for me to talk to my mom when I was a kid, too. She always told me not to worry about things so much, instead of just listening to what I had to say. I made the same mistake tonight, and I promise I won't do that anymore. I'll just zip my lips and listen.

"I love you, no matter what, and I always will."

She rakes her front teeth over her lower lip, listens for movement.

"Hannah?"

Slowly, she gets to her feet, curls one hand around the doorknob and knocks lightly with her knuckles.

"Babygirl, can I come in?"

THIS IS THE WAY I DIE

I want to be broken, to be shattered then reshaped into something new. Something with bulletproof skin, eyes that can see in the dark, lungs that can breathe in water as well as air, and an impenetrable heart. I want to be made monstrous, beautiful, frightening.

You wield the scalpel, the clamps, the bone saw. I am offering myself as the subject of your experiment. Yes, I know it will hurt. Yes, I know there is no guarantee. I may end up terrified or warped and deformed or as fragile as spun glass, but all things carry a risk.

Know that I am not a victim. Know that this is my choice.

~

I 'm drowning when I come to you. You make no mention of my sodden hair, the water dripping from my fingertips onto your floor, the squelching sound of my footsteps, but I know you see them. You see everything.

You see: A girl of indeterminate age, her shoulders slumped but her eyes holding tight to a defiant spark.

You think: The spark is fragile, hanging on by a tiny thread, and you could snip it quickly if you chose, so quickly I wouldn't notice until I collapsed into a pile of nothing, a not-thing.

You fear: The words from my mouth, the conviction in my voice.

You've been waiting for someone like me for a very long time.

~

"What's your name?" you say.

"Why?"

You raise your eyebrows. "I should call you something, shouldn't I?"

I bite my lower lip and finally say, "Lola Mae Blue."

One corner of your mouth quirks into a half-smile. "Lola Mae Blue. I like it."

When you take my hand, you say nothing of the chill in my skin. The heat of yours feels strange, alien, as if my own flesh has forgotten what it's like to be warm. I'm suddenly afraid of the warmth, afraid of burning up, burning down to ash and cinder, so I gently tug my hand free from yours. Your lips part for an instant but close before a word escapes.

Your eyes are proud, yet hesitant, when you show me your work-shop. The lights are bright, startlingly so. A metal table with a raised edge and a small hole for drainage takes up the center of the room; the tools of your trade are spread out on a bench in the corner; schematics and designs cover the walls; the smell of disinfectant lingers in the air.

The air conditioner turns on with a whoosh. I see goosebumps on your forearms; I have none of my own.

~

You show me your sketches, your ideas. I point here and there. You erase lines, draw new ones, darken others. When you finish, you hold up the sketch, a small smile on your face. I look for a long time, but there's something missing, something I can't define. It's beautiful and strong, there's no doubt about that, but it's somehow …

empty. Powerless. You see the hesitation in my eyes and flip to another sketch.

You stop to make coffee, ask me how I take mine. Before you take a sip, you pick up the pencil again. After a time, the second sketch is discarded like the first, but with a low growl instead of a frown. Another sketch and then another meets the same fate as the sun drops below the horizon and the house grows dark.

You make more coffee. You don't have to ask this time; when you hand me my mug, the coffee is perfect.

We start on another sketch, then you frown and toss the sketch-book aside. "They're not good enough," you say, and pull out a new sketchbook, the blank surface of the pages awash with possibility. You tuck the pencil behind your ear, pick up your mug. "Talk to me," you say, your voice little more than a whisper. Your eyes catch mine; I look away first.

"About what?"

"Tell me what you want, what you're afraid of. Show me how to see things through your eyes. The other sketches were concepts. This is about you, not something vague."

I exhale. Glance down at my hands. Slender fingers, short nails, and a tiny scar near the base of my thumb, a scar from a wound I can't remember. I have many like it. I'm not sure if I truly don't remember, or if I've chosen not to remember. Sometimes letting go is for the best.

We sit in silence for a time; I can't find words to fill it up. Finally, you bring me a blanket, ask me to hold out my hands and when I do, you drape the fabric over my palms.

"Close your eyes and tell me how it feels."

I laugh, but the sound is harsh at the edges, almost manic in its desperate attempt to sound normal.

"Please," you say. "I'm serious. Tell me."

So I do.

Soft, silky, surprisingly heavy, warm. Boring. Boring. Boring. I have no idea why you think this will help, but I like the way your brow creases when you work.

The pencil scratches across the paper, pauses, and scratches again.

"Tell me about the color," you say.

"It's grey," I say. "Like a storm or dryer lint."

Your eyes widen. How can I explain to you that everything is grey?

"Show me," I say, when you stop sketching.

"Not yet."

~

The next night, you place an old coffee mug in my hands. There are chips in the handle, a crack in the side, circular stains marring the pale inside.

Again, you say, "Tell me."

Again, I do.

Fragile, brittle, worn, tired.

~

"Is Lola Mae your real name?" you ask.

"Does it matter?"

"Do you have family? Friends?"

"Again, does it matter?"

"It matters to me."

"It doesn't to me."

I know you want more, as evidenced by your parted lips and the creased V between your eyebrows, but you let it go.

~

A pencil, complete with teeth marks. Yours, I presume.

Concentration, thoughts, choices, decisions.

~

A book, the cover tattered and creased. I flip through the pages, inhaling the scent of old paper and a story I've never read.

Words, forgotten, broken promises.

I blink once, twice. Your face is carefully blank, a study in statuary. I put the book aside and steeple my fingers beneath my chin.

"Will you show me now?"

"Not yet."

"Why," you ask one night, flipping a pencil from finger to finger. "Why do you want to do this?"

"Does there need to be a reason?"

"I'd think so, yes."

"There are a hundred. Is that enough?"

"Tell me."

"No."

A knit scarf. I take each end and wrap it around my hands. Stretch it out.

Pain. Hurt. Drowning. Dying.

I stand. Let the scarf fall. "Enough," I say. "Enough. You don't need to know these things. You don't need to know anything about me, only that I'm here, only that I've come to you."

You stand, put your hands on my shoulders. You're close enough that I can smell your skin, a mix of sweat, coffee, and graphite. It's too much. You're too close. I step back, away, holding my breath. I run outside, bend forward with my hands on my thighs, tell myself to inhale. Exhale. Inhale. Every movement makes my chest ache; something so biologically simple shouldn't be so fucking hard.

I make coffee and step into the living room, wondering what you'll have me tell you tonight, wondering how I'll tell you that this isn't part of the bargain, this dissection isn't part of the process. But you pat the sofa beside you instead and hold out the sketchpad.

The first sketch is hard to take. I want to turn away, but I force myself to look. You've drawn me with my shoulders sloped, my chin tucked. Defeated. Tired. The second sketch shows me curled in a small ball. The next shows me standing at a window. The next, me with hands outstretched and tears on my face. The next shows me standing, half my body concealed behind a shadow, not my own, my face twisted in fear.

I don't understand these sketches. This is not why I'm here. You know this. Before I can speak, you hold up your hand, show me the last sketch.

She is not me. Not yet. She is strong, proud. There's a light in her eyes, apparent even in the smudges of charcoal. The changes, the modifications, are perfect. The anger inside me slips away. I touch the paper as if somehow I can reach through and touch her, bring her into me, become. I want to smile, but my mouth has forgotten the shape.

"Are you ready?" you ask.

"Yes."

~

On the table, I wonder if I should be afraid, but I refuse to remember what fear tastes like. Surely I've swallowed enough for ten lifetimes.

You decide to start with my hands. I ask why, and you look surprised.

"I'm not sure," you say. "It seems like the best place to start. Is that okay?"

"Yes."

I feel the sharp sting of a needle, then nothing at all. I wake to pain, as if my hands have been dipped in acid. The bandages are

THIS IS THE WAY I DIE

dotted here and there with Rorschach designs in reddish brown. You feed me, bathe me, brush my hair.

Strange, this being taken care of, yet I sense no obligation in your touch, only kindness, concern, a gentleness that frightens me even as it comforts. Is this why you started with my hands? So I could learn to trust, to accept that I am worthy of this?

When it's time for you to unwrap the bandages, I draw in a sharp rush of air. These hands are capable and warm. I touch my face, my neck, and then move about the room, touching walls, windows, curtains. The textures—rough plaster, woven silk, smooth glass—fill my skin, feed a strange hunger, a need to impress everything with my fingerprints.

You come to stand beside me, take my new hands in yours. Mine are strong enough now not to pull away. I run a fingertip across your knuckles.

"Are they okay?" you say.

I nod, terrified that I'll cry if I speak a word.

～

All the mirrors, including the one over the bathroom sink, are gone, their vacancies marked by lighter rectangles of paint and holes in the plaster.

"I want you to wait until we're done. Is that okay?"

I look down at my new hands. "But I can—"

You press a finger to my lips. "Please."

"Okay."

～

My eyes are next. You buy a cane, and I spend a week walking while it tap-tap-taps in front of me. I fall once, twice, but eventually I don't need the cane, only one outstretched hand. Then I don't need to even extend my hand; I know where everything is and sidestep all the sharp edges.

You unwind the bandages, and I blink against the sudden sting of light. I cover my eyes, peer through the spaces between my fingers. It's a shock to see that your eyes are blue, nearly the same shade as the sky outside.

The blanket draped over the back of the sofa, the same one you had me hold, is red. I sit on the floor with it in my lap, tracing patterns in the weave. I feel you watching and when I glance up, you offer a smile.

∾

My mouth and lungs follow.

I smile, tracing the shape of my lips with one finger. Strange, yet familiar, like a ghost of someone I once knew. I laugh and it sounds real, which makes me laugh even harder. Soon, you're laughing at me and I'm holding my stomach because it hurts in a painful way that feels inexplicably good. When the laughter slips away, the smile remains.

"Tell me," you say. "Tell me where you came from. Tell me something, anything."

I open my mouth to tell you no; instead, other words break free. I tell you of my mother, my father. I tell you how I ran away for the first time at eleven; the last, at seventeen. I tell you of the streets, the fear, the people who hurt, the people who tried to rescue, those who merely turned away—a cruelty more cutting than anything else. I tell you of a thousand things I've never spoken to anyone else about.

When my voice dries up, I step outside and breathe without effort. For the first time in a long time, the only thing in my lungs is air, not water. My eyes burn with tears, and I let them fall.

∾

"It isn't my real name," I say one night while we're eating. "Or, no, it is my real name, but I gave it to myself."

"Will you change it again? When I'm finished?"

I put down my fork. "I don't know."

~

We slip into a routine: I break; I heal.
When you replace my spine, my height increases by an inch. My shoulders stop slumping forward, my chin doesn't seek out my chest. My new legs move with purpose, my arms, unafraid to reach out.

~

"How did you know?" I ask you.
"Know what?"
"Why I came here?"
You shrug. "I just did."
"Are you sorry?"
You shake your head hard. "Not at all. Never think that. Please, never think that."

~

Under the fluorescent lights in your workshop, your tools gleam like a promise, offering hints of my reflection in blade and handle both. At the end of the bench, there's something covered with a cloth the color of old pennies, but as I reach for the fabric, you touch my arm.
"Not yet," you say. "Please."

~

When you replace my skin, the pain is fire hot and star bright, and I can't even find my voice to scream.
You lead me to the guestroom, bring me warm soup and extra

blankets, kiss my forehead as if I were a child. The touch of your lips turns my arms to gooseflesh, and when you step back from the bed, your eyes are wide. Mine, too.

You close the door behind you; I turn my face into the pillow and sleep more deeply than I have in forever.

This new flesh is so strange, so perfect. No scars. No blemishes. No memory of anyone else's hands. It will not bruise at a slight or a glance. I press a finger against my forearm, take it away and watch the color rush back in. I touch my face, feeling the differences there, too: the lack of tension, the tiny lines at the corners of my eyes, lines borne of laughter.

～

After the last external scar fades to nothing, you take my hand and lead me to a standing mirror you've covered with a sheet. I close my eyes and listen to the whisk of fabric as you pull it free. I take a deep breath. Then another. And I open my eyes.

The Lola Mae staring back at me holds infinite possibility in her gaze, gleaming with the ferocity of Godzilla. She could topple cities, set the world afire. Her shoulders are strong; her limbs, powerful. She could tear apart the strongest bonds, shatter the bones of an oppressor with little effort. Her lips hold resolve; her chin, pride. No one could break this woman. No one would dare even try.

She is so unlike me that, for a moment, I can't remember how to breathe. But I'm not drowning. I'm dreaming awake. Aware. She is all the me I always hoped for, all I feared belonged only to pretty fantasies I sometimes indulged when the nights were long and wrapped in solitary confinement.

Yet my fingers tremble. I am paralyzed by thoughts that someone will see through the reconstruction, will see the girl who used to live within, will smell the vulnerabilities of the still-fragile heart inside and exploit every one until the external shell crumbles away to nothing and the truth is revealed: this is all window dressing, and bereft of its clothing, this mannequin is still powerless.

I turn to you and touch my chest, unable to give my fears voice. You press one finger against my lips.

"It's not ready yet," you say.

❧

We walk hand in hand by the lake behind your house, not speaking, just being. We whisper in the dark. I tell you I always wanted to learn to paint. I tell you I want to climb a mountain and stare at the clouds. I tell you I want to read Romeo and Juliet. I laugh, embarrassed by these things, these frivolous wants. You touch my cheek, stare into my eyes.

The next morning, I find an easel, tubes of vibrant colors, brushes. Then hiking shoes, bug spray, and an old volume of Shakespeare's tragedies.

❧

A song comes on the radio, one I remember my mother singing before she slipped into a bottle and forgot her voice. I burst into tears. You wipe them away, put your arms around me, and we sway together, moving in time to the notes.

When the song stops, we keep moving, my head on your shoulder, yours arms holding me close.

❧

I ask about my new heart, and you say, "I need a little more time, please."

❧

You're out running errands when I creep into your workshop. My fingers shake as I remove the cloth. The heart is finished—

smooth and perfect and free of scrapes and gouges. Made of bright and shiny metal, it knows no pain, no sorrow, no memories.

I lift it slowly, carefully, and it thumps steady and strong in my hands. I picture it behind my ribs, a captive bird inside a cage. But this heart is also a blank slate, and once you place it in my chest, there will be nothing left for you, nothing left *of* you, inside. I bow my head and cry.

When my tears dry, I touch my chest. Are the changes enough? Am I enough? After a time, I nod. This one piece, then, I will keep. All the broken shards; all the stitches holding it together; all the bruises; all the fear.

I place the new heart back on the table, cover it, and turn out the light.

∾

We have a late dinner outside beneath a darkening sky. We drink red wine. Laugh. I slip my hand into yours. Such warmth. Such safety.

"I love you," you say.

I answer with a kiss. My heart whispers the words so quietly you can't hear.

∾

I leave in the small hours of the morning. You're fast asleep, one hand tucked beneath your cheek like a child. Will you weep when you discover I'm gone? Break things in a rage? Acknowledge that this is the only way it could have ended?

I leave the new heart behind. Not as a token for you to remember me by—I wonder, fear, how long it will continue to beat in my absence —but for me to remember where and who I've been.

I am afraid, unspeakably so, yet perhaps there is strength, not weakness, in this fear. And I know I could stay. I would be safe here, perhaps too safe. If I stay, I'm afraid I'll never be anything other, more, than your creation. I was lost and you led me from the shadows—you saved me—but I have to make the rest of the journey on my own. I know I will carry you, us, inside every step of the way, but I was never yours to keep.

Still, I give one last look over my shoulder and as the air dances a melody across my skin, I wonder. Then I let it go. I let it all go. There is power in this, in saying goodbye.

I've been waiting for someone like me for a long time.

THE HANDS THAT HOLD, THE LIES
THAT BIND

*T*he thorn breaks through Callie's skin, rising from her left shoulder like a small, jagged periscope. No pain, no blood, only a strange fluttery sensation whispering the length of her spine. The barb, about the length and width of a fingernail, is a shade darker than her skin, its shape a tiny shark's fin, the skin around it slightly ridged.

She covers her mouth, holding in a laugh because it's not funny. It's not funny at all. She takes a deep breath, stares at the posters —*The Avengers* and *Star Wars*—on her bedroom wall for a long time, then at her shoulder again. The thorn's still there. This time she does let out a laugh because it's ridiculous. Lots of weird things happen when you're twelve—pimples, boobs, shopping for bras with your mom, your dad leaving and moving to the opposite side of the country—but thorns aren't one of them. At least they're not supposed to be.

Her laugh stutters to a halt. She has a thorn. In her shoulder. Call Mia, she thinks. But two months ago when Callie got her period in Ms. Llewellyn's class, Mia told everyone. More than half the girls in seventh grade—including Mia—already had theirs. It shouldn't have been a big deal, and Callie still doesn't understand why Mia did it;

they've been best friends since preschool. This, though? This puts her in freak territory.

The tip of the thorn is bone hard and sharp and probably would've cut through the strap of her tank top if it emerged beneath it instead of right next to the edge. The shivery feel in her back returns. She bares her teeth, growls softly, then shakes her head. Growling? That makes her an even bigger freak. Tears prick her eyes, and she squeezes her lids shut to try and hold them in. This can't be happening.

"Callie?"

Callie's gaze snaps wide-eyed to the doorway. Her mom's face goes still and sheds its color. Instinctively, Callie covers the thorn with a cupped palm, but it's too late.

"No," her mom says, her face dropping its mask, turning all flint-hard eyes and twisted lips. "Don't touch it." She moves so fast that Callie steps back until her thighs hit the mattress, panic flooding her mouth. She wants to get away from those eyes, that mouth, but there's nowhere to go.

Her mom's face shifts again to something with slightly less menace. "Okay. We'll take care of this. Everything will be fine," she says, her hands butterflying to her chest. Then she nods, as though in answer to some silent question, and grabs Callie's upper arm, fingers digging in hard.

"Mom, let go, that hurts." She can't remember the last time, if ever, her mom touched her this way, or even with anything other than a brief hug. Even before Dad left.

"Be quiet and come with me."

In the bathroom, her mother lets go and points to the toilet. "Sit."

"Why?" Callie says, rubbing her upper arm.

"Because I said so."

"What if I don't want—"

"Sit. Down."

Callie closes the lid and sits, knees pressed together, mouth dry, while her mom rummages in the medicine cabinet and pulls out antibiotic ointment, an adhesive bandage, and tweezers.

"What are you going to do?"

"What needs to be done."

Callie covers the thorn again.

"I said don't touch it!"

The tears return, and Callie's heart races so fast she's afraid it will leap from her chest. "What is it? And why are you so—"

"I said be quiet," her mom says between clenched teeth.

"Not until you tell me—"

"Enough! It has to come out. This isn't debatable. It has to come out now before it can take root."

Sorrow glitters in her mother's eyes, too, and that isn't new—she's been crying almost every day since Dad left—but these are different somehow. "Take root? What do you mean?"

Her mom presses the back of her hand to her mouth, but Callie hears a sob trying to escape, a strange, animalistic sound. The hardness flashes in her eyes again.

"Mom, I'm scared. Did I do something wrong?"

The harsh edges fall from her mother's face as quickly as her hand falls. "No, no, nothing like that. The, the, it has to come out, that's all. Everything will be fine. I promise." She brushes hair from her forehead and takes up the tweezers.

"I can do it," Callie says.

"No. I'll take care of it."

But her mom pauses, her fingers trembling, the tweezers a few inches above Callie's shoulder. Silence hangs heavy and thick. Then her mom starts humming, a strange rhythmic sound that makes the hairs on the back of her neck rise.

"Mom?"

She doesn't respond. Puts tweezers to thorn. Callie glances away. It feels as though her mom's pulling something out from deep inside, and it burns both fire and ice. Callie tries to hold in a cry. Tries and fails. Her mom hums louder, but Callie hears something else, something she can't define. A voice, yet not a voice, and it's not coming from her mom. It's not coming from anywhere, which doesn't make sense. Then it's gone, and the only things she's aware of are an ache in her shoulder and a strange feeling in the pit of her stomach.

Eyes glassy, her mom squeezes a pearl of antibiotic ointment over the now bleeding wound and affixes the bandage before Callie can get a closer look. "Thankfully, it was a small one. It shouldn't even leave a scar," she says with a smile so artificially bright and cheery that Callie recoils.

Her mother seemingly pays no attention. Callie reaches for the thorn, now discarded on the edge of the sink, the wider end speckled with blood, but her mom gets to it first. Their gazes lock and hold. Again, the false smile.

"What is it?" Callie whispers.

"It's nothing. We don't need to talk about it. Everything's fine now."

"It isn't nothing. It was inside me, and I don't even know—"

"No one, not even Mia, can know about this." She grabs Callie's arm again, gives it a small shake. "Do you understand?"

"But—"

"Do. You. Understand?" Her fingers dig in deeper with each word.

Callie nods. "Will it happen again?"

Her mom flinches but leaves the bathroom without answering, taking the thorn with her. Callie rubs her arm, where her mom's grip left bright red fingermarks, and then her shoulder. She nudges the bathroom door shut with her foot and peels one end of the bandage free. The wound, already beginning to scab, looks normal, as far as scratches go. What scares her more than the unanswered questions, the strange anger, or what she thinks she heard, is that her mom was upset and angry, but she wasn't surprised. Not completely.

∿

Callie bounces the eraser end of her pencil on the kitchen table. Her homework is long finished, leftovers warmed and eaten. *Working late*, her mom's text message said. Callie wanted to talk to her this morning, but she was already gone when Callie woke up. As if *that* wasn't suspicious at all.

She runs her index finger across the bandage. What if another thorn pops out? What if it happens in school? What's she supposed to do, run out of class before anyone notices? Right.

She's already looked online. She found a couple of books with the words *girl* and *thorn* in their titles, including one she already has—and it has nothing to do with random thorns popping out of anyone's skin —and a bunch of tattoo pictures. She didn't really expect to find anything saying hey, here's what you do when thorns start growing out of your skin, but it would've been nice to find *something*.

If her dad were still here, she knows she could talk to him about it. He wouldn't brush her off or treat her like a little kid (or pretend a thorn was nothing major, nothing to talk about); he never did. Chest aching, she rests her head atop folded arms on the table, thumbing the edge of her open sketch pad. She misses the way he hugged her at night before bed, the way they'd sit next to each other on the sofa reading. She misses hearing his voice, misses hearing him call her *punkin*. She doesn't miss the fights he had with her mom, or the way he worked late a lot, and maybe he didn't talk to her as much when things got really bad, but that wasn't her fault. You don't divorce your kids. You *don't*.

She cocks her head closer to the wound. Listens. After a few minutes, she makes a face. What was she expecting anyway? Whatever she thought she heard was probably her imagination. She pulls off the bandage, digs her thumbnail in, and hisses in pain as she scrapes off the scab. No matter what her mom said, she wants a scar. There *should* be a scar.

When her mom finally comes home, she's wearing her I-had-a-bad-day-at-the-office-and-hate-everyone face, and her eyes are still draped with the hard, flinty veil, so Callie keeps her mouth shut. Even though she worked late, her mom's makeup is perfect and her clothes aren't wrinkled. She's all high cheekbones, sharp comma collarbones, and fair hair where Callie's round-cheeked, soft and dark, her eyes a touch too far apart, her mouth a little too wide. Maybe not ugly, but not pretty, not like her mom. She doesn't really resemble her dad either. One time he joked that she was the mailman's child, and her mom got mad and didn't talk to him for the rest of the day. Callie thought it was funny but knew better than to say so.

~

*H*i, Dad, it's me, Callie. Um, school's going good I guess. I hope your new job is too. Is it really warm there? Do you get to go and swim in the ocean? Probably not because you're so busy with work, but I would if I were there, even if I were super busy. Anyway, I wanted to say I love you and I miss you. Call me back soon, okay?*

~

*C*allie sleeps late on Saturday morning, and when she goes downstairs, her mom's outside, still in her pajamas and robe, smoking a cigarette, something she only does when she's really stressed.

"Mom?"

She exhales a plume of smoke before she turns around. "What?"

"Can we talk about the, the ..." Callie lifts her shoulder, tips her chin in its direction.

Her mom shakes her head. "No."

"That's what you said last night and the night before and the night before that, you wouldn't even talk to me. Why can't we talk about it?"

"It's gone, isn't it? Go inside, Callie. There are waffles in the freezer."

"But I thought I heard—"

"Enough!"

She turns away but not before Callie sees her face twist into the angry mask. Callie stomps inside. All she wants is to know what's going on. Why can't her mom tell her the truth? She digs under the bandage again, not even wincing when she peels off what's left of the scab.

~

The wound leaves a small pink scar. Callie wears tank tops and keeps her hair in a ponytail, but if her mom notices the mark, she doesn't say a word. Not that she's said much of anything at all lately.

The house is way too quiet with only the two of them, as though her dad packed all the conversation in his suitcases and tucked the laughter and smiles in carefully taped boxes. Callie told her mom that once; she pursed her lips and said it was better than all the arguments.

Callie would rather have all the fighting in the world than the empty space where her dad should be.

~

Mia's mom brings them glasses of apple juice and grilled cheese sandwiches with the crusts cut off. When she leaves the bedroom, Callie and Mia both roll their eyes, but it doesn't stop them from eating or drinking.

Mia flops on her stomach, crumbs stuck to her lower lip. "Did you see Vivica today?"

"Yeah, why?"

"Her cousin pierced her cartilage, here." Mia points at the top curve of her ear. "Her mom apparently had a fit and grounded her for forever, but she let her keep the earring in. Isn't that dumb?"

Callie shrugs. "It's Vivica's ear. If *she* likes it ..."

"My mom would kill me, and yours would kill you, too. Hey, what's this?" She pulls a sheet of paper out of Callie's math book. "Did you draw it?"

"Yeah, but it's nothing really." Callie says, pinching the inside of her cheek between her teeth. The drawing shows a girl with thorns on her shoulders and arms. Thorns big enough to impale someone with.

Mia traces the figure's outline. "She's cool. Is she a superhero or a villain? Are those things part of her costume or part of her?"

"I don't know. She's just something I made up. I wasn't really thinking about it."

"She looks bad-ass, like Black Widow, only better. You should totally draw more. Maybe make a real comic with her, and the spikes should be part of her, not just her costume."

"Whatever. Can I have it back? I need to get home."

"But it's early."

Callie tucks the drawing in her book. "Yeah, but I told my mom I'd do some laundry before she got home." She keeps her eyes downcast so Mia won't see the lie within.

"Bor-ing."

"Better boring than my mom pissed off," Callie says.

She takes her time walking home, not that it matters much; Mia only lives two streets away. Callie passes a bunch of little kids playing on a front lawn, their mothers watching from the porch. On her street, Will Brecht is riding his bikes in lazy figure eights from sidewalk to driveway. He's her age, but he goes to private school. Their dads were friends, but their moms, not so much.

Her phone buzzes and as she's pulling it out of her pocket, it slips and tumbles into the grass. Insects dance from neck to tailbone, and the tip of a thorn emerges on the inside of her wrist.

"Oh," she whispers. "Oh, no."

It doesn't hurt, but it's bigger than the first one—half the length of her thumb and nearly as wide—and it looks sharper, too. The creeping in her back grows stronger, radiating out to her shoulder blades.

"Callie, you okay?"

She blinks in the sunlight, hears a low sound coming from deep in her throat. Will is on his bike in front of her, his face screwed up in confused amusement.

She blinks again and shivers. "Just dropped my phone."

"You sure?"

"Yeah."

Will bikes away, casting several glances over his shoulder that she pretends not to see, and she forces herself not to run. Once safely inside her house, she drops both phone and backpack on the kitchen floor and half-sits, half-falls, into a chair, shaking. Pinching the thorn between finger and thumb, she gives it a tug. Hisses in a breath. A tiny drop of blood appears at one corner, but the thorn stays put.

Freak, freak, freak, she thinks. But another part of her, a secret voice deep inside, says, no, not a freak. Something else. Something different. Maybe even something better. She barks a laugh. Right.

She texts her mom: *It happened again. Will Brecht almost saw it. Now will you talk to me?*

I'll be home as soon as I can, comes the reply. *Stay inside until then.*

What does she think Callie's going to do? Run around showing it off to the neighbors?

When her mom rushes in and sees the thorn, her face turns inscrutable. (But at least it's not angry.) Callie has the tweezers, a bandage, and the ointment already on the table. Good little soldiers awaiting their mission.

Her mom starts humming. This time, Callie watches the whole process. Her mom doesn't yank the thorn out straight, but bends it a little to the side, pulling hard enough that her knuckles turn white. Callie swallows the pain and hears the not-voice again. It's as quiet as the echo of a whisper, but it's definitely not her imagination. As soon as the thorn is completely out, it falls silent.

"Mom, what *is* that? What's wrong with me?"

Her mom exhales sharply, wipes away the blood, and applies ointment. "Nothing's wrong with you," she says, but the words sound as though she's choking on them.

"Yes there is. I have thorns. I'd call that something super wrong. Am I sick? Dying?"

"No, you're not sick." She puts on the bandage. Scoops up the paper tabs and the thorn. "And you're not dying. It's not like that."

"So what is it then? I'm not a kid anymore, and I have a right to know."

"All you need to know is that they have to come out, and that eventually they'll stop."

"When?"

"I don't know. A few years maybe."

Callie snorts, knowing her mom hates it when she does. "So I'm supposed to what, not worry about it for a few years? Not say anything? I mean I can't ask anybody else when *their* thorns stopped, right?"

Her mom grabs her arm, even tighter than she did the first night. "You can't say anything to *anyone*. Do you understand me?"

Callie yanks her arm away. Stands so fast the chair clatters to the floor. "Right. Say nothing, and what if it happens when I'm in school or with Mia? Still say nothing? Be a good girl and run home to Mommy? I bet Dad would talk to me about it. I bet *he'd* tell me the truth."

Her mom makes a sound that's half-sob, half-laugh, and Callie races upstairs, slamming her bedroom door shut behind her, frustration snot-thick in her throat. She stays in her room the rest of the night, ignoring her mom when she calls her for dinner.

Funny how she doesn't call a second time.

～

When the second wound begins to heal, Callie scratches it open so it will scar, too. "Hello?" she whispers when blood starts to flow, but the only thing she hears is the wet scritch of the scab tearing free.

～

Callie's in Mr. Andersen's English class when the third thorn emerges, just below her navel. Still shivery, she reaches beneath her t-shirt, pretending to scratch. The thorn feels smaller than the others, but it's still razor-sharp. A sound creeps into her throat; she shoves it down before it can escape. She should ask to be excused and call her mom, but she doesn't. No one can see the thorn where it is, plus she has a science test after lunch and making it up will be a pain. Fear traces a cold spiral on the nape of her neck, but it doesn't feel terrible. Not exactly.

When she gets home, her mom texts that she has to work late. Once she *does* get home, Callie thinks about telling her, but when she opens her mouth the only thing that comes out is a short, clipped, "Hello."

～

H i, Dad. It's me, Callie. I, um, I know you're busy with work and stuff, but maybe you can call me when you're not so busy? I miss you a lot. A whole lot.

～

O ne day turns into two; two turns into three. The thorn doesn't grow any larger, doesn't change color, doesn't do anything except force her to sleep on her side instead of her stomach. She's careful to wear loose-fitting t-shirts and lower slung jeans. Careful, too, not to touch her abdomen when her mom's around.

On the fourth day, Saturday, her mom's sitting at the kitchen table, hands curved around a coffee mug. On the placemat: tweezers, a bandage, ointment. Callie pretends not to see them, but her heart beats heavy and her palms go damp. She opens the refrigerator, takes out the orange juice.

"Where is it?" her mom asks.

"What?" Callie says over her shoulder, as she pulls out a glass.

"Don't play dumb with me, Callie. Where is it? I know it's somewhere. I can see it in your eyes. I can—"

"What?"

"Don't do this. Where is it?"

Callie digs impressions of her front teeth into her lower lip, turns around, and lifts her shirt.

"When did it happen?"

"Yesterday." Callie averts her eyes.

"Yesterday when?"

"I don't know. After dinner sometime."

"After dinner."

"Uh-huh."

"So last night, not just yesterday. I was here after dinner, so why didn't you say something?"

Callie shrugs her scarred shoulder.

"This isn't a game, Callie. You have no idea what could happen."

"How could I since you won't tell me?"

Her mom's mouth goes all lemon pucker, but she doesn't say anything, just picks up the tweezers with shaking hands. "No, don't sit down, stand there and hold still."

Callie crosses her arms, glaring at her mother as she kneels.

"What were you thinking? I told you they had to come out."

It's Callie's turn not to answer, but it's a short-lived victory. Her mom hums and the tweezers tug, the pain bright and sharp. Callie squirms, biting back a yelp. The voice, if it *is* a voice, whispers something low and unintelligible.

"Hold still a minute more. There."

The end of the thorn glistens with Callie's blood and something that resembles an eyelash thin tail. Her mom's gaze darkens. "Are you sure it was last night?"

"Yes Mom, it was last night." Callie punctuates her words with a roll of the eyes. "So will you tell me now what's really going on?"

Her mom wraps the thorn in a napkin and tucks it in her pocket. Covers the wound with the ointment and bandage. "No, you're too young."

"Right. But I'm not too young to have it happen. It isn't fair not to tell me, and it isn't fair for you to be all pissed off about it when I don't even know what's wrong."

"We are not having this discussion. I've told you everything you need to know."

"You've told me nothing."

"And that's all you need to know."

"I heard it. The voice. Who does it belong to? Where is—"

"You heard nothing."

"I bet if Dad were here—"

"Well, he isn't. He left us."

"No, he left *you*, Mom."

"Oh, honey. He left us both." Her mom looks as though she wants to say something else, but she closes her mouth, shakes her head.

"He's busy, that's all!" Callie says. "He'll call me once he isn't. I know he will."

Her mom reaches out, but Callie moves before she can make contact. She storms from the kitchen and stomps up the stairs as hard as she can. Her dad did *not* leave her. *She* wasn't the one who argued with him all the time. *She* wasn't the problem.

∾

When the final bell rings at school, the hallways become a river choked with broken branches. Callie pushes through the crowd to her locker with Mia at her heels.

"Are you okay?" Mia asks.

"Yeah, why?"

"I don't know, you just seem different, that's all."

"Different how?"

"I don't know. Just different different."

"That's *so* helpful."

"Sor-ry," Mia says.

Callie touches her abdomen, rubs the ridge of bandage there. "It's just stupid stuff with my mother."

"Want to come over and do homework?"

"Sure." Callie almost hopes a thorn shows up for Mia to see; then her mom will *have* to tell her the truth. But she thinks of the kids at school, what they'd say, what they'd do, and pulls a face.

Her mom's still at work when she gets home. Surprise, surprise. In the bathroom, she puts her nose close to the mirror. Thinks of Mia's words. Same old face in the mirror, though. Same Callie. And she isn't sure if she's hoping to see something else or not.

Instead of finishing her English homework, she draws another girl with thorns and uses a red pen to add drops of blood. When her mom finally comes home, she hides the picture in her underwear drawer.

All night, she catches her mom looking at her. Not regular looking, but looking too long and too hard, and Callie fights the urge to run and check the mirror again every time. She ends up retreating to her bedroom and runs her hands along her arms and legs and torso. Nothing out of place. Nothing different. No thorns.

~

U nable to fall asleep, Callie kicks off the sheets. Turns on her side. Flops on her stomach. Her mom's television is still on, which wouldn't be a big deal if she shut Callie's bedroom door after peeking in on her. (Callie could've told her to shut it, but she was pretending to be asleep.)

She climbs out of bed and pauses by the door to listen. It isn't the television. It's her mom. Callie creeps down the hall, careful to avoid the spot near the bathroom where the wood creaks. Her mom's door is open a tiny crack because the latch broke a month ago and Callie's dad's the one who always fixed stuff. Her mom's cross-legged on the bed, facing away from the door, a small box open beside her.

"Leave her alone," she says. "Please."

Someone—or something—speaks in return, too low for Callie to hear the words, but she recognizes the voice.

"You *can't*. She's all I have. She doesn't deserve this. Please let her go, let us both go."

Another response Callie can't hear. Her mom drops something into the box, closes the lid, and gets up, box in hand. Callie retreats to her room, her arms all over goosebumps while anger threads through her veins.

Why does the voice want her? *What* does it want? And why won't her mom tell her the truth?

~

After school, Callie drops her backpack on the kitchen table and heads to her mom's bedroom. There used to be a framed picture of Callie and her dad on the dresser, and another one of her parents together, both wearing Mardi Gras beads and wide smiles, but the pictures are gone now, only odd empty spots hinting they'd ever been there at all.

One by one, she opens the dresser drawers, checking underneath the clothes and in the corners, being as careful as possible not to mess anything up. There's nothing under the bed but storage boxes full of winter clothes. She finds things in her mom's nightstand she'd rather not see and slams the drawer shut, her cheeks flaming.

One side of the closet contains her mom's clothes; the other, only a few white plastic hangers her dad left behind. An empty suitcase, winter boots, and a box of old photographs of her mom as a child sit on the top shelf. Callie huffs out a breath and crosses her arms, tapping the nearest shoe box with her toes and dislodging the top, revealing not shoes but more old photos. The box next to it holds shoes, as does the one next to that, but in the far corner, almost buried by the hems of hanging dresses, she finds another with photos in it and hidden under the pictures, a small wooden box that rattles when she shakes it.

Inside, resting on the bottom, are the thorns. But there's too many, way too many. No voice, though. Only a brittle clacking as the thorns slide over and around each other.

She scoots out of the closet and dumps the thorns on the floor. They're all varying sizes and shades, all sharp. There's a wet shimmer on the bottom edge of one, and her finger comes away streaked with red. She's pretty sure it's blood, but no way she's going to taste it to check.

It isn't one of her thorns, of that she's sure. Hers are a different color. Only one, the one from her abdomen, has the little tail and her stomach twinges. She takes the thorn that came from her wrist, easy to tell because it's so big, and lowers it to her skin, lining the edges with the scar.

The weird feeling takes hold of her spine, and the scar opens, with neither blood nor vein within but a vast darkness. The space between the almost-connection wavers; the voice drifts into the air. A lullaby, a promise of something else. The sensation in her back intensifies, hot and cold at the same time, a touch shy of pleasure, a whisper from pain. The voice gathers weight, its presence in the air a strong perfume, and then it whispers her name.

She cries out and pulls the thorn free. For one long moment, it won't come loose, tethered by an invisible force, and for an even longer moment, she doesn't want it to. Then it gives way, as though severed with a blade. She rocks on her heels, and her skin closes, the scar exactly as it was. Heart pounding, she balls up one of her mom's scarves and uses it to sweep all the thorns into the box.

Did the other ones come from her mom? If so, she has to know what they mean. And why would she keep them if they were so bad? Callie rubs her wrist, then yanks her hand away, afraid her skin will open again and swallow *her* up.

～

*H*i, Dad. It's Callie again. I guess, I guess just call me back when you can? I really miss you. Oh, and there's something really important I want to talk to you about. Mom won't tell me anything, and I know you will, even if you don't really know. Just call me, okay? Pretty please?

～

*C*allie's washing her hair when her fingers find the thorn in her scalp. Her hands drop to her sides. She last washed her hair two days ago, and this morning when she brushed it, the bristles caught on what she thought was a tangle. Has the thorn been there the whole time? She didn't feel it come in, didn't feel anything strange at all. She rinses out the rest of the shampoo without touching her hair, and pads to her mom's room clad only in a towel, tweezers in hand.

"I have another one."

Her mom's mouth works, but nothing comes out. She nods, scrubs her face with her hands. "Let me have the tweezers."

"Not until you tell me what they are."

"Callie, it's late and you have school tomorrow. We don't have time for this."

"It isn't that late."

"Maybe this weekend ..."

"Right, and I'm supposed to believe that?"

"Callie—"

"Tell me what they are, what they mean! Just tell me this one time, and I won't ask again!"

Her mom's shoulders slump. "They don't mean anything."

"I don't believe you. If that was true, then you wouldn't be so upset."

"I'll tell you this much," her mom says, mouse-whisker quiet. "If we leave them in, they'll change you. They'll destroy you. Please, no more questions tonight. Let me take it out and have done with it."

Callie bites the inside of her lip hard enough to draw blood, but she keeps her mouth shut while her mom parts her hair.

"We won't be able to put a bandage on it, but it's a small one so it should be okay."

"Fine."

Humming tunelessly, her mom yanks out the thorn, and the voice whispers one word: *Liar.* Her mom's mouth tightens for a brief moment and her cheeks turn pink, but she says nothing at all.

~

The letter from her mom to her dad is marked *Return to Sender.* Callie traces her dad's name on the envelope, knowing she shouldn't open it, but her mom won't ever know if she rips it in little pieces and buries them in the trash afterward. She carries the letter to her room. Shuts and locks the door.

Michael:

For the record, Callie still doesn't know the truth. She wouldn't be trying to call you if she did. If I'd known this was the way things would end up, I would've told her from the beginning that you were her stepfather.

I know I said I didn't want you involved in her life, but I was angry. We both said a lot of hurtful things. I never thought you'd take off and move away.

What you're doing is cruel. She loves you. You're the only father she's ever had.

Lydia

Callie rocks back and forth on her bed, holding the letter to her chest. It can't be true. It can't be. He *is* her dad. He's always been her dad. Her mom's lying, like she is about the thorns. Sobbing, she calls her dad, but he doesn't answer—he's busy with his stupid job and she hates hates hates it—and she's crying too hard to leave a message this time.

She wipes her eyes, hides the letter between her mattress and box spring, pushing it way into the middle, and races into her mom's room. When she returns, she has a thorn pinched between thumb and index finger. With her door locked again, she holds the thorn above the scar on her wrist until the space between wavers and her skin opens.

"Tell me what you are. Tell me the truth," she whispers into the darkness. "Please."

~

On Friday nights, Callie's mom always drinks two glasses of wine to unwind. Callie pulls the stopper from the half-empty bottle in the fridge and pours in the sleeping pills she pilfered from the medicine cabinet at Mia's house and crushed with a meat tenderizer. She only took two; she doesn't want to hurt her mom, just make sure she goes to sleep, and she doesn't know how quickly they work. In the movies they work in an instant, so her mom might never get to the second glass.

After dinner, her mom pours a glass before she dons her pajamas and curls on the sofa with a book. Callie sits on the other end, her own book in hand, sneaking peeks from the corner of her eye. When the glass is nearly empty, Callie extends a hand. "I'm going to make popcorn. Want me to refill your glass?"

"Yes, thank you." Her mom sounds sleepy, but Callie can't tell if it's regular sleepy or not.

Some of the pill dust has settled to the bottom of the wine bottle, and Callie shakes it until it's all mixed up again. Still awake, her mom takes a sip when Callie gives her the glass, makes a small face, but takes a second sip a few minutes later.

When the glass is still two-thirds full, her mom touches a hand to her forehead, darts a look, her lids heavy and her brow creased, at Callie. Callie tosses popcorn in her mouth, tries to pretend it's an ordinary night.

"Callie? What ..." her mom says, her words slurred.

Her eyelids flutter shut. Callie tosses the bowl of popcorn on the table and runs upstairs. When she returns, her mom is still asleep, her mouth slightly open. Callie's hands shake as she lifts her mom's pajama top. There, on the skin of her abdomen, almost hidden by the faint tracery of stretch marks, are tiny scars. The voice told the truth.

She takes a thorn from the box and holds it above her mother's skin, moving it slowly from side to side. One of the scars opens, revealing the same darkness Callie saw in her own. She hesitates a moment and the voice says, "Don't worry."

Her mom's eyes open. She tries to lift one hand, but it flops back down. "Callie? What are you doing?"

Callie sets the thorn in place, grabs another. "They said you'd be okay. They said if I did this, they'd leave me alone."

"No, oh, no," her mom says, her words tangled and thick. "They only tell you what they want you to hear. Listen to me ..." Her head lolls against the sofa cushion, and a soft moan slips from her lips even as her eyes close once more. Callie continues to return each thorn to its proper place. When the box is empty, her mom moans again, louder this time, and her mouth works. "You have to, to take them out before ..."

Callie bites the side of her finger. The air fills with a low hum punctuated with small cracks. Her mom's body twitches. Her eyelids snap open and inside them, neither iris nor pupil, only an oily, moving darkness. The thorns begin to grow, twisting into knots as they extend into vines, and Callie scrambles off the couch, her heart racing. This isn't right. This isn't what the voice said would happen. She grabs for her mom, almost touches her, but the vines split once, twice, three times, waving in the air as though caught in a breeze and pushing her hand away.

They wrap around her mother's limbs and torso with the sound of sandpaper on stone, and it doesn't take long before her mother is completely covered. And still the vines twist and grow.

"Mom!" Callie shrieks. "Make it stop!"

She didn't know. Her mom has to believe that. She didn't know. She tries to grab the vines, but they slither from her grasp. The tips melt into the air, creating a dark outline, like a doorway to somewhere else. Her mom's hand breaks free from the brambles, and their fingertips touch.

"Hold on, Mom. I—"

Callie hears a cry, a muffled *hurry*, and the vines make one last twist. The black rushes in, Callie's ears pop, and then her mom is gone. The black hangs in the air, vaguely human-shaped, then it vanishes, too.

"I didn't know. I'm sorry, so sorry. Come back, Mom, okay? I want you to come back."

She sinks to the floor, tears coursing down her cheeks. No. Everything will be fine. She'll fix it. She'll make it right. She holds a thorn against her wrist.

"You have to give her back," she says. "Please, I want my mom. Please give her back."

But the scar remains shut, the voice silent.

～

We're sorry, the number you're trying to reach has been disconnected. Please check the number and try your call again.

NOT MY CIRCUS, NOT MY MONKEYS:
THE ELEPHANT'S TALE

*L*adies *and Gentlemen, Children of All Ages ...*
Every circus has a story, and every story has its secrets. Those of us taxed with bearing the burden of such things do so with no sense of pleasure, only duty. We remember so that others, in time, may forget.

I.

Here, the music: a calliope. The notes instantly recognizable; the tune age-old and clichéd. The instrument itself, its brass pipes pitted and dark, is carried within an open-sided wagon, the wheels painted in once bright shades of yellow and red. There is no way to adjust the volume, so the music is always too loud, too brash.

I've always hated the sound. It brings to mind the sharp pain of a cattle prod, the shouts, the forcing of my cumbersome body into positions it wasn't meant to hold. And for what? The momentary pleasure of others, the applause, the indignity? All small cruelties of a life lived in captivity.

But we are all captives in one way or another.

And so the spotlight swings a great arc, back and forth, back and forth, until it stops to reveal:

The Ringmaster:

Time has left his top hat with a curious, half-deflated appearance, and there's a tiny V missing from the brim. If you ask, he'll blame a Siberian tiger with an incompetent handler. The truth is, he'd indulged in too much popcorn and tripped up the steps, but to admit that would be to concede fallibility and appearances are paramount. Always.

He's taken to sneaking a handful of kernels in the morning, carefully brushing his teeth afterward to remove the evidence from his teeth. At night he doesn't bother to hide such things. He's in charge of the Big Top after all, and if the red and white stripes on the tent are dull, if the fabric is frayed at the edges, it's no one's business but his own.

The Contortionist:

Pale and lachrymose, she never stays still. She flits from one room, one space, to another, leaving a trail of glitter behind. Her fingers are always on the verge of trembling; her lips hold an apology at the ready. For nothing. For everything.

She rarely speaks and when she does, her voice is high-pitched, her words either sharp enough to leave marks on the recipient or light enough to drift in the air like wisps of cotton candy. When she catches a glimpse of her reflection, she jumps, unsure who the face belongs to but unable to remain still long enough to peer behind the silvered mask.

The Mirror Twins, Acrobats Extraordinaire:

Two girls of fifteen, long of limbs and torsos, wide eyes in elfin faces. The eldest twin (by a mere three minutes) has a tiny mole on her right cheek; the youngest has the same on her left.

They slip and glide through hallways and rooms, their feet making no noise whatsoever, something they've spent their lives perfecting. They exist in their own sphere, a small ring within the larger whole. They share a bedroom they've painted pale green and do their best to avoid the Ringmaster, having learned all too well the sting of his whip when he's reminiscing. They wear matching scars on the backs of their thighs when they were unaware he was still awake one night. But they were younger then and not so careful.

The twins see the Contortionist in passing, but the passage of time has turned those meetings into small, unhappy accidents. They can't bear to see the way she folds her body, the way her joints seem boneless. (And she cannot bear to see her own failure in their eyes.)

The Animals:

Me, a scarred beast with broken tusks. I keep to myself in the corners, sleeping most of the time. In truth, I've not the energy for much else, but even when I sleep, I'm aware of the performers around me. I see and hear everything, even the secret thoughts not meant to be shared.

On my back I carry a gilded cage, filled with dark, shadowy shapes, nebulous things you can only see from the corner of your eye. Best not to look too long or too hard. Best to forget about me; best to let me tend to the business of remembering.

The tiger sharpens its claws on the linoleum in the kitchen and the legs of the dining room table. It sleeps in patches of sunlight, but it never sleeps unaware, and if you step too close it will remind you it still has teeth.

The tiger neither remembers nor forgets. That's not his job. The tiger merely *is*. A beast and nothing more.

And now we come to the monkeys. They're fractious, as monkeys often are, sneaky, and prone to throwing shit when the whim strikes. Their greatest fear is to be forgotten—how many circuses have you attended where the monkeys take the center ring? Relegated to the places just out of the spotlight's reach, they never get such an honor, but you can hear them, chattering and shuffling about and scratching the fleas from their fur.

Even when you can't see them, the monkeys are always there.

A confession: When I was young, before the stripes on the tent began to fade, I tried to crush the monkeys beneath my feet, but they were too fast.

Other Acts:

Occasionally the clowns arrive, jumping free from their impossibly tiny car. Cue the wide smiles, the laughter, but as time goes by, they appear less and less, and more times than not, when they pile back into the car, one clown doesn't fit and is left behind. He'll sit on the back porch, smoking a cigarette and wiping the grin from his mouth with a dirty bandana before he hitches his pants and heads off, drawn, no doubt, to a more appreciative circuit.

The magician and his assistant stop by here and there, pulling flowers from sleeves and rabbits from hats. (The tattered paper blossoms shed their petals within moments. The tiger eats the rabbits before they can multiply.) The magician speaks in theatrical cadence; the assistant in a girlish voice at odds with the deep lines bracketing her eyes and mouth. Sometimes they bring giant lollipops for the twins or a bag of peanuts for the Ringmaster. They never bring anything for the Contortionist, and they never stay very long.

II.

The Ringmaster spends most of his nights slouched on the sofa. The tuxedo he wears no longer fits properly: the buttons strain; the seams are a deep breath away from splitting their threads; the satin cummerbund, a water-stained and faded shade of once-crimson, cuts a divot into his body; the matching bow tie nowhere in sight.

When I was a lion tamer, he says, holding tight to a tattered whip. His words are slurry and disjointed, and he doesn't finish the sentence. He rarely does, preferring the sharp snap of leather to fill in the missing spaces.

He gobbles popcorn by rote, ignoring the pieces that spill down his front. His eyes glaze over, but he keeps chewing. When he can't eat any more, he stands on unsteady feet and bows, sweeping the hat from his head in a grandiose manner. Only then does he truly smile, the expression bearing an uncanny resemblance to the tiger's maw.

The Contortionist curves her body away from the smile, but she's never quite fast enough and her apology spills atop the popcorn. A second too late for that as well. She closes her eyes and thinks of a young woman she once knew, a woman who danced with a bear. She thinks perhaps the performance ended badly, but if so, at least it ended.

The monkeys shriek, and the tiger bares its claws, its eyes gleaming. I want to intervene. I want to wrap my trunk around the Ringmaster and squeeze every drop of life from his body, but I know it isn't my place. Maybe if I were younger or stronger, I'd do it anyway.

In their room, the twins exchange a glance and cast their eyes down, pretending they don't hear a thing.

Tomorrow will be better, the youngest says. And when we have our own circus, it will be different. The eldest says nothing, simply shakes her head.

When the eldest twin thinks the youngest is asleep, she peels the sequins from her body, wincing at the sting, but even when her eyes fill with tears, she wears a smile. Each bit of pain means she is a little more her, a little less them. (Most of the time, she doesn't consider her sister part of *them*.)

When the eldest falls asleep, the youngest creeps from her bed and gathers the discarded sequins. One at a time, she places them on her own skin, overlapping them to conceal the spots that have lost their shine.

The twins share almost everything, but they never speak of the sequins.

Intermission

The pole in the center of the tent takes on a lean.
　　　The tiger stretches and lets out a noxious cloud of gas.
The monkeys hoot softly to each other.
And the weight on my back grows heavier still.

II. ...Continued

The Ringmaster stands atop his chair and brandishes his whip. His voice reaches out and up, demanding attention. I was the greatest performer on earth, he says. Now look where I am. Look at this. Look at *you*.

The Contortionist curls into a tiny ball, rolling this way and that to avoid the frayed end of the whip, but it catches her about the ankle and the Ringmaster slowly reels her in. She tries to think of the dancing bear again, but she knows—even when she pretends not to—that performance ended with an accident and blood, so she scrambles for the edge of the safety net and holds on, holds on, holds on.

The tiger roars, the monkeys screech and beat their chests, and the twins cower in their room, covering their ears. The youngest cries; the eldest refuses.

I'm reminded of the ropes, the bullhooks, the electric shocks. A sense of desperation, of knowing that while this won't last, it will never end.

When the house finally quiets, the eldest twin plucks the last sequin from her arm and opens the bedroom window. She holds out her hand, but the youngest has too many sequins and cannot move.

You can't go, the youngest says.

I have to, the eldest says. *We* have to. Please.

The youngest frowns. But we belong here, she says.

If you believe that, you're no better than they are, her sister says.

In that moment, the youngest sees not her mirror image but a stranger. The eldest opens her mouth to speak again but decides against it and slips over the windowsill. The youngest crawls to the window and watches as the eldest disappears into the shadows. She opens her mouth to scream her sister back, to bring her home, but her mouth is filled with sawdust instead of a voice.

I know she doesn't understand, but her sister was afraid that after the last sequin was gone, she'd keep plucking, peeling herself away until there was nothing left.

Captivity breaks us in different ways. Nevertheless, it breaks us all in the end.

III.

The Ringmaster says nothing of the eldest twin's disappearance, merely snarls. The Contortionist weeps, wipes her tears, and weeps some more. The monkeys caper about in graceless figure eights. The youngest twin moves slowly, her limbs no longer flexible. She doesn't yet know the choreography of a solo act and is terrified at the prospect. She finds a few sequins beneath the eldest twin's pillow and tucks them beneath her own, to give back to her sister upon her return. (For of course she'll return, she thinks.) At night, she keeps vigil at the window, her hands tucked beneath her chin, her thoughts drowning out the sound of the Ringmaster and his whip.

One morning, she discovers the Ringmaster still and silent in his chair, surrounded by half-chewed bits of popcorn, the whip coiled on the floor. The Contortionist appears a few minutes later and comes to a stop for the first time in years. The two stare at each other for a long time, and even the monkeys are curiously silent.

If I could speak, I'd tell them the Ringmaster died with an unfinished word on his lips, but they might wish to believe it an apology instead of a curse. Is a final word even important if no one hears? Is a final apology meaningful if every preceding action says otherwise?

The youngest twin realizes the tiger is gone, leaving behind only a steaming pile of dung. She cleans up the mess and uses a small throw rug to cover the stain.

(I saw the tiger leave, too, his services no longer required. I was glad to see both beasts go.)

The magician and his assistant arrive, sans flowers or lollipops. They don't mention the absence of the tiger, but they speak in strangely hushed voices, the assistant constantly dabbing her eyes with a handkerchief, until the Contortionist tells them to leave. Then they shout and stomp their feet—and a rabbit tries to crawl from within the folds of the handkerchief—but they finally leave.

The youngest twin never sees them again.

In the weeks that follow, she finds the Contortionist curled up on the top shelf of the closet, next to a box labeled *Our Wedding*; beneath the kitchen table, clutching an empty popcorn container; and sitting atop the closed lid of the toilet, clad in an old robe, holding the whip on her lap and whispering that the show must go on.

But when the youngest twin tries to talk to her, she doesn't even acknowledge her presence.

Second Intermission

The pole continues to lean.

One side of the tent partially collapses, spitting a plume of dust into the air. A tiny bit of sunshine creeps in through a tear in the fabric.

The clowns wait at the far end of the tent, holding red rubber balls in hand, hoping they'll have a chance to resurrect their act. If there's ever been a chance to recapture the laughter, surely it's now.

Then the Contortionist sews the rip shut with ugly, uneven stitches, and the clowns make their exit, leaving behind a smudge of greasepaint and one oversized shoe.

The monkeys race in mad circles, kicking up clouds of sawdust in their wake.

And I remember even as I wish to forget.

III. ...Continued

The Contortionist leaves for a day and when she returns, she isn't alone. The Strongman doesn't speak to the youngest twin, nor she to him. It doesn't matter because he isn't strong enough and a few weeks later, he's gone. The youngest notices that another monkey has joined the crew; this one is sullen and simply glares at her as if his existence is her fault. The other monkeys keep their distance from the newcomer because his smell is questionable.

The Contortionist brings home The Human Cannonball next and he *does* talk to the youngest, but his eyes are too bright, his speech far too animated, and the Contortionist seems to move faster than she ever has.

The Human Cannonball doesn't linger too long either.

After the Fire-Eater and the Daredevil, or perhaps he was only a Sword Swallower in disguise, come and go, the Contortionist stays in her bedroom for three weeks straight. The youngest twin leaves food on a tray outside the closed door, but she's never sure who really eats it. She suspects the monkeys.

She's right.

The Fire-Eater left behind two things: a bruise on the Contortionist's cheek that turned a sickening shade of yellow-green before it disappeared completely, and a leopard. The leopard neither changes color nor does it vanish. The scrawny beast sits curled in a ball beside the refrigerator and bares its teeth from time to time, but it ignores the youngest twin. She ignores it as well.

She retreats to her own room, closes her eyes, and talks to her sister, pretending everything is as it was, even though she knows the show has been wrong for a long time and was even before her sister's defection, yet at least she knew the rules and regulations.

Her sequins begin to fall with each breath, each step. She picks them up, but they no longer stick to her skin, and, eventually, she leaves them on the floor.

She finds a box of old marquee posters tucked away in an old cabinet. The posters contain no monkeys, no tiger, no elephant, only four smiling performers, their costumes perfect and new, the stripes on the tent behind them shining bright.

The youngest twin has no memory of such things, but she hangs one of the posters on her bedroom wall and pretends to remember.

The Grand Finale

Sometimes the youngest twin hears the Contortionist moving around, but she's erected her own tent and the youngest can't find the entry. She no longer whispers to the eldest at night, no longer believing in a return.

Wielding a chair in one hand and a broom in the other, she chases the leopard into the yard. She tosses bananas there, too, and when the last monkey tumbles out, she slams the door behind them and sweeps the sawdust from the floor.

In the morning, the leopard and the monkeys are back. Traces of sawdust, too.

She doesn't bother to try a second time; they're as much a part of this circus as she is, no matter who arrived first. She didn't invite them in, and she doesn't have the authority to cancel their acts.

She takes up juggling but can't keep the balls in the air; she tries using the light fixture in the dining room as a trapeze, but there's no one to catch her when she falls; she even finds the Ringmaster's top hat and tries it on, but it slips over her eyes.

The Contortionist remains inside her own tent.

The youngest twin takes the poster from her wall and tears it into confetti. She packs a bag and leaves the sequins under her pillow.

On her way out, she presses a kiss to my head and releases the buckles that hold the cage on my back. It falls, spilling its contents out in a dark pool. While I'm grateful for the release of the pressure against my spine, it doesn't matter whether I bear the cage or not. Some things, once carried, always linger. She'll understand this one day. But I nuzzle her hand in thanks nonetheless.

The monkeys try to follow her, but she shoos them back. You are not mine, she says. You are not mine. The leopard blocks her way, but she says, you are not mine either, and brandishes the broom until the cat pads away. She pauses by the Contortionist's tent to say goodbye, but her face falls, as if realizing the Contortionist already said goodbye a lifetime ago so she takes a deep breath and steps outside instead.

Yet she doesn't move for a long time. I feel her fear and know she's only a second away from returning, and it shames me to admit that I'm angered by her inability to move. This is not my circus, but I've been bound here by duty stronger than any chain. She has a chance to break her fetters, and I don't understand why she won't take it.

Then I see the tears cascading down her cheeks. I swallow my anger and rise, ignoring the creaks in my knees and the pain in my joints. I nudge her with my trunk, and she jumps, one hand pressed to her mouth. She bows her head against my side. I touch her again; she shakes her head.

I bend down, flick my ears, and nudge again, this time pulling her toward me. For a long moment, she does nothing; then she climbs on my back and I rise once more.

A sense of unease fills my belly. Who will bear witness to the Contortionist if not me? Who will mark the occasion when she finds the will to leave her tent?

I toe the ground with one foot. Perhaps the Contortionist needs no witness. Perhaps the end of her routine belongs to no audience save her own. Perhaps this is her way of breaking her own shackles.

The youngest twin sits with her back straight, her hands holding me tight, trusting that I won't let her fall, and so I walk. I'll carry her until she's strong enough to walk on her own, and I hope she'll never need to strap a cage to my back. But for now I'm content to move, to stretch my legs, to support her so she can hold her head high. We are no longer captives, she and I, but willing participants.

The spotlight narrows its beam and follows as we head away from the Big Top, and when we step beyond the light's reach, the music, the dreaded, endless calliope, finally, finally, comes to a stop.

THE JUDAS CHILD

A kid in a baseball cap and a Ninja Turtles t-shirt is sitting on the park bench, swinging his legs. The boy stands off to the side until he's sure there are no grown-ups nearby, and then he flops down on the bench, hiding his misshapen left hand while pretending to pick a scab from his knee with the other. Turtle leans forward, the hat's brim turning his eyes to shadow. The boy guesses he's eight, maybe, or close enough. Not too skinny either and that's good. The monster doesn't like it when they're skinny.

"Did you get hurt?" Turtle asks, his gaze skimming the scars on the boy's arms and legs.

Even faded with the passage of time, the scars are ugly and pitted, as though his flesh was repeatedly gouged with a small ice-cream scoop. The boy used to try and hide them, but not anymore. "I was in a car accident," he says.

"Did it hurt?"

"A lot." The boy peers over both shoulders. The park is still empty save for the two of them, and best of all, it's surrounded by bushes and trees. The branches sway in the breeze, rattling like a knocked-over pile of bones. In between flashes of green and brown, he catches glimpses of small brick houses with wrought iron-railed concrete

porches and brightly painted front doors. It's probably a nice neighborhood, a place where people have parties and cookouts in back yards,
where they walk their dogs on the sidewalks and nobody gets mad.

Once he took a dog, a skinny thing he found eating out of a trash
can, to the monster, but it ripped the trembling animal into pieces,
roared in the boy's face, and squeezed his hand until it crackled and
popped like cereal in milk. Then it made him clean up the mess.

(It's hard to dig a hole with one hand, not much easier to fill it in.)

It's spring, which means Turtle should be in school. He doesn't
look sick, and if it were a holiday the park would be crowded and the
boy wouldn't be here. Questions linger on his tongue, but he swallows
them down. Best not to know. The answers wouldn't matter anyway.
"Want to see something neat?" he says, keeping his voice friendly but
low. Saying things the right way is important.

Turtle scrunches his face. "What is it?"

"A monster."

Turtle grins, revealing front teeth his mouth hasn't grown into yet.
"There's no such thing as monsters. Really, what is it?"

"What I said, a monster." The boy shrugs. "You don't have to
believe me if you don't want to." He stands, tucking his left hand in his
pocket, like a secret you don't want to share. "See you later, okay?"

"Wait," Turtle says. "Is it really a monster?"

"Yeah, but it's not really that exciting. It's dead and disgusting
and stuff."

"I don't care," Turtle says, slipping off the bench so fast he almost
slams into the boy. "I want to see it."

Kids always trust other kids. It's not the boy's fault that Turtle's
parents didn't teach him not to talk to strangers. None of it's his fault.

～

When the boy was nine, a crack in the earth opened and he fell
in. He didn't know there was a monster waiting at the
bottom, but it wouldn't have mattered. The monster was clever. It
built its lair in such a way that it only took one misstep. The boy fell

end over end, scraping knees and elbows and chin along the way, and landed hard with all the breath knocked out of him. That's why he didn't scream right away. He couldn't. Then he got a good look at the monster, at the ink-stain scales, the whip-thin tail, the ragged, filthy claws, the eyes the color of every nightmare that ever was, and all that emerged was a whispery little moan.

When the monster bared its teeth, yellow and chipped and crusted dark at the gum line, the boy found his voice. He tried to get away. He did. He should've tried harder, should've screamed louder, but he was only nine and small for his age. No match for a monster the size of five men. He never stood a chance.

Its teeth were in his skin and his flesh was sliding down its gullet before the boy could scream a second time. He thought it had bitten off his whole hand, but it had only taken the very tip of the pinkie finger on his left hand.

(That was long before the squeezing.)

Its jaws snapped again, taking a piece from his right arm, just below his elbow. It moved closer still and the boy shielded his face with his arms, sick to his stomach at the shock and pain, the smell of blood and the sticky feel of it soaking through his clothes.

The monster nudged his arms away with its snout and opened its mouth wide enough to reveal shreds of the boy between its teeth and worse, old skin, not the boy's, that smelled rotten and foul.

The boy said, "Please don't hurt me anymore." His words hung in the air for a long time before the monster made a low, choking sound. It sounded like a laugh, and then it sounded like a cough. But mostly like a laugh.

Then the beast gathered him in its horrible arms, scales scraping skin wherever they came in contact, and the boy knew it was going to keep biting him until there was nothing left, so he closed his eyes and hoped it wouldn't hurt too much.

It carried him through tunnel after tunnel, deeper and ever deeper into the earth, the boy crying and bleeding the entire way. When they reached a large circular cave with a low ceiling, the monster dropped him onto the dirt floor, curled up in front of the entrance, and went to sleep, its gravelly snores—so much louder than his dad's—filling every crack and every corner.

The boy scooted as far away as possible, his back pressed hard against the rough wall. Although he was deep underground, his parents would find him. Grown-ups could do anything. He was sure of it. He just had to be brave until then.

He pressed the base of his hands against his eyes so the tears wouldn't leak out. He hoped his parents hurried up because he wanted to go home. He missed the *Star Wars* poster on his bedroom wall, his Transformers, his mom's homemade chocolate chip cookies. He even missed the way his dad always burned everything he cooked on the grill, but that made him think of skin and fat and teeth and his head went swimmy. But everything would be okay. He'd go to sleep and when he woke up, his parents would be there and the monster would be under arrest and he'd be safe.

～

"Do we have to walk far?" Turtle asks as they leave the park and turn down a side street that curves like a C.

It's the best way to go; there's only one house on the whole street —right in the middle of the C—and the lady that lives there is old and wrinkled and walks one slow step at a time. When she comes outside to fetch the mail, she holds the envelopes right up to her face, so the boy knows she can't see very well. Not being seen is one of the rules.

"Nah, not too far," the boy says. "Just to the end of this street and in the woods a little bit."

"Does it stink? The monster, I mean. Like really bad?"

"Yeah, it does."

"Like rotten eggs? Or poop?"

"Even worse."

"What's it look like?"

"It has big teeth and long claws."

"Like a bear?"

"Kinda, but it has scales, not fur, and it's bigger and stronger and scarier."

"How do you know it's stronger than a bear if it's dead?"

"Monsters are always strong."

"My mom says there's no such thing as monsters. She has to say it every night to my sister cause she thinks there's one in her closet that comes out when she sleeps."

"Grown-ups always say that."

"Yeah, and my sister's afraid of everything. I'm not. Not even monsters."

The street ends where the woods begin. The trees are dense, the ground a tangle of thorny vines and twigs that crackle beneath their feet, but the boy leads Turtle off to one side, onto a narrow, half-hidden path, prepared to grab him if he balks. Sometimes they hesitate; sometimes they get scared. Turtle doesn't stop though.

"What's your name?" Turtle asks.

The boy traces the tip of his tongue across his teeth. Names are dangerous. If you don't have one, it can't be taken away. "You first."

When Turtle says a name, the boy muffles his ears so he can't hear it, but after, he says, "Hey, that's my name too."

Turtle narrows his eyes, slows his steps. "You're lying. I bet you're lying about the monster, too. I bet you're lying about everything."

"No, I'm not. We're almost there. You'll see." The boy smiles. He's very good at wearing the right smile. He's also very good at lying.

∾

The monster bit and consumed; the boy bled and scabbed and scarred. He learned how to go away someplace else in his mind, someplace where there were no monsters, no teeth, no pain. He told himself that one day the make-believe world would become so powerful it would destroy the real and take its place, but it was a lie too big to believe.

He guessed his parents figured he was dead. Their faces became fuzzy and indistinct until he was sure they were only ever a dream. He gathered his name and those almost-memories, tucked them far away so they couldn't creep back in. So they couldn't hurt. Sometimes in the dark they tried to sneak back in, and that hurt more than the monster's teeth.

One day the monster bit his upper arm, spat out the flesh, and paced in circles, snapping its teeth and drooling. Some time later—minutes? Hours?—there was another bite, another glob spat onto the dirt. The boy didn't understand what was wrong. He thought the monster would kill him, but it seized him, its claws digging into the fresh wounds, drew him near, and whispered in his ear, telling him what it wanted him to do. The boy said no. He said no a thousand times, but although he was much bigger than when he first fell into the monster's lair, he was still only a boy and, eventually, he said yes.

The sun hurt his eyes the first time the monster sent him outside. He stood for a few moments with the unfamiliar warmth on his skin, listening to birds chirp and insects buzz. The air was so sweet his heart hurt. It felt like another world, another planet. He could run away—he *should*—but he was too afraid to find out his dream parents weren't real after all, and if they were, they wouldn't want this scarred, damaged boy who wore a ghost of their son's face. No one would.

It didn't take long to find what the monster wanted. Pale hair, freckles, dirty sneakers, and a Transformers sweatshirt; walking on the sidewalk, dragging a stick. When the boy asked if he wanted to see something neat, Autobot said yes. He held the boy's hand tight. The boy didn't want to remember that part, but he couldn't make himself forget it.

He covered his ears with his hands and hummed under his breath so he wouldn't have to hear the wet tearing of skin, the sharp crunch of bones, the cries for help. When it all stopped, there was nothing left but a pile of shredded clothing, and the boy made up a story that the stains were spilled hot chocolate and the clothes, dirty laundry.

Autobot was only the first. The dog came next, and then the others. Too many to count; too many to remember.

The tears and screams never lasted very long, even when it felt as though they lasted forever. One day the boy didn't put his hands over his ears, and the sound wasn't as terrible as he feared. After a while he stopped paying attention at all, stopped looking at their faces, stopped thinking of them as anything other than meat.

The boy knew this made him a monster too.

~

D eep in the woods, the sun struggles to reach the ground, but the gloom doesn't seem to bother Turtle. He keeps following the boy along the path, talking about his sister, his mother, his school, his favorite toys. The boy wishes he'd be quiet instead; his voice makes the boy's head hurt.

"I thought you said it wasn't far," Turtle says. "We've been walking *forever*."

"We're almost there." The boy points to a darker shadow in the ground several feet away. "See that hole there?"

Turtle stops, crosses his arms over his chest. "I don't see anything."

"It's hard to see from here. Look closer."

Turtle squints. "I see something, but it isn't a monster. Are you sure you're not lying?"

"I'm sure. It's a hole and the monster is inside it."

"You didn't say anything about a hole. Do we have to go in it?"

"It isn't very deep. Geez, if I knew you were such a scaredy-cat, I wouldn't have told you about it."

"I'm not scared." Turtle says, puffing out his chest before stomping over to the hole.

The boy exhales through his nose. When he has to carry them, they scream and kick and punch, and he's always afraid someone will hear. Nobody pays attention to kids walking together, but they do if they think one of them is hurt, especially if they think one of them is hurting the other.

Crouching, Turtle pokes at the dirt. "It looks dark in there."

"It only looks that way from here. It isn't that dark inside."

"I don't smell anything either."

The boy begins to scoot into the hole feet first. "Do you want to see it or not?"

He doesn't wait for an answer, and Turtle follows him in.

The monster is on its side, perfectly still, and the boy can't hear it breathing. Maybe it really *is* dead. His heart thrums hard and heavy. Maybe this time he told the truth, and if the monster's dead, he won't have to do this anymore. The hope tastes like chocolate chip cookies, and he smiles wide enough to make his cheeks hurt. He reaches for Turtle's hand, but Turtle takes a step forward, his eyes huge.

"Holy crap, it's real."

The monster opens its eyes. It stretches, chest rumbling, claws scratching furrows into the ground, tail sweeping clouds of dirt-dust, and fixes both of them with its gaze. The boy's smile crumples and falls apart, and something inside him does the same. Turtle shrieks and makes for the entrance, but the boy clutches his upper arms, holding him in place.

"I'm sorry," the boy says as he brings his mouth close to Turtle's ear. "Don't worry. You'll get used to it too." And he shoves him toward the monster.

"No," Turtle yells, reaching out for the boy as he falls. "Please don't leave me here! You can't!"

But the boy scrambles up and out of the lair, skinning his palms and knees on the way. He runs through the woods, making no sound at all when tree branches smack his face, when his feet slip on loose rocks. He passes the old lady's house, the wrought iron-railed porches, a barking dog, and a man cooking a slab of meat on a grill. The smell makes his stomach clench, makes him think of teeth tearing into flesh, but he doesn't want to think about that. He doesn't want to think about anything at all.

So he keeps running.

S IS FOR SOLILOQUY

*H*ere is the bridge where we first met. Do you remember? The clouds were heavy in the sky and we were both in a hurry to beat the rain and our shoulders bumped and we went spinning in opposite directions. The book in your hand—George Orwell's *Animal Farm*—dropped nearest to me so I picked it up and spun myself back to you.

I told you it was one of my favorite books and when the rain started we were still standing together. Your eyes were the bluest I've ever seen and I couldn't stop looking at the curve of your lips. You didn't stare at my breasts even though my raincoat was open and I was wearing a V-neck sweater with a kiss of cleavage on display. That impressed me as much as the book. It meant you were smart as well as intelligent.

Before we parted ways I called my phone with yours so you'd have my number and when you called me two hours later I answered on the third ring.

Here is the coffee shop where we had our first date. We were so deep into our conversation that we didn't notice the time or the baristas preparing to close for the night until one tapped your shoulder and cleared her throat. Apologies spilled from our lips so fast we made her laugh and we held hands as we walked outside. Your skin was warm and when you squeezed right before you let go I squeezed back.

Here is the front door of my apartment where you kissed me for the first time. Not after the first coffee date but the second. You walked me home and our hands brushed together more than once but you didn't link your fingers with mine and I couldn't bring myself to do the same. When we kissed your lips were soft and hesitant and in spite of myself I was trembling. After we whispered good night and I'd locked the door I giggled like a schoolgirl and couldn't stop. Not even when I hated the sound and the implication. I was better than that. Older wiser etcetera etcetera.

Here is the front door of your old apartment where we first made love. Obviously not at the door like our kiss but inside the apartment. I laughed then too and then cried which made me laugh again and then you started laughing and even though I said I had to go I fell asleep in your arms.

You woke up first and made pancakes and bacon.

Here is the office building where you worked. I remember how you griped about your boss because he was demanding and thought overtime was something you should be grateful for. I remember how grateful you were when you decided to go freelance and put in your notice.

We celebrated that night with steak and red wine and a movie. Try as I might I can't remember what we watched and I suspect we didn't watch very much.

I drank too much wine but not so much that I wasn't aware when you crept out of bed in the middle of the night and crept back in several hours later. I didn't say anything to you about it though.

Here is the bookstore where we spent a lot of Sunday afternoons. You told me you loved me for the first time in the science fiction and fantasy section. (I waited a few days before I said the words back because I was worried you'd think I was simply echoing yours and that I didn't mean them. I did then and I still do. I hope you remember that.)

I remember you once got a phone call that filled your eyes with storm clouds and you left the bookstore so fast you forgot to say good-bye. I'd like to say it was when I got home and watched the news that I first started to worry I'd been wrong about you but I think that came later.

Here is the theater where we saw the time travel movie that you hated and I loved. Well you hated the parts of it you saw because your mother called and you had to leave fifteen minutes before it ended. I offered to go with you but I hadn't met your mother yet and you said you didn't want it to happen like that.

I still haven't met your mother. I'm not sure what that means but I know it means something.

Here is the bar where we met for drinks that night last spring. I know you remember. Everyone remembers that night because every television screen and every channel broadcast the same footage. Like something from a movie there was an explosion and two masked people in costume fighting an extraordinary fight of impossible flying leaps and jumps and spins. After the chaos came a victory. A person in silver tight enough to reveal six-pack abs was dragged away in hand-cuffs they assured us were unbreakable while a person in a patriotic shade of blue—and yes it was tight enough to show off their muscles as well—brushed dust from their shoulders.

Cut to a scene of a police car on the side of the road with two unconscious police officers sprawled on the ground and a pair of empty handcuffs on the back seat.

Cut again to a man in a red costume standing behind a podium. He said it was time to come out of the shadows. Time to tell the truth. (Funny how he didn't take off his mask though.) How there were people like him with special strengths and most of them used those powers for the good of society. I couldn't help but laugh at that part because he was so earnest it had to come from a script. No one really talks like that.

Then he said there were some who only wanted to profit from their talents but he insisted there were only a few and they would all be caught and imprisoned and we had nothing to fear. He didn't use the word villain or hero but everyone knew what he meant. The bar exploded into conjecture and arguments and even hysteria from a blond guy in the back who wouldn't stop saying it wasn't possible in this weird raspy voice until his date slapped him across the face like Cher did in that one movie.

You shook your head and traced aimless circles on the table with one finger. You said it was hard to believe. Said it was like something from a comic book. I agreed.

Here is the restaurant where I waited for you until you called to say something had come up with a client and you were going to have to work late. I brought dessert to your apartment to surprise you and you weren't home. I thought of leaving the dessert—Tiramisu your favorite—on the doormat but I didn't want you to know I'd been there. Didn't want you to think I was checking up on you.

I went home and watched T.V. More footage from around the world. Bank heists explosions car chases kidnappings rescues heroes villains masks. The charred remains of a secret lair. Construction of new prisons. Men and women who could fly. Who could walk through walls. Who could lift cars over their heads and stop bullets with the palms of their hands. And the man in the red costume—the official spokesman of the good guys—always there assuring everyone that his team had everything under control. The villainous element didn't work together so their position was much weaker and it was only a matter of time before they all fell.

But good guys trying to catch bad guys didn't have anything to do with us and I turned off the television and sat in silence.

Here is the flower shop where you bought roses to apologize for breaking our date at the restaurant and for working late so many nights and for not answering my calls. I forgave you and we made love but when I woke in the middle of the night you were gone.

You'd left a note that said you loved me but had to get up early for work and were afraid you'd sleep too late at my apartment.

Here is the grocery store where our carts collided in the ice cream aisle. You were surprised to see me because I usually did my shopping at night. I'm sorry you said. I've been so busy with work. I'll call you tomorrow.

But you didn't call.

Here is the park where you told me to meet you. I waited and waited but you never showed never called. I finally gave up and headed home.

There were sirens in the distance and a news van rushed by but I ignored them. No matter what the man in the red mask says the villains always get away. I think it's supposed to be that way. If there weren't any villains there wouldn't be a need for heroes. Supply and demand.

Here is the stretch of pavement where we last spoke. I was coming to see you I said. I smiled and reached for your hand but you said you didn't have time to talk and you pulled away before our skin made contact. I asked why you stood me up at the park. You said not every-thing was about us. But nothing was about us. I didn't even know if there *was* an us and I begged you to tell me what was wrong. You said nothing was wrong and you had to go.

When you walked away I couldn't bear to watch. How could something so good go so wrong so quickly?

And now here is an alley. I know it's a strange location and it's starting to rain—only a light mist but it will turn my hair into a halo of frizz—but I didn't check the weather beforehand I'm sorry. Or maybe I'm not sorry because it feels like the day we met. I can see you standing at the opposite end and while you wait you're darting glances at your watch because you haven't seen me yet. I asked for only a few minutes of your time and I was afraid you wouldn't come but now that I know you're here I need a minute to gather my thoughts.

Because here is where I tell you the truth and the truth is almost everything has been a lie.

Our first meeting wasn't accidental—I'd been watching you for several weeks. The night I drank too much wine I merely pretended to be drunk. When you left I timed your absence and checked the news reports the next day. And I know you never worked in that office building. It was a cover story. A few phone calls confirmed that.

Watching that first televised footage with you was unbearable. There was so much I wanted to say and so much I'd been planning to say but I was waiting for the right time. The footage with the empty handcuffs was staged by the way. They didn't want the public to know the cuffs weren't as unbreakable as they thought. But I think you already know.

Every time you disappeared there was a fight between a hero and a villain. Every. Time. So I know you've been lying to me but you're clever and I can't figure out the last piece of the puzzle and it's the piece that's most important.

If you're a hero everything changes.

If you're a villain everything changes.

The media has it all wrong. We're not as bad as they want us to be. Maybe we don't rescue the masses from burning buildings or out of control trains but that doesn't mean we're bad people. They're right about us working alone but it does get lonely after a while. When you come up with a great plan there's no one to share it with and no one to help go over all the small details that can so easily get overlooked. Drowning your solitary sorrow after a defeat in a bottle of red wine or a half-gallon of mint chocolate chip ice cream is no fun. Celebrating a victory by yourself gets old too and all too soon it resembles the post-defeat routine only with more expensive wine and gourmet gelato instead of ice cream.

So. I have a proposal. I think you and I would make a great team because we do—I love you so much—and if we work together we could defeat anyone and do anything. We'd be unstoppable.

If I'm right.

If I'm wrong here is where I kill you or you kill me or we both try at least. More than likely neither one of us will die but we'll create a great deal of damage in the attempt. (I really hope you brought your mask but if not I brought an extra. Anonymity is paramount where the public is concerned.) Our fight will be amazing—and did I mention I love you?—and will probably make the evening news if we start soon enough. I'll get away of course. I always do.

Here is where all the lies end and everything else begins.

THE FLOATING GIRLS: A DOCUMENTARY

The floating girls are all but forgotten now. It's easier to pretend they didn't exist, to pretend it didn't happen. But there are parents who still keep bedrooms captured in time, complete with clothes folded in bureau drawers and diaries tucked beneath pillows, everything in its place, waiting, and there are friends who still gaze at the sky, wondering how far the girls floated and if they ever fell.

Some of us haven't forgotten. Some of us never will.

Twelve years ago, three hours after the sun set on the second of August, nearly 300,000 girls between the ages of eleven and seventeen vanished. Eyewitness reports state that the girls floated away, yet even now, many of those eyewitnesses have recanted their stories or simply refuse to talk about it at all.

The girls lived in cities, in the suburbs, in the country. They lived in first world and third world countries. They were only children; they were one of many siblings; they were of all ethnicities and religious backgrounds. They were everyone and anyone, and after that night in August, they were no more.

I've found plenty of evidence decrying the phenomenon, but there are lists of the girls who disappeared. Those who claim it's all bullshit provide other lists, girls who vanished and were found years later: the runaways; the girls involved in ugly custody battles, who were spirited away by either custodial or non-custodial parents; the girls whose decomposing bodies were recovered from forests, old drainpipes, beneath concrete patios.

But none of those girls were floating girls, only gone girls. The reports always conveniently leave that out.

I wonder about the evidence I haven't found, that doesn't exist. It seems like there should be so much more. And how many girls who vanished were never reported? And why just girls? Why just *these* girls?

As far as I can tell, very few scientists or statisticians studied the phenomenon itself. No one counseled the families; no one dug through the chaos to find the facts. Like certain religious or political scandals, everyone wanted to brush it under the rug.

Maybe it made a strange sort of sense at the time. I don't know.

~

Jessie and I grew up next door in a tiny corner of suburbia. You know the sort: backyard cookouts, running through the sprinklers, drinking water from the hose, playing tag. Perfectly charming. The sort of childhood that screams ideal. The sort of childhood that could take place anywhere, in any town, not just our little corner in Baltimore, Maryland.

Our backyards were separated by a row of hedges with spaces in between perfectly sized for someone to walk through. We would flit from yard to yard—mine had the swing set and the sprinkler; hers the sandbox and hammock—and house to house—split foyer for me, rancher for her—nearly inseparable, spinning circles and holding hands while we chanted *Jessie and Tracy, best friends forever.*

My strongest memories are of the countless hours we spent catching fireflies. We'd keep them inside glass jars with holes poked in the lids so they wouldn't die and invent stories that they were princesses trapped in the bodies and the lights were their way of calling for help because they couldn't speak. And every night before we had to go in, we'd let them go, watching until they blinked out of sight, pretending they were off to find their mothers, their princes, the witches who'd cursed them.

I think you only truly make that kind of friendship in childhood. When you get older, you know better than to let people in. You know they'll only disappoint you in the end.

~

V ideo interview with Karen Michaels of Monmouth, Oregon, March 17, 2010:

[A woman sits in a cramped, dingy kitchen, a lit cigarette clutched tightly between two fingers, an overflowing ashtray by her side. She grimaces at the camera and looks away. Her face is worn and heavily lined, her shoulders hunched forward.]

"Thank you for agreeing to talk to me, Mrs. Michaels. I know this is difficult."

[Mrs. Michaels takes a drag from her cigarette. Exhales the smoke loudly.]

"Call me Karen, okay?"

"Okay, Karen. I know it's been a long time, but can you tell me what happened that night, August second—"

[She waves the hand holding the cigarette.]

"I know what night you're talking about."

[Another inhale from her cigarette. Another exhale.]

"Nina had problems with sleepwalking when she was a kid. Used to drive me crazy. For a couple years, I had to lock her bedroom door from the outside to keep her in the house. You got kids?"

"No—"

"That's right. You already told me you didn't. Who knows, maybe you're lucky. Anyway, that night, the night Nina floated, it had been years since she walked in her sleep. I heard her go down the steps, and I followed her. She went out the front door and stood on the lawn, staring down at her feet, like this."

[Mrs. Michaels stubs out her cigarette and stands with her arms straight and her head down, her hands held out a few inches from her body.]

"I thought she was sleepwalking again, that's all, so I stayed on the front porch. I was getting ready to go get her, grab her arm, and take her back in because I had to get up early in the morning. But then she went up, just up, like a balloon. I, I—"

[Video cuts off. Returns. Mrs. Michaels is wiping her eyes.]

"Are you sure you're okay?"

"Yeah, sure, I'm fine. I, so she went up, and I thought ... I don't know what I thought. I ran and tried to grab her, but she was already up too far. I touched the side of her foot, but I guess, I guess I was just too late."

[She grabs another cigarette and lights it. Her voice is barely audible when she speaks again.]

"I let her go. I didn't know what else to do, so I let her go."

[Her head snaps up. She looks straight into the camera.]

"Everyone told me not to talk about it. It's like she never existed at all. But she did, and no one cared that she was gone. No one. Do you really think this thing, your project, will help?"

"I'd like to think it will, yes."

[She makes a sound low in her throat.]

"Will you tell me what Nina was like?"

"She was like every other kid. Listened to her music too loud, left her dirty clothes on the floor, griped about her chores, but she didn't run around wild or anything like that. She didn't drink or do drugs or cause me any grief."

"And what was your relationship with Nina like?"

"Normal. I mean, we had fights, but nothing really serious. She was always in her room, reading or listening to music."

"What about with her siblings, her father?"

"Everyone was fine. Everything was fine."

[There's a long pause, and she looks away with tears in her eyes. Video ends.]

❧

Jessie's father died the year we turned eight. I remember black clothing, tears, confusion, and the smell of flowers. At some point, she and I snuck out into her backyard and played in the sandbox. I don't remember what we talked about or if we talked about anything at all, but I remember how we slipped out of our dress shoes and wriggled our toes through the warm top layer of sand to the cool beneath. I remember the scent of honeysuckle thick in the air.

❧

Recording of a telephone interview, July 28, 2012:
"You're not going to use my name, right? I don't want you to use my name."

"No, I won't."

"Good. Okay."

"Tell me what you think happened on the night of August second."

"All I can tell you is what I saw. The kid was hanging in the air in her backyard, looking like some kind of angel, only not the kind you can see through. I mean, she wasn't wearing anything like an angel would. I think she had on some kind of dress, but nothing like you see in pictures of angels or anything like that. Then she went straight up. Craziest damn thing I ever saw. I kept thinking it was the beer. I only had a couple, maybe three, but ..."

"Did you do anything?"

"What could I do? Hell, by the time I figured out my eyes wasn't playing tricks, she was high up. I mean really high."

"And you told the authorities what you saw?"

"Yeah, I told them. Lot of good that did. They said I was crazy. Or drunk. People can't float. But I know what I saw, and that girl just floated up and away."

"Did you know anything about her?"

"No, she was just the kid who lived next door. She kept to herself, the whole family did. I mean they were nice enough, just not real friendly."

"Is there anything else you'd like to say?"

"You're not going to use my name for this thing, right? I don't want my name used."

"No, sir. As I said before, I won't use your name."

~

Jessie and I started to drift apart the summer she turned eleven, about a year after her mom remarried. I'd ask her to come over and catch fireflies, and she'd say no. I'd invite her to spend the night, and she'd say no. I spent countless nights crying, trying to figure out what I'd done wrong, because best friends didn't stop talking to each other unless something was wrong.

My mother sat me down and said, "Tracy, honey, that's what happens with friends sometimes. Don't worry. Maybe she's just going through a phase. You *are* becoming young women, you know."

She was only trying to help, but I wanted everything to go back to the way it had been, not the way it was.

~

Video footage, dated August 2, 2002:
      Video opens with a scene of a back yard, complete with a hot tub, a fire pit, and tables and chairs setup for a party. There's a break in the video; when it returns, the sky is dark and a party is in full swing. No children are present. The camera captures several people saying hello to the cameraman, there's another break in the filming, and then the camera is stationary, capturing a wide view of the partygoers.

5 minutes, 06 seconds: A pale blotch can be seen in the far left corner, above a row of well-trimmed hedges.

5 minutes, 08 seconds: The pale blotch is larger, the shape completely visible over the hedge.

5 minutes, 10 seconds: While the partygoers continue to drink and laugh, the blotch continues to rise.

Video editing enhancement of the last few seconds before the blotch disappears from the film clearly shows a young girl in her early teens, her face solemn, rising up through the air.

[Note: Records state the video was taken by Jack Stevenson of Denver, Colorado. Repeated attempts to contact Mr. Stevenson have been unsuccessful.]

∾

By the time I was twelve, the drift between Jessie and I had become a crevasse. We weren't even on speaking terms. She was just a girl I used to know. As kids do, I'd made new friends and sure, her rejection hurt and sometimes I'd look over the fence to see if she was outside, but I was a kid, just a stupid kid.

How was I supposed to know?

∾

Photograph A: Photo shows a baobab tree and a girl beside it. On closer inspection, the girl's feet are hovering about a foot from the ground. The girl is looking away from the camera. The back of the photograph reads August 2, Shurugwi, Zimbabwe.

[Note: Photograph provided by one of the girl's family members, who asked to remain anonymous. For that reason, the name of the girl is also withheld.]

Photograph B: The central image is the Eiffel Tower in Paris, France. On the far right of the photo, a girl is suspended in the air, her arms held in the distinct way described by many others, her face serene. Using the tower as a point of measure, she is approximately 1,050 feet in the air.

[Note: *Image found on a website claiming it was manipulated digitally, however, no evidence of alteration can be found in the image itself. The girl in the photograph has not yet been identified.*]

Photograph C: Photo of Trakai Castle, south of Vilnius, Lithuania, taken by Algimantas Serunis of Chicago, Illinois, while on vacation. A girl's head and shoulders are visible above the westernmost tower of the castle.

[Note: *The girl has been tentatively identified as Ruta Gremaila. Attempts to contact her family have been unsuccessful.*]

$\sim$

When I was fourteen, Jessie showed up at the back door one night. I was blaring music and eating the last of the mint chocolate chip ice cream, knowing my dad would pretend to make a big deal about the empty container and my mom would roll her eyes at both of us. My parents weren't home, and yes, I've wondered more than once if it would've made a difference.

"Yeah?" I remember saying.

"I was wondering if maybe you'd want to hang out for a little bit?" she asked, her voice whisper-thin, her eyes all red and puffy, like she'd been crying. Behind the red, though, there was a strange emptiness, a hollow where laughter had once lived.

I remember being surprised, more at her request than her eyes. Although I'd made new friends, she hadn't. She skulked through the halls at school like a ghost. She sat alone in the cafeteria at lunchtime and with her shoulders hunched in class. She wore baggy clothing and kept her head down so her hair almost covered her face, and she always walked home alone.

"I can't, sorry. I have a math test tomorrow I have to study for."

"Oh, okay." She stood for a minute, toeing the doormat with the tip of her shoe. "See you around then?"

"Sure."

But I lied. There was no math test. I just didn't want to talk to her.

~

Video footage of interview with Sheriff Joseph Miller, Brookhaven, Pennsylvania, September 9, 2008:

"No, none of it's true. I have no idea why you'd even want to talk about it."

"So why do you think everyone reported the same thing?"

"I don't have an answer to that."

"Maybe it's because it really happened."

[He glares into the camera.]

"Look, it didn't happen. A bunch of kids ran away, a bunch more people got upset and invented some story about floating."

"But didn't three girls from your own town vanish?"

[His expression changes, and he crosses his arms over his chest.]

"Yeah."

"Don't you think that's suspect?"

"Sometimes kids, especially girls, run away together. It happens."

"And what if I told you those girls weren't even friends, didn't even go to the same schools?"

[He sighs heavily, looks at some spot in the distance, and shakes his head in dismissal.]

"We're done here. Some of us have real work to do."

~

On August 2, 2002, the summer Jessie and I were fifteen, I was in the back yard on a blanket, staring at the stars, waiting for one to fall so I could make a wish. My parents were out at the movies, and other than the crickets chirping, the neighborhood was quiet.

Jessie's kitchen door opened—it had a funny little squeak that all the oil in the world wouldn't fix—and Jessie walked out into the yard. The lights in her house were off, and she was little more than a shadow flitting across the grass.

I hunched down on the blanket and watched through the hedges. She stood still in the middle of her yard for several minutes with her head down, her hands fisted at her sides. I thought about calling her name—I know I did—but then her hands relaxed, her arms extended slightly, and she lifted her chin to stare straight ahead. Then she lifted off the ground.

She was a foot in the air before I realized it wasn't an illusion, before I was able to do anything other than blink. I scrambled to my feet, told her to stop, and raced through the hedges, scratching my upper arms all to hell in the process. I shouted her name and called out for my parents, for her parents, for anyone.

Jessie never looked down, not once. I stood right underneath her, waving my arms and yelling at her to come back, until my legs couldn't hold me up anymore and my throat was too thick to speak.

My parents found me in the back yard when they got home. I was on the blanket, sitting with my grass-stained knees pulled to my chin, crying. I told them how Jessie just floated and kept floating until I couldn't see her anymore, until she was gone.

I saw the disbelief in their eyes. My father went over to Jessie's house, knocked on the door, and came back shrugging his shoulders after no one answered. My mom pressed her hand against my forehead, proclaimed I had a fever, and sent me to bed. I stayed there for three days.

Jessie's parents told the police she ran away.

∽

Video footage of an attempted interview on August 18, 2011 with John Gelvin from Brawley, California, whose daughter, Rosie, age thirteen, is still listed as missing. Documents show she was reported as a floating girl. Other documents show that Child Protective Services had been called on at least one occasion before Rosie's disappearance, but no further action from CPS can be found.

"Sir, you said you saw Rosie float."

"No. I didn't. You're mistaken. She ran away."

"But I have a report here, a police report, that says—"

[He spins around and begins to walk away, speaking over his shoulder.]

"Leave me alone. Just leave me alone."

❧

I tried to tell people the truth. My parents continued to blame the fever. When I told Jessie's parents, her mother's eyes filled with tears, the silent, terrifying kind; her stepfather told me to leave their house and never come back. They moved away a few months later and didn't tell anyone where they were going.

People at school thought I was crazy, even after the other reports came out. Jessie was just another troubled kid who ran away. It happened every day. No big deal.

If I'd been an adult, if I hadn't see Jessie float away, I wonder if I would've been as dismissive. Possibly. Probably.

I tried to tell the truth so many times, but no one would listen.

❧

Graffiti on the side of a building in Rapid City, South Dakota, June 8, 2013, in the section of the city known as Art Alley:

SILENCE IS A FORM OF HELIUM

[Note: According to a local artist, who asked not to be named, the graffiti was originally written on the building in September of 2002, and she's been repainting it as needed ever since. When asked if she knew the identity of the original artist or thought that the statement was related to the floating girls, she declined to answer.]

❧

E ventually I stopped talking about it, about Jessie. I didn't forget her, but it was too hard to keep trying to explain what I saw to people who refused to believe it. I finished high school, moved out of state for college, dropped out in my second year, and came back home.

When my parents decided to sell their house and move to Florida, I found a box of photos in the attic, pictures of me and Jessie when we were young, pictures of us holding our firefly jars, grinning crazy kid smiles, those smiles that scream innocence. Our eyes were filled with laughter and happiness and hope.

And I remembered her eyes the night she came over, the night I turned her away. We all have a secret spot, a tiny light, inside us, and it doesn't take much to make that light go out. It doesn't take much to extinguish that light forever.

As I carried the photos out to my car, I decided to do something. I'm not sure if I decided to do it for Jessie or for the others or for me, but I don't think it matters.

I'm not a fifteen-year-old girl anymore, and I've spent years digging for proof, searching for the truth. Maybe now people will listen, and maybe they'll start talking.

∼

E xcerpt from "A Study into the Phenomenon of the Floating Girls," dated November 2002, author not cited:
Given a lack of concrete evidence to the phenomenon, and with evidence that a percentage of the girls were from troubled homes and had a history of running away, we can only conclude there was no phenomenon, only a strange set of coincidental circumstances.

It is also noted that there was a heavy incident of fog in the northwestern states, which may explain the visual oddities noted there.

Reports from other countries are sketchy at best with most being reported well after the disappearances in the United States, leading this researcher to determine that they were copying the phenomenon, perhaps in hope of cashing in on the notoriety. More research is needed.

[Note: There is no evidence that any further research was conducted.]

~

I live twenty minutes away from the house I grew up in. Kids still play in sandboxes, they still catch fireflies and run through sprinklers, they still promise to be best friends forever. At night, I stare at the sky and wonder if the girls are still floating. I think they are, and we just can't see them.

I tell Jessie I'm sorry, but the words seem so fucking inadequate. I should've been there for her. I should've listened. And after, I should've kept talking. Hell, I should've screamed and shouted. But I didn't.

No one did.

For Jessie
Tracy Richardson, Director
The Floating Girls Project
Baltimore, Maryland
2014

TAKE A WALK IN THE NIGHT, MY LOVE

He is a good man. Remember that. He is a good man.

~

There's something in the bed, something that scratches your skin when you move your legs, and you whip the sheets aside, fearing an insect, or worse—a spider. Dirt, coarse and abrasive, clings to your feet and ankles, between your toes. You hiss in a breath, shake your husband's pajama-clad arm.

Half-asleep, he mumbles, "What's wrong?"

"There's dirt in the bed." Your voice is little more than a whisper.

He rolls over, wiping grit from the corner of his eye. "What time is it?"

"Just after six. Look," you say, pointing to your feet.

He sits and untangles his legs from the sheets. No dirt there, only on your side, on your skin. Your arms break out in gooseflesh, even though it's mid-spring and your bedroom is warm.

"Did I get out of bed last night?" Your voice is thick with unshed tears.

"Not that I'm aware, but you know me, I sleep like a stone," he says. "Maybe you were sleepwalking."

"I've never done that before, have I?"

He shrugs and shakes his salt and pepper hair from his eyes. "I don't think so."

The bright sunlight, welcome after several days of unceasing rain, makes the lines fanning the corners of his eyes and bracketing his mouth appear deeper than usual, makes the fifteen years between the two of you more than evident.

He takes your hand, but you slip free and swing your legs over the side of the bed. There's a smattering of dirt on the floor as well. And in the hallway, and on the stairs. You make out the curve of a heel here, the smudge of a toe there. You pinch the bridge of your nose before descending, still clad in your nightgown. More dirt leads from the back door, which is shut and locked as it should be. Through the window, you see impressions on the stone patio as well.

Beyond the patio, the grass of the large, sweeping lawn shimmers with dew. Several acres separate the house, a brick two-story, four-bedroom built in a neoclassical style, from the towering pines at the edge of the property.

His footsteps are soft behind you.

"Look," you say, pointing.

He takes your shoulders in hand. "Maybe ... Maybe it's ah ... hormonal. You *are* turning fifty in a few months."

You feel the smile softening his words and lean back against his chest. "So I'm getting old? Is that your official diagnosis, Doctor?"

He clears his throat, scuffs one foot on the floor.

"Healthy adults don't just start sleepwalking," you say. "They don't. Not even with changing hormones."

He kisses the top of your head. "Are you sure you don't remember getting up?"

You bark a laugh. "For what? To go outside in the yard? It isn't even trash day," you say, regretting the words as soon as they're past your lips. They sound absurd. As absurd as the thought of sleepwalk-ing. And yet, a quick memory flashes in your head—you turning back the sheets and slipping from bed as quietly as possible, your fingers trembling and mouth dry.

He turns you round and kisses your lips, softly, sweetly. "If it bothers you that much, you can always call the doctor."

"Not confident in your diagnosis?" you say, smiling a little.

He kisses you again. "Honestly, my love, I'm sure it's nothing to worry about."

$\approx$

You're brushing your teeth and then you're in the back yard. You blink in the darkness, take a step back, the grass soft beneath your bare feet, and press fingers to temple. Lilac perfumes the night air, and the chirrup of crickets and the distant hoots of an owl give it voice.

The taste of mint lingers on your tongue. You're in your night-gown, your hair still pulled back from your face with a fabric head-band. You shake your head, as though you can shake this away. You were in the bathroom. The *bathroom*. And then you were here, with no memory of the journey in between. Your stomach clenches, painfully so. You can't sleepwalk when you're wide awake so how did you get here? And why?

Behind you, the door opens with a bang. He's wide-eyed and worry-lined, crossing the lawn in long strides until he's at your side. He reaches for you, then lets his hand drop. The lines on his face deepen. His mouth works, but nothing emerges, and a lump grows in your throat.

Finally, he says, "Julia?"

"I ..." you manage. "I don't know what happened. I was inside, I was brushing my teeth, and then, and then—"

Tears spill over your lashes, stealing your voice away. He takes you into his arms and you breathe him in, holding tight. *I'm not well*, you think. It's the only explanation.

The tears continue to fall, and when they stop, your voice is a sandpaper rasp, "I think I should see the doctor now."

He hugs you closer. "We'll make that happen," he says into your hair.

$$\sim$$

S everal days of tests pass in a blur. Bloodwork, an EEG, a CAT scan, an MRI. Words run through your head all the while—epilepsy, meningitis, brain tumor. When the doctor says there's nothing physically wrong with you, you laugh. You can't help it. He prescribes rest and Valium to help calm your nerves, and while you're sure you don't need the latter, you take the prescription anyway.

On the drive home, you twist your hands in your lap and stare at the passing scenery. Old houses, older trees, luxury cars. Everything feels wrong, as though you're an actress on an elaborate movie set, in a role you've not prepared for. Your spine grows cold and you shudder, digging half-moons in your palms with your fingernails.

"Julia, is everything okay?" he asks. "How are you feeling?"

"Disjointed," you say, turning your gaze toward him, taking comfort in the planes of his face. "As though I've something on the tip of my tongue, something I should know, but don't."

While waiting at the stoplight, he meets your eyes. His are dark brown, the sort that appear almost black in certain light. You're a lucky woman; he's a kind and gentle man, not at all like most of the plastic surgeons portrayed on television, all filled with ego and arrogance and grand delusions of perfection.

You remember when you first met at a small coffee shop on the other side of town. How your heel slipped on a lid someone had dropped on the floor, and he grabbed your arm just in time to keep you from falling. You shared a table that day and three months later you said I do, though it didn't feel like an impulsive decision. It felt like the right one. You loved him, loved the light in his eyes when he looked at you. No one had ever looked at you that way. You still feel the same, even after twenty-five years.

Right now, though, fear coils in your belly, a fear both strange and yet familiar. Not of him, but of something else.

He rubs your thigh. "Julia, my love, all shall be well."

You nod.

All shall be well.

~

The Valium makes you foggy headed and you brew a pot of coffee stronger than usual, hoping it will cut through the haze. Unfortunately, it's barely drinkable, even with copious amounts of milk and sugar. Still, you take small sips, trying to swallow as quickly as you can before the bitterness sets in.

You wander the house, trailing fingertips across the dark wood furniture. Family heirlooms, most of it, and it fills you with calm. In the library, your favorite room in the house with its built-in shelves and comfortable furniture, you select a book at random and sink into the corner chair, your legs curled beneath you.

Yet the Valium dulls your focus and after a time, you set the book aside in favor of a photo album—the two of you on holiday, an island in the Caribbean, the name of which escapes you at the moment. Fruity drinks with paper umbrellas, bright turquoise water, white sand. Breakfasts in bed; making love beneath a swirling ceiling fan, your bodies coated in sweat; walks in the moonlight. The smell of the sea, of hibiscus blooming in red profusion.

Barbados. The word swims into your mind and you nod to yourself. Yes, you were in Barbados. You turn another page in the album, revealing several photos of only you, sitting in bed with a sheet draped across your hips. You squint at the picture and slip it from its plastic sleeve, holding it close. There's a scar on the right side of your abdomen.

You push down the waist band of your pants, trace your fingers over the smooth, scarless skin. You check the photo again and the strange fear settles in your belly. Scars can't disappear. You check your abdomen yet again. There are creams and ointments to make them less apparent but there's nothing on your skin. Not a dimple, not a bump, nothing.

At dinner, you ask, "Did I have my appendix out?"

He swallows his food, takes a quick sip of wine. "No, why?"

"Here," you say, sliding the photo from your pocket and pushing it across the table.

He picks it up with a frown.

"Doesn't it look like I have a scar?"

He lets out a breathy laugh. "It looks like it, yes, but it's a shadow. From the sheet, see?"

And it *is* a shadow. It's so obvious your cheeks warm.

"We can arrange to have your appendix out though, if you really want to. That would be rather silly, though, wouldn't it?" Although his face is serious, his eyes shine with mirth and then the corners of his mouth lift and a laugh bubbles up from your throat.

When the laughter begins to fade, he says, "Eat, my love."

You cut a piece of steak. Chew. Swallow. "We should go back there."

"Hmmm?"

"To Barbados."

"Okay," he says. "We will."

He smiles, but it doesn't quite reach his eyes.

"Is dinner okay?" you ask.

"It's wonderful," he says. "As always. I'm a little tired, that's all."

~

Someone is calling your name, over and over again. You freeze in place, blinking in confusion. You're in the driveway, almost to the gated entrance, dressed in your nightgown with your purse slung over one shoulder. Light rain dances across your skin, plastering your hair to your cheeks and neck, and the stones of the driveway dig painfully into your bare feet.

"Julia!" he calls again and you turn.

Even in the darkness, his face seems pale and drawn.

"Where were you going?"

"I'm not sure," you say, and then you are. "My mother. I was going to see my mother."

"In the middle of the night, dressed like that? You must have been dreaming."

"Yes, I think I was."

"Here," he says, extending one arm for you to loop yours through. "Walk on the grass so you don't cut your feet."

Halfway to the house, you say, "Can I go see her, though? My mother? Obviously not tonight, but it's been a long time, hasn't it?"

His forehead creases. "You mean her grave?"

The fear returns to your belly. Your mother's dead?

"We can take flowers to the cemetery this weekend if you like," he says.

"Yes, I'd like that," you say. "I'd like that very much."

Back in bed, he kisses your cheek and tells you to sleep. As your eyelids begin to slip shut, a moment of panic burns bitter on your tongue. You can't remember your mother's funeral. You should remember something like that, shouldn't you?

∾

You shake a Valium onto your palm but pause with your hand halfway to your mouth. There's too much to do today for you to be dull-witted so you drop the pill back into the bottle.

After you finish the dusting and the vacuuming, you put another load of laundry in the washer and stand in the doorway of the laundry room, your arms slack at your sides, unsure what to do next. An odd sensation washes over you and leaves you cold. The house feels wrong. Everything feels wrong. Mouth desert dry, you walk to the powder room and stare at your reflection. Have your cheekbones always been so sharp, your lips so full? You run the water until it's cold enough to hurt and splash your face again and again.

"Love?"

You jump and spin around, your hands and face still dripping.

"What's wrong?"

"I'm ... I'm," you say. "I'm scared. I don't feel right. I—"

"Shhh," he says. "Everything's fine. You're perfectly fine. There's nothing to be afraid of."

And like that, your fear is gone, but even that feels wrong, because while you may no longer be afraid, you remember feeling that way.

"Julia, come," he says. "It's nearly lunchtime."

~

You're in the back yard again. Alone. You have a fork in one hand and your mouth tastes of balsamic vinaigrette.

"Julia?"

"What happened?" you say.

"You got up while we were eating and came outside."

"Didn't you try to stop me?"

"I did, but you pulled away." His eyes are sad. "And, I wanted to see what you'd do."

You take a step back. He doesn't even have the decency to look ashamed.

"No," he says. "It isn't like that at all. I thought it might help me help you. I would never do anything to hurt you, Julia. You know that, don't you?"

You nod, but there's something odd in his face, something ... sly. He's doing this to you. You don't know how or why, but he is. The question is, what exactly is he trying to make you do?

~

When he leaves to run errands, you wait until his car pulls out of sight before you go into his study. It smells of well-worn leather and something musky, his aftershave lotion perhaps. Bookcases line the walls and you trace your fingers over the spines. Medical journals, all of them, detailing surgical techniques. You turn on his computer, but it's password protected and all your guesses are wrong. In the bottom drawer of the desk, there's a small Moleskine notebook, not much larger than the palm of your hand, its cover creased and worn. Heart racing, you open it, revealing small, cramped writing. On the first page is a list of names and notations you neither recognize nor understand:

Dr. James Braid – the father of – Scottish – 18/19ᵗʰ century

Emile Coué – 19ᵗʰ century – placebos – autosuggestion

Franz Mesmer – mid-18ᵗʰ century – animal magnetism – man in black cloak

Milton Erickson – chronic pain – 1957 founding of TASoCH – patient need not be aware, as long as cured

Caligari – 11ᵗʰ century Italian mystic – somnambulist (Cesare) – murders

You flip to another page, hoping for something that makes more sense.

The first stage of hypnotherapy is going well. The patient is calm and relaxed, performing simple tasks as requested, responding to questions with the appropriate yes or no answers.

You frown. Hypnotherapy? But he's a plastic surgeon. Retired now, but still. He flattened stomachs, augmented breasts, erased wrinkles on aging faces. Was this something he studied previously? Something he did on the side? If so, he never mentioned it either way. He never said a word.

Neither the writing nor the paper look new, and the page edges are feathered, as though the book has been thumbed through many, many times.

The methods, while unorthodox, do work. The findings, of course, can't be published because there are many who would deem them unethical.

You flip ahead.

Although the unpleasant memories cannot be eradicated, they have been suppressed. Asking about those memories evokes no recollection, only traces of confusion that further sessions are expected to nullify.

You turn to yet another page. Same handwriting, but blue ink instead of black. No dates or names anywhere. What did he do them and how does it relate to you? Did something happen to you? Something he doesn't want you to remember?

At this point, there is no introduction of new information so as not to muddle the thought process needful for—

He clears his throat and you look up, dropping the book onto the desk. Your hand butterflies to your chest. He leans against the doorway, his face calm.

"What are you doing to me?" you say.

"Loving you, that's all."

You shake your head. "No, that isn't all. The sleepwalking, the blacking out. You're doing something to me. I know you are." You point to the book. "Hypnotherapy, that's hypnotism. Is that what you've been doing to me? Hypnotizing me? Why? Why would you do something like that to me?"

He nods toward the book. "I left it there for you to find, hoping this time I was wrong and you wouldn't go looking. It was the only way I could be sure, even with the rest."

"This time? What do you mean?" He steps close and you raise your hands, ball them into fists. "You stay away from me. You—"

He says, "Be still," and your arms fall to your sides. You try to lift them, but they feel as though they weigh a hundred pounds and you can't make them budge at all.

"I'm sorry, my love," he says.

Your mouth won't work although words are shrieking in your head to be released. Why can't you move? Why is he doing this to you?

"Walk with me," he says, his voice like good whiskey.

You don't want to walk with him, don't want to cross the room at his side, but your legs make the decision for you. He pulls a key from his pocket, slides a bookcase aside, revealing a door. But you've lived in this house for over twenty years. How has he hidden this from you?

He opens the door and flips a switch, bathing the revealed staircase in a warm glow. "Careful now," he says. "Hold the railing while you walk down."

Your traitorous hands and feet do his bidding.

"Despite what you might be thinking, I'm not trying to hurt you. I didn't think we'd have to do this again so soon, but the mind fights so to break free."

In the room sits a chair with padded restraints, a projector, a screen.

"Don't worry. You should know by now that this part won't hurt. I might have to do something about that scar, but you won't remember a thing, I promise you that. Funny that you've never noticed it before." He touches your face, his hand warm, and you want to pull away but you can't. "You cling so tightly to your old life. I never thought that would happen. I don't think ..." He shakes his head. "Sit, please."

You do and he buckles the restraints around your wrists and ankles, not so tight that they hurt but tight enough to hold you in place. He kneels in front of you and strokes the back of your hand. "Maybe this time you won't try to remember anything else. Maybe this time we can finally be happy together. We made it nearly a year. That's longer than before. That has to mean something. That has to mean I'm doing everything almost right." He gazes into your eyes and you tell yourself to scream, to shout, but nothing happens.

"Speak," he finally says.

"Please. I don't understand any of this. Let me go. Don't do this. Please don't do this to me."

"Julia was a wonderful woman. You should be proud I chose you to fill her shoes." His eyes go soft and far away as he continues to stroke your hand. "My wife, my everything."

But *you're* Julia. You're his wife. Aren't you?

"Where is she?" you say, your voice trembling, both wanting and dreading the answer. "What happened to her?"

"She was sick," he says, his mouth tight. "That's all you need to know."

"No, please. If I'm not really her, then who am I? Please tell me that much."

"You were no one," he says. "Now relax."

Tension bleeds from your shoulders. You open your mouth, but he says, "Hush" and your voice disappears.

He turns on the projector and an image of you flashes on the screen. No, you scream silently. That isn't me. He said she was sick, but what did that mean? Did she die? Did he hurt her? You need to know. You deserve to know.

"Your name is Julia Anne Allan," he says, his voice honey-sweet and you feel as though you're falling into a dark, endless hole. You don't want to listen to him, but his voice is so soft, so steady, so sure.

"You were born on August fourteenth ..."

~

You finish loading the dishwasher and head into the library, your favorite room in the house. On the very top shelf on the far wall, a book is pulled halfway out—*Rebecca* by Daphne du Maurier, your favorite.

You take it and sink into the corner chair, curling your legs beneath you. A bit of paper sticks out from the end of the book and you tug it free. A letter, folded in three, the edges slightly tattered, the folds feathered almost to splitting. You rest the book on your thigh and unfold the paper.

April 5, 2010

Dear Julia:

If you're reading this, then everything is going according to our wishes. I chose you, you see, not him, and you agreed. Please don't be afraid. This letter is nothing to be afraid of. There's nothing to be afraid of.

There's much I could tell you of you, of how we met, but it isn't important to know that now. Suffice to say, you were in trouble and needed a friend, I needed a way to ensure that my life's work would continue, and I didn't want him to be alone. Fortuitous that we were similar in age, coloring, and build. Fortuitous that he could make alter-ations to correct the dissimilarities.

I know you thought I was joking at first. I know you didn't think it would work, but if you're reading this, then I'm hopeful it did. After all, Rebecca *is my favorite book. You told me you'd never read it before.*

I know it might be difficult, but you need to be patient and under-

standing. After I got sick, I taught him everything I knew, but when you condense years of learning into months, there are bound to be small missteps along the way. He won't give up, and I have faith all shall be well in the end.

Though you might wish for more details of your former life, the three of us agreed that, should you ask, not telling you would be for the best. It would only upset you. I decided to write this letter—and he doesn't know about it so you must keep it that way—in case you were afraid, but remember, you have nothing to be afraid of.

Truth be told, at first he wasn't as keen on the idea as I'd hoped, but once I convinced him it was his idea, once I convinced him he loved you as much as he loved me, the rest of the pieces fell into place.

He is a good man. Remember that. He is a good man. I wouldn't have put you in this situation, nor would you have put yourself here, if he were not.

Remember, you are Julia. You are his wife, the love of his life, the woman he'd do anything for. Even this. You are Julia, and there's nothing to be afraid of. Now refold the letter, put it back in the book, and forget you ever read it.

FALLING UNDER, THROUGH THE DARK

*K*ara's sitting at her desk when she falls. There's no time for panic; it happens too fast. One moment she's working. The next, she's in the water. Gravity and the force of the fall plunge her into the depths and everything blurs. She wants to yell but her body needs to conserve oxygen and won't allow it. Natural buoyancy kicks in and she bobs to the surface, eyes still burning from the chlorine.

Now her heart starts to race and she breathes in huge gulps of air, her mind already fumbling for statistics. Facts. *Every day an average of ten people die from drowning, and of those, two are children fourteen and younger.*

Even as the edges of her world sharpen back into shape, the water pulls again, but *nearly 80% of drowning victims are male* keeps her afloat.

She rubs her palms together and focuses on the sounds of the office: the rhythmic hum of a printer ejecting paper, a snippet of conversation from another accountant's cube, a quick trill of laughter, music from someone's speakers set too low to discern anything save its existence. The prosaic, the expected.

Of course, because the falling is only in her head and her heart.

There are many ways to drown; not all of them require water.

"Grab hold of something when the attack starts," Doctor Harris said. "It will help your mind realize what's happening isn't real. Close your eyes so you see darkness instead of distortion—that works with car sickness, too—and breathe slow and even."

But his recommendations require thought, and in those five to ten seconds, there are no thoughts, only the sensation, the shock. He told her it would pass—the old time and wounds and healing song and dance—and offered a prescription, an offer she didn't take.

She doubts he'd approve of her methods.

She keeps statistics running through her head until the end of the day—she doesn't fall again—and drives home, the sky a study of pink and orange. Her cell phone rings on the way, but she ignores it, knowing it's Colin. They've said everything that needed to be said and everything that didn't. She has nothing left for him.

Walking into the silence of her apartment, she fights the urge to call out that she's home. Old habits don't like to relinquish their hold. She turns on the television instead for background noise. Bare walls gleam marble pale. Boxes she hasn't bothered to unpack collect dust in the corners. After setting a can of soup to heat, she listens to her voice mail. Colin asks if she's received the papers from his attorney, asks if she's signed and sent them back yet, asks how she is. The last feels like an afterthought. She grimaces, erases the message, and drops her phone beside a teetering stack of unread mail on the kitchen table.

Through the sliding glass door leading to a small balcony, she has a view of the South River, a tributary of the Chesapeake Bay. In spite of the autumn chill in the air, boats still move across its surface.

It takes longer to drown in salt water than fresh, allowing a greater chance of rescue.

She closes the blinds. Every flat surface in the living room holds a collection of framed photos: Ben's wispy hair, his sweet smile, his trusting eyes. In spite of the photos, the apartment isn't home, but a waystation. She fled to this apartment three months ago, unable to bear the house, the pool in the backyard, unwilling to meet Colin's eyes, to bear his scrutiny as she pored over statistics, unable to explain her compulsion.

A stack of books perches on the corner of the coffee table; another pile rests on the floor, some still bearing their library markings though they're long overdue. She's read about local drownings, accidental drowning, suicide drownings, the science of drowning. A description of horrible experiments done with dogs to gauge the behavior, the stages, gave her nightmares for weeks. She ripped out the pages and ran them through the shredder at work.

She knows as much about drowning as she does accounting. Knows more than she wants to know. Knows, too, that if her mind can turn Ben into a statistic, she can convince herself it all makes some kind of sense. At least that's what she tells herself.

Kara closes her eyes. Memories flicker like frames in a movie: the unlatched gate, Benjamin face-down in the pool, a shout, a scream, the ambulance, the police, the questions, the disbelief, the distillation of the events into a single word—*accident*.

But the word assigns no culpability. It's nothing more than a panacea for blame. She uncurls her fingers, wincing at the half-moons sure to leave bruises in her palms. Her gaze flicks to the kitchen, to the stack of mail. When Colin admits he left the gate unlatched, allowing their three-year-old access to the pool, she'll sign whatever he wants, but forgiveness isn't something that can be won with mere words.

~

Strange how the mundane becomes a kind of torture. Ben loved the grocery store, loved to sit in the cart and babble, arms reaching for any brightly colored object, be it a box of sugary cereal or a package of bendable straws. Now Kara moves through the aisles with military precision, a list in hand and no deviation. If it wasn't important enough to remember outside the store, it's not needed at all.

When she moved to Annapolis from Edgewater, only ten minutes away, she worried she hadn't moved far enough, but she hasn't run into anyone from her old life yet. Not that they'd recognize her with her formerly long hair shorn into a pixie and the lines cutting brackets around her mouth and across her forehead, lines that appeared seemingly overnight. The change is significant enough that her reflection in the morning still startles her.

The sales clerk gives her a half-hearted smile and an equally half-hearted hello. A mother and child wheel behind Kara in the line. His wispy hair reminds her too much of Ben's, and she keeps her gaze fixed on the clerk's busy hands.

Then she falls. The world distorts and she can't do anything but let the water take her down. The sales clerk's mouth moves, but her words are muffled and indistinct. *Someone who is drowning will not thrash about.*

She bobs to the surface, plummets again and—

They become still and the people around them may not even realize something is wrong.

—she can't breathe because she's holding her breath and she can't *un*hold it—

"Ma'am, your change?"

—and she's too deep and she catches a glimpse of something else, something small, and then it's gone and—

One in five—

she breaks the surface again, but the water is swirling around her ankles, trying to pull her back. The clerk's mouth is open, her brows raised. The mother is standing in front of her son, shielding him as though Kara's attack might be communicable.

"Panic attack," she wants to say, a lie that everyone will accept. Instead, "One in five," emerges.

The clerk blinks. "Ma'am?"

Kara grabs her bags and bolts, not caring that the clerk calls after her about her change, not caring that she draws wide-eyed alarm from everyone she passes. *One in five who die from drowning are children fourteen and younger. One in five. One in five.*

The water recedes, but the smell of chlorine clings to her mouth and nose. In the car, she rests her head on the steering wheel, her eyes closed and burning. The chemical reek hangs heavy in the air, and the cuffs of her pants are wet. She lifts damp fingers to her nose, inhales the caustic bite.

What did she see? *Who* did she see?

No one. She saw no one. She saw nothing. It's all in her mind, never mind her pants. The moisture and the smell are more mental trickery. She scrubs her hand on her thighs and thinks of Doctor Harris, who she hasn't seen in a month, thinks of the prescription, but she knows there aren't enough pills in the world to put her shattered pieces back together again.

∾

While the bathtub fills, she balances on the edge, her robe loose around her shoulders. Try as she might, she can't shake what she saw (or didn't see) from her mind. Rationally, she knows it couldn't have been Ben, but what if? What if she has a second chance to save him and put everything back to right? What if her sorrow has made it possible? The heart can make almost anything real.

Easing into the bath, she takes a deep breath and scoots down so she can slip beneath the surface, her eyes open. Soon enough, a nest of claws and barbed wire makes a home inside her chest, but breathing is the art of the living. She can't count herself among that privileged group, even if she isn't precisely dead.

At the funeral and after, if she heard "I'm sorry for your loss" one more time, she was sure her teeth would turn piranha and rend flesh from bone, but they didn't and she didn't. She nodded and said, "Thank you," all the while screaming inside.

Her lungs are doing the screaming now. She fights to stay under, but her body refuses and she lurches up, gasping for air.

Wrapped in a fluffy towel, she laughs broken glass and brambles. It isn't funny, but it is. The attacks started a week after Ben's accident and now that she wants to have one ... Her cell phone rings from the kitchen, the sound jarring, and—

She falls.

Into the blur, the inability to breathe, and everything turns grey.

Something moves there with her, no, not something, but someone—Ben, drifting, his hair floating above his scalp in pale tendrils, his arms outstretched. Kara reaches, her mouth opens to say his name, and—

Among ages one through four, most drownings occur in swimming pools.

—she shoots to the surface and falls to her knees, coughing out a mouthful of water. She scrubs the taste of chlorine from her lips with the back of her hand. Not caring that her sopping towel is dripping a puddles on the floor, she curls into a nautilus, sobbing.

She can't do it. She can't. She's not afraid of the water. She's afraid she won't be able to save him. She's afraid she'll have to let him go.

Again.

∾

T he knock at her door is soft but insistent.

"Kara, I know you're home," Colin says. "I saw your car in the parking lot. Please, can we just talk? We really need to talk about the house, and I just, I just want to know you're okay. This is hard on me, too, okay? You're not answering my calls anymore and—"

Kara scoots as far into the corner of the sofa as she can, pulls her knees to her chin, and covers her ears.

The five stages of drowning: Surprise, lasting five to ten seconds; Involuntary Breath Holding as the body tries to protect itself; Unconsciousness as the body begins to shut down; Hypoxic Convulsions due to the lack of oxygen; Clinical Death when the heart finally stops.

∾

F rom her balcony, she watches the river. The air has turned from chill to cold, and only a few boats are out on the water. She empties her mind. Wills herself to fall, again and again, but nothing happens.

She closes her eyes. Thinks about Ben running around the yard. That day, he brought her his new water wings, fresh from the package, still deflated and smelling of plastic, and said, "Want to swim now, Mommy," and she said, "In a bit, little man. We have to finish with the pool first." He pouted but went to play with his trucks.

She wasn't being mean, but she and Colin were cleaning the pool and the decking, getting things ready for the season. A little early, but the weather was warm enough. Then she ran into the house for something and when she returned, Colin wasn't there.

And Ben was in the pool. Somehow he'd managed to put on the water wings, not understanding that their superhero logo wasn't enough to keep him afloat.

She falls. Down and down into blur and shadows, and she sees that it's not a pool but a vast ocean of the deepest black, a chasm with no bottom. Although she can't see Ben, she senses him in the darkness, waiting.

Consciousness is usually lost within three minutes of submersion.

And she's back in the here and now. Her lips pressed in a thin line, she summons an image of Ben and falls again. *Four minutes without oxygen* brings her back. Water sluices from her skin, runs across the balcony, drips off the edge.

~

She drives over the South River Bridge into Edgewater, humming along with the radio. Her fingers tremble when she makes the turn onto her old street; her stomach twists when she pulls into the empty driveway. It takes five minutes before she can make herself get out of the car, jingling the keys in her palm. If Colin changed the locks, this trip will be in vain, but she doesn't think he did.

She's right. The inside of the house is dark; all the curtains in the back are drawn, blocking the view of the yard there. The house itself looks ... lost. There are divots in the rug from the sofa she took, and her gardening magazines still sit on the end table. Over the fireplace, there's an empty space where a family portrait once hung. She can still smell Ben in the air, though, and she pinches the bridge of her nose between her finger and thumb.

Some factors that influence risk of drowning are: lack of swimming ability, lack of barriers, lack of close supervision.

French doors in the family room lead to the back yard. Her steps are quiet and she darts furtive glances over both shoulders while she crosses the patio and lawn. A waist-high white fence surrounds the pool, the gate closed and latched tight. Colin hasn't closed the pool yet. Leaves and dead bugs float on the surface, rendering it a scene from a Shakespearian tragedy.

Most drowning children do not yell for help.

Kara's hands curl into fists. While she fell in love with the flower beds and the kitchen, Colin fell for the pool. Growing up, his best friend had one, and he recounted a thousand summer days spent playing Marco Polo and Fish Out of Water, games he said he'd play with their children.

She remembers laughing because they'd just decided to start trying for a baby the previous week. The thought of being an actual parent was still too nebulous. She wants to remember that she was worried, but she wasn't. She believed in the protective power of the fence, the gate, and the lock. And Colin promised he'd teach their children to swim.

Drowning is responsible for more deaths among children ages one through four than any other cause save congenital birth defects.

She passes through the gate. Strips to her underwear and bra, her skin pebbling. She swallows hard, fighting the urge to run. You can drown in grief as easily as you can in a swimming pool. Either way, you emerge on the other side irrevocably changed. Damaged.

If she falls and Ben is there, she'll do whatever it takes to save him. If he isn't there, she'll call Doctor Harris and take him up on the prescription. She'll return Colin's call and sign the papers.

Children aged one through four have the highest drowning rates.

She can't stop shaking, but maybe she owes Ben her fear. Maybe she owes it to herself, too. She steps to the pool's edge. Clears her mind and thinks about Ben's smile. His laugh. The way he'd tug on her shirt and say, "Carry me, Mommy." She takes a deep breath and thinks about that day, thinks about him saying, "Want to swim now, Mommy," and—

She falls. The world turns wavery, light streaming through the water in rays of pale. Because she isn't surprised this time, she counts the seconds. Gets to nine when her feet touch the bottom. Then the concrete crumbles, opening into a chasm, and she stops counting, keeps falling, past black stone walls, marked with pale horizontal striations. The sort of lines you'd make on a doorframe to mark a child's growing height. And from the walls, a steady thump, a great heartbeat.

She twists her body, knowing she doesn't have much time, but she's surrounded by shadows and murk. No Ben. Fear and a growing tightness in her chest turn her movements frantic, then she sees him drifting toward her, his eyes open, his mouth curled into a smile so familiar it makes her chest ache anew. He's wearing his water wings and they're filled with air. Safety. Is this magic or madness or something undefinable? Perhaps a bit of all three.

She reaches for her son, and Ben holds out a hand, fingers splayed. For a brief moment, she feels the warmth of skin against skin, then only stone. The water ripples and when it stills, a tableaux comes to life on the wall of the chasm: the house, the back yard, the fence. She and Colin are standing inside, near the pool. Ben is sitting on the grass, his water wings beside him, arranging his toy cars in a circle.

He says, "Want to swim now, Mommy."

The other Kara says, "In a bit, little man. We have to finish with the pool first."

Then Colin runs into the house—

No, that isn't right. Colin didn't go inside the house. *She* did.

She wills her eyes to close, but they won't. Everything wavers again, clears, and now the other Kara's scooping debris—a bird's nest that fell from one of the trees—from the pool. Colin calls her name from inside the house, she puts the net aside, and dries her hands on her shorts. She passes through the gate and—

Four minutes without oxygen and the brain cells begin to die.

She doesn't want to see this anymore, but her body won't move. She can't make it move.

—says to Ben, "I'll be back in just a second," the other her says, moving toward the house, but there's something wrong. She needs to turn around, she has to stop because the gate didn't click. It didn't latch.

Her mouth opens. Water rushes in. The ache in her chest turns to a thousand jellyfish stings. Colin was already inside the house. *She* left the gate unlatched.

No, no, no. Colin left it unlatched. Not her. Please, not her. In the shadows of her mind, she sees herself running into the house, sees Colin standing by the pool, but the image breaks apart.

Even if the heart can make almost anything real, it doesn't make it the truth.

The tableau bleeds back into the stone. Her body convulses, and her elbow strikes something hard, knocks it away. All around her float framed photographs, Ben's smile peeking out from every one. Her body convulses again; the resulting waves send the nearest photo spiraling.

Another image flickers across the rock—Ben floating face-down, the water wings deflated and torn, tattered ends floating like strands of seaweed.

She screams into the water. Pounds against the rock with her fists. She didn't mean it. It was a mistake, but she can fix everything. She just needs another chance to make things right. She won't forget to lock the gate this time. But Ben's image fades, and she knows it's too late. All the apologies in the world won't bring him back.

The pain inside her swells. Breaks. The steady thump from the chasm's walls begins to slow; the stone begins to melt into nothing at all. She drifts down and down, and then there are hands beneath her arms pulling her up, dragging her out. Voices tell her to breathe, just breathe, and she can't find the words to tell them that she wants to, but she can't remember how.

THE SERIAL KILLER'S ASTRONAUT
DAUGHTER

*T*hey teach you a lot of things in school, in training. One thing that's missing: *What To Do When Your Father's a Serial Killer.*

~

Harrison is quoting from *Aliens* again, something about hell and express elevators. It was funny the first time. After ten months? Not so much.

And we aren't traveling down to anywhere; we're orbiting about 220 miles above Earth on this space station. No xenomorphs, no artificial humans, no acid for blood.

Barring any unforeseen circumstances, I'll make my return trip to Earth in two months and get back in time for my father's execution.

Peachy.

~

Picture this: four days ago. A broadcast from the station. Your basic *hello, how are ya, this is what we're working on now* kind of thing. The folks back on Earth love it.

Harrison, Wallace, and I have the handheld camera floating with us in the corridor outside one of the service modules. The plan is to show the kids how we do maintenance work here in microgravity. Usually the press isn't involved, but the Russians unveiled a new research project into changes in bacterial virulence before the camera switched to us. By now, half the chairs are empty. Our crew isn't the celebrity type.

On a different station we might be. People still love to watch astronauts play instruments or pranks, random shit like that. This space station is owned by a private company, though, and for supposed confidentiality reasons, the public isn't given unlimited access. No song and dance routines or selfies or status updates on social media allowed.

In some ways, it's better this way; we can do our jobs without having to perform for the masses. But the company isn't fooling anyone. They do it so they can control the public's interest. I have to admit, so far it's working.

A reporter, short and blonde with a cruel twist in her smile, raises her hand, is picked by the Earth-side moderator. (I know the smile. I know the type. Perfect lawn, perfect house, perfect happy fucking family, all the while spreading venom like it's goddamn hummus on a pita.)

"Is the news about your father affecting your work in any way?" she says.

Camera cut to the confusion on my face. I'm thinking she has me mixed up with Harrison. His father's in the hospital with heart trouble, but Harrison is a six-foot black man and I'm a five-foot, six-inch white chick.

"I mean, it must be a shock," she continues, "to know that Mark Coyne, killer of twelve women, is your father."

The pressroom erupts in chaos—shouts, flashing lights, waving arms. Cut to my face again. More confusion. A hint of anger. The broadcast cuts to the moderator who is asking for the next question. While that happens, I head out of the corridor, out of camera view, with Harrison and Wallace both looking at me with twin expressions of what-the-fuckery.

Film at eleven, right?

~

The first marriage proposal is a gem: *I FEEL like I know you 4EVER. Your eyes, the smile, plz say yes. I know you're daddy will luv ME.*

I delete it. Proper usage of the apostrophe is hard, but still. The second proposal, written in a far more eloquent manner (and he promises me a lifetime of happiness and love and undying devotion), comes a week later, followed less than twenty-four hours later with the third and fourth. Of those two, the less said the better.

Great, now I have groupies. Like father, like daughter?

(Yes, serial killer groupies exist. Don't bother looking that shit up; it'll make your head spin.)

I don't even know how the fuck they got my email address. I know nothing's *really* private if you look hard enough, but shit ...

~

The folks at the top have been curiously silent, save for one missive I received an hour after the reporter dropped her bomb. It told me that under no circumstances was I to participate in any other planned broadcasts and that further instructions would be forthcoming. Basically, shut your mouth and keep working.

Typical. Still, it makes me uneasy. I know it's only been a week, but I expected a slew of messages. I guess the company has more important things to worry about. I hope so anyway.

~

The reporter who broke the story about my father sent me an email after the broadcast. She says she held onto the information for three months, but *he* was going to go public if she didn't. I'm guessing she planned it that way so she can say she didn't intend to fuck me over career-wise.

Right.

(I got that from Harrison, by the way. I hope I conveyed the correct inflection. Yes, I know it's from *Alien*, not *Aliens*. Harrison is an equal opportunity quoter. And yes, I'm thinking about *Alien* again. The one character just says "right" over and over and over again. Annoying. It's even more annoying when Harrison does it. And he does. All the time.

Don't get me wrong. I like the movies. Seriously, what's not to like? Ripley is a badass female character who takes on a monster alien and kicks its ass. In space. And in the second film, there are two badass females. Even if Vasquez, the marine, doesn't get to survive. At least she goes out on her own terms and with a hell of a bang, too.)

And no, the reporter didn't apologize for blindsiding me with the intel.

Here's the skinny: my mother dated my father. Briefly. They never broke up, he just vanished. She found out she was pregnant, and, obviously, decided to keep me. Ten years later, he got caught.

I never knew my father, never knew who he was or anything about him. I have my mother's last name. My mother says she didn't know, didn't match up the face from her memory to the one in the news reports, and he used a fake name when they dated. She found out the same day, the same way, I did.

Apparently the reporter, who's writing a book, tracked my father's backstory down after he fessed up on some of his aliases. Bam. Hello, birth certificate. My mother used his name, in case I ever wanted to track him down.

After the thousandth emailed apology, I told my mom to stop. It wasn't her fault. She's lucky she didn't end up as one of his victims, but they were all blonde and very young. My mom had dark hair and wasn't quite so young. Maybe he just wanted to try and act normal for a while. Maybe he was hiding. Maybe it doesn't matter.

Twelve dead women, all with families and loved ones, and the media has decided to focus on me. No, it doesn't make sense, but it makes a hell of a headline, so they say. Most people don't remember the names of the victims anyway.

And somewhere in the middle of this whole mess, the press is having a field day. I've become the serial killer's astronaut daughter. I don't know who the hell *she* is, but she isn't me.

~

My official title is Technical Mission Specialist. A space mechanic, if you will, but Harrison, Wallace, and I call ourselves cumscrubs, on account of the special grease we have to use up here.

Crass nickname aside, I've been a regular on this station for the past ten years. Usually it's twelve months up, six back, but I've had shorter stints in both places. It sounds cheesy, I know, but they recruited me after my high school science fair. I'm reliable, I play well with others (mostly), and I do my fucking job.

On this mission, we're here with the Commander, the Flight Engineer, a couple Science Officers, and a few Russian Cosmonauts, including a doctor. Wallace, Harrison, and I try to stay out of everyone's way while we make sure all systems are in the green. The others stay out of our way, too.

Wallace and I are running diagnostics on the interior of a docking module; Harrison running the same outside. (Don't tell the bosses, but we rock-paper-scissored for it.)

I pause, wipe a scrim of sweat from my brow, and tip my head in Wallace's direction. "Did you see the latest? They're painting me as some Jezebel with sociopathy in her veins. Wondering if I'm safe to be here with all of you, or if that shit is genetic and I'm one step away from snapping and killing all of you. I'm being crucified for something I didn't do, for someone I'm *not*."

"Why are you even watching that shit?"

"How can I not?"

"My advice to you," Wallace says, "is to stay quiet and dignified. Let it blow over. Two months and we're out. The novelty will wear off."

"Quiet and dignified? Are you fucking serious? I'm an astronaut, not a fucking Barbie doll. Would you stay quiet and *dignified* if you were going through the same thing? And do you really think things will be better once we're back? That'll make this shit look like a picnic."

He doesn't answer. It doesn't surprise me, though. Don't rock the boat—that's Wallace's way of doing things.

∾

Another news broadcast, this one solely Earthbound: him, the blonde reporter, a room in the prison—cinderblock walls, metal table bolted to the floor, shackles around his ankles, handcuffs on his wrists.

She says, "Would you like to talk to your daughter?"

He smiles a fucking Cheshire cat grin. Pity it doesn't reach into his eyes. (The genetic gods are cruel bastards 'cause my eyes look a lot like his.) "I would, very much so."

I bite the inside of my cheek so hard I taste blood. "Fucker." I exhale the word.

I hear Harrison's voice in the corridor outside the module and turn off the vidscreen fast.

∾

I stare into the mirror for a long time. My eyes. His eyes. Mine don't look so cold, so dead. At least I don't think so. I look at the palms of my hands, move my fingers. Weird. I never noticed that hands look a lot like facehuggers, the nasty spider-like progenitors of the alien. Yeah, that's another reference to the movies. I can't help it, though.

Harrison plays them all the motherfucking time, and they stick in your head.

The facehuggers gave life, although not birth, to the alien, but the only similarity between the two was the acid blood in their veins. (Think human head-sized creepy crawler versus a huge monster with a nightmarish double mouth.) I know *his* DNA is inside me, but there's even less of a similarity between our life forms. I've never thought of hurting anyone. I mean, yeah, I've been pissed off enough to want to punch someone in the face, but not like ... that. Not like him.

~

A few more marriage proposals, emails from people asking me how it feels to be his daughter, another message from the blonde reporter (I delete that without even reading), a quick note from my mom, asking if I'm okay. I look down at my grimy hands, my coveralls smeared with grease. Yeah, it looks about like you think it would.

Then I see the email with the Department of Corrections address. It sits in my inbox, daring me to open it. Delete it, I tell myself. Have the IT folks block the address.

He asks how I'm doing, what I'm doing, tells me he sees a lot of himself in me. I run my tongue around the still sore spot in my cheek. At the end, he adds a P.S. *Tell your mother I said hello.* No comments about who, what, where he is.

I didn't even know prisoners on Death Row were allowed email. Then again, somebody like him, the cops probably want him to have access, then they can take a peek whenever they like to see if he's saying anything that might help. I can't imagine what that would be, though. They're just going to kill him in a couple months, case closed. Hell, maybe no one, not even the cops, gives a shit what he's saying for that very reason.

I've read the details of his crimes, bad enough, and imagine there's plenty worse they haven't leaked to the public. I have a feeling the reporter will include all the juicy details in her book. People love reading about shit like that the same way they love slowing down when they pass a car accident.

I don't say a word to the guys about the email. Harrison, Wallace, and I have been working together a long time and we shoot the shit about everything. But this email? No fucking way.

I stab the delete button hard; if he emails me again, I won't read it.

～

When Wallace pulls me into the communications mod, Harrison is already there, his face grave. "Sit down, okay?" he says.

I see *his* face, paused on the screen. (Strange, I always thought I looked like my mother, but in this frozen shot, I see a lot of myself and I fucking hate it.) "What the hell, guys. This isn't funny." I glare at Wallace. "Correct me if I'm wrong, but didn't you ask me why I was even watching this shit? So what gives?"

He has the decency to look embarrassed before he holds up one hand. "I know, but you need to see this."

The blonde is there, sitting by his side. He looks to her. She nods. He gives a hesitant half-smile, looks right into the camera.

"I've had an epiphany, and I've decided to be completely honest for the first time in my life. I owe this to my daughter, working up on the space station. She really is an amazing woman." He pauses to clear his throat and look down at his lap. "I want to come clean about the ... about some other victims I haven't talked to anyone about yet. But on one condition. I'll give the information to my daughter when she returns to Earth."

A sharp intake of breath—mine. "Motherfucker," I whisper.

A strange numbness spreads through my limbs. It isn't bad enough that he's got the press thinking we were some sort of family? That he was involved? Now he wants to tell me about the women he killed? Uh-uh. No way. Is this some kind of payback for not responding to his email?

Wallace puts a hand on my shoulder. Harrison does the same on the other side.

"That's some real pretty shit," Harrison says.

"Why the fuck would he want to tell *me*? I'm not a cop."

They both just shake their heads.

"I'm not talking to him about *anything*," I say. "This is all so fucked up. It's ridiculous."

Wallace nods.

Harrison exhales through his nose. "Yeah, yeah it is."

~

Along with the proposals, the people wanting to be my friend or offering prayers to support me in my time of need or telling me to kill myself before I hurt anyone, there are a slew of messages from the media, all wanting interviews, all wanting to know what I'm going to do. What. The. Fuck.

And the worst?

The messages from families of missing women that fit his preferred type. They're all begging me to help them: *our only daughter, Patty; our sister, Evie; my best friend, Tilda.*

I can't fucking help them. I can't.

~

Another message comes in from the top. Brief and to the point: No contact whatsoever with Mark Coyne. As if I needed the reminder. As if I'd want to talk to him about anything at all, let alone his crimes.

~

Dear Daughter:

Not sure if you're keeping up with the latest celebrity broadcasts, but you and I are the biggest stars right now. Maybe in an alter-

nate universe, I could've helped your Mom raise you, could be sitting with her right now watching all the reports about you. I hope you write. I'd like to get to know you before it's too late.

No comment about wanting to tell me about other dead women.

My eyes flick back to the *Dear Daughter* again and again.

Delete.

∾

I run into the Commander in between the laboratory modules. She smiles but not before I see the pity in her eyes. I don't smile back. Fuck her *and* her pity.

∾

I head over to the Russian side of the station, flick the side of my neck the way they showed me. They grin, hand over the vodka. It burns like a bastard on the way down, but I don't cough or sputter. They laugh, give me a high-five.

"Your father. *Durak*, yes?" one says.

"Means like dumb-ass," another says.

The others laugh. Another high-five. Another swig of vodka all around.

∾

D*ear Daughter:*
        I've been reading about your schooling, your training, every-thing. I'm really proud of all your accomplishments. Hey, maybe you could contact your Mom for me, ask her to respond to my messages? Maybe the three of us could do an interview together? Elise Paulson, she's the reporter who's writing the book about me, would be willing to put everything together. Just let me know, okay?

Delete.

I'm trying to loosen a bolt that refuses, no matter how much lube I smear around it. "Come on, motherfucker," I yell, wielding the wrench like it's a sword. I attempt to anyway. The microgravity turns the movement into some weird underwater ballet-like thing. Under different circumstances, it would probably be funny as hell, but Harrison doesn't laugh. He puts his hand on my arm, takes the wrench, and steeples his fingers beneath his chin.

"What's going on?" he asks.

"Nothing, I can't get this fucking bolt loose, that's all. I think the threads are stripped."

"Not what I'm talking about and you know it."

"You mean other than the shit about having a serial killer for a father? Or that he wants to talk to me about his kills?"

"Is that it?"

I stare down at my hands for a long time. "No. He keeps emailing me."

"What the fuck?"

"I know, right? And get this, he opens the emails with Dear Daughter. Fucking ridiculous. No, I'm not answering the emails, if that's what you're asking."

"But you're reading them." No question in his words, but it's there in his eyes.

I shrug.

"We have IT guys for a reason. They can block that shit."

"I know."

"This is what he wants, you know?"

"What do you mean?" I wipe my nose with the back of my hand, leaving a smear of grease that makes me grimace. Shit smells like the ass-end of a man who hasn't showered in a month, maybe two.

"You know I studied a bit of psychology, right?"

I nod.

"They're all manipulative bastards. He's trying to fuck with your head, and it's working." He adds the last bit in a soft voice so out of sync with his usual cockiness, I can't help but laugh—one quick bark.

"I just want this shit to go away," I say. "It's like a bad reality show. Daddy Issues in Space or some shit like that."

His turn to laugh. "But he ain't your daddy, little girl, just some guy who provided a bit of squirt." He picks up the tube of grease, lets a little out to float in the air. I bat the glob away.

"Nasty."

"But true. He's behind bars. You being his kid makes for drama and he's milking it for all it's worth. What else has a man waiting to die got to do, especially a man like him?"

"Sitting up here, saying nothing while the media goes nuts is making me crazy."

"So don't say nothing."

"Harrison, you know I can't do anything without *their* approval. Besides, I don't even know what I'd say. I just hate letting it go, you know?"

"What are they going to do, come up here and get you?"

"No, but I'm already under contract to come back in another year. I can't do anything to fuck that up."

He hands me back the wrench.

"So you're not afraid of me at all? Maybe worried that I'll go sociopath on your ass and kill you with this thing?"

He laughs. "Right. Get back to work, grunt."

"You don't think I should talk to him about the other victims, do you?"

"You don't even have to ask me that to know my answer," he says, his voice serious.

∾

Downtime on the station: watching Sigourney Weaver take out a bunch of aliens with some kick-ass weaponry. The screen is tiny, the sound shit, but it's better than nothing.

From Harrison: "She's the best damn character ever. Hardcore tough."

From Wallace, accompanied with a punch on the arm: "Like you."

Me: "And they still put in a scene with her in her underwear."

Harrison snorts. "It doesn't take anything away. Shit, it's just underwear."

Right. I've got grime under my nails that will never come out and I like it that way. Know why? It says I'm real, I have a fucking purpose. I'm not somebody's tits and ass on display like a window mannequin. They did that shit to the baddest fictional woman in the universe. Hell, they even did it to the female marines in the second movie, but that's sort of forgivable because the guys were in their skivvies, too.

You won't catch me in my underwear. I sleep in my fucking coveralls.

∾

In microgravity, it doesn't matter if you sleep upside down or sideways; it's all the same. I'm in my sleeping pod, staring at the dark of my eyelids, but sleep refuses to come. I creep out, float like a ghost down the corridor to the commo mod. Bad idea, I know.

It's one of the late-night shows. An expert is talking about someone being a liability, about the press being too much for any PR firm to handle, about the likelihood of contracts not being renewed. It takes a few minutes before the reality sets in. They're talking about me.

I float back to my sleeping pod. Pretend not to care. Pretend to sleep. They can't possibly terminate me over this, can they? It's not like that man had a hand in raising me, and I haven't been talking to him.

A few years back, a pissed off ex-girlfriend of one of the Flight Commanders released a sex tape. Tame stuff, really, but the media went crazy. Know what happened to him?

Nothing. When the press died down, he was already on the station orbiting Mars. His contract has been renewed without a hitch ever since. Men are forgiven for their transgressions; women crucified for theirs even if *theirs* don't belong to them.

Film at motherfucking eleven.

~

Dear Daughter:
So how much time does it take to readjust to being back on Earth? Just wondering when I can plan on talking to you. I want to talk to you about a lot of stuff, not just the stuff I mentioned on television, but normal dad-daughter stuff.

Delete.

~

I pause outside the commo mod when I hear the tinny sound of a broadcast.

"Has she responded at all?"

"No, she hasn't. I've done all I can." His voice is properly contrite.

"Will you consider talking to anyone else?"

"I don't know. I just don't. I guess in some ways this felt like a way for me to atone to the victims and their families, to my daughter, to everyone."

"Is it true that your lawyers are filing for a stay of execution based on the potential new information?"

"I really can't comment on that."

The news flips to a legal expert, weighing in on the chances for a stay. Apparently, it looks pretty good.

Whoopee-fuckin'-do.

~

When I come out of the toilet, the Commander is there. I step aside, thinking she has to use the shitter, but she touches my arm instead. I pull away but the microgravity kills any shot of it being a yank. Yes, we all fucking float up here, Mr. King.

"We're doing a broadcast on Friday," she says in a soft voice. "If you wanted a few minutes with the camera, we'd all be okay with it."

I choke back a laugh.

"I'm serious," she says.

"Do the boys up top know about this?"

She smiles. "No, and they don't need to until after the fact."

We stand there, just looking at each other.

"You've gotten a raw deal. We all know it, but you need to take control."

Another laugh from me, but it sounds pretty damn close to a sob, too close to one for comfort.

"Look, I've had to put up with a lot of shit to get where I am. I've had to keep my mouth closed more times than I can count, and I regret it. You have a chance to show them you won't just do what we've always done."

"We?"

"Women, especially women in male-dominated fields."

I bite my tongue. I doubt any other woman has a clue what I'm going through. A serial killer dad definitely qualifies as a unique situation.

"And don't think I'm just throwing you out to the wolves. I'll support you in any way I can."

I find that hard to believe. Why the hell would she sacrifice her career for someone like me? "I'm not exactly feminist spokeswoman material, you know."

"And why not? Why not you?"

"I'll think about it, okay?"

She nods. "Good."

Her gaze holds mine for a little while before she heads back the way she came. Maybe the situation really doesn't matter at all, but fuck, I'm a mechanic, not anyone important or influential.

~

Another email from him comes in. I delete it without reading, then empty my trash folder so I can't change my mind.

~

Harrison and I are sitting at the kitchen table with lasagna in foil packs—it's tastier than it sounds—when I clear my throat.

"Do you know about the broadcast?"

He nods. "You going to do it?"

"I don't know. I mean, maybe. Either way, I'm pretty sure I'm fucking done because of him and the media. Never mind that *they* recruited *me*. Never mind that I've been coming up here for ten years. Hell, I've spent more time here than down there."

"So, you going to sit around and mope? You've been quiet, hoping this will all blow over, right? And it hasn't, so you need to protect *your* ass. Saying nothing makes you look—"

"Weak?"

"You've never been the shut up and stay that way type, you know? I get why you've been quiet, job on the line and all that, but this is your life, not anyone else's. You're a badass astronaut, woman. Shut that shit down. Shut it down hard. Be like Ripley."

I grin around a mouthful of lasagna. "Be like Ripley?"

"Damn straight. Fuck the boys at the top. They're trying to protect the company, but this isn't about them. It's about *you*. Ripley wouldn't take any shit and you don't have to either. What are they gonna do? Come up here and smack your hand?"

"If I do this, though, they'll *never* send me back up here."

"You never know. They might surprise you."

"It is so fucking unfair. I'm damn good at what I do."

"We *all* know that."

O n Thursday, Harrison, Wallace, and I rock-paper-scissors for
the last trip outside. I win. (I know they made their choices a
split-second after I made mine. Long enough, you know? They're good
guys that way.)

After I check and tighten all the bolts that need it, I look over my
shoulder. Earth. Home. I wish like hell I could stay up here for
another twelve months, because then he'd probably be dead and some
other drama would take over the news.

I look over my other shoulder, out into the deep dark of space, my
gloved hand on the locking clip that holds me to the station. No matter
what, this is as peaceful as it's going to get.

I stay outside as long as possible, too long, but neither Harrison nor
Wallace give me any grief about it.

F riday:
Harrison grins when I come floating down the corridor. I can
hear the Commander's voice as she talks to the Earthbound.

If I were a man, none of this would matter. They'd brush it under
the rug, say whatever, he had no hand in the raising of said child and
boom, media shitstorm over.

If I do this, my entire career could very well be over. If I *don't* do
this, my entire career could very well be over. I didn't ask for any of it,
but fuck it. I'm not staying quiet and dignified. I'm not keeping my
mouth shut.

When the Commander finishes, Harrison swings the camera in
my direction. I won't ever tell him, but Ripley's never been my favorite
badass character. If you watch the way Vasquez walks around in *her*
underwear, you can tell she really doesn't give a fuck and, right now, it
seems better to channel her instead.

I straighten my spine. Take a deep breath.

Let's rock.

UMBILICUS

*T*ess places the last of Emily's clothes in a box, seals it with a strip of packing tape, and brushes her hands on her shorts. Stripped of its profusion of books and games and art supplies, Emily's room is a ghost.

The box goes into a corner in the living room with the other things earmarked for donation. In her own bedroom, she stands before the wall papered with newspaper clippings, notes, torn pages from old books, and turns away just as quickly, pinching the bridge of her nose between her thumb and index finger.

The small window air conditioning unit growls like a cat that swallowed a dozen angry hornets; a similar sound sticks in her throat. Everyone has to say goodbye eventually, her mother said once from a hospital bed, three weeks before her heart failed for the last time.

With her mouth set in a thin line, Tess begins removing the thumb tacks, letting the paper seesaw to the floor, catching glimpses of the pictures—a school photo with an awkward smile, her own face caught in grief's contortion, a stretch of beach—and the words—*depression in children, somnambulism, unexplained juvenile behavior*—and the headlines—*Suicide? ... Not Sleepwalking, Her Mother Says ... Body Not Found, Presumed Dead ... Presumed Dead ... Presumed Dead ...*

She drops the thumbtacks from her palm onto her dresser and rips the papers free, tearing them into pieces before she lets go. When the wall is nothing more than a study of pinprick holes in plaster and the floor a mess of tattered white, she grabs a dustpan and brush and a garbage bag. Sweeps everything in, refusing to pause even when Emily's face appears.

Utter madness to try and find reason in the unexplainable, and Tess knew, without a doubt, she'd never find an answer. Let the doctors claim Emily was depressed—ignoring everything Tess told them to the contrary—and committed suicide, but they weren't there that night. They didn't see what happened, the way the ocean receded—

(*the shape in the water*)

—the way Emily kept walking, murmuring a word too low for Tess to discern.

She pulls a face. Ties a knot in the bag. Emily was only seven years old; the word *suicide* wasn't even in her vocabulary.

Tess tosses the bag near the front door on her way into the kitchen to wash her hands. On the television in the living room, a commercial is listing side effects for a medicine to treat high cholesterol, side effects the stuff of nightmares. Background noise, its only purpose to swallow the silence.

"Mommy?"

The voice is muffled, but Tess would know it anywhere. She whirls around, soap bubbles dripping from her fingers, her heart racing madness in the bone-cage of her ribs, and pads into the living room.

"Mommy?"

Now it's coming from behind. Tess races back into the kitchen. "Emily?"

Nothing but the rush of water, then she hears another voice, too low to decipher, speaking under—inside—the water. Her stomach clenches.

Not possible, not possible at all—Emily is gone and all the pennies in the world tossed into a fountain won't bring her back—but Tess grips the edge of the sink hard enough to hurt. "Emily?" she says, her voice catching on the second syllable.

Only water splashing on stainless steel answers. Reason kicks in. Tess turns off the faucet and steps back from the sink, wiping her hands on a dishtowel. Through tears, she glares at the boxes piled in the corner—a sandcastle built by sorrow's hands.

From the kitchen window, she can see a small playground just beyond the parking lot. Two children are on the jungle gym, their mothers sitting on a nearby bench. Occam's Razor, Tess thinks. Sound travels in odd ways.

~

With one hand in her pocket and the other clutching Emily's favorite teddy bear, Tess takes the narrow pathway leading to the beach. Her apartment, the second floor of a converted house, is far away from the tourist trade, and the night is quiet and calm.

The soft whisper of her footsteps in the sand is masked by the susurration of the night waves kissing the shore. Once upon a time she loved the ocean, loved the feel of sand on her skin, loved the sound and smell of the surf—it's the reason she moved to Ocean City the summer after her nineteenth birthday, why she stayed after David took off, leaving her with no warning, no money, and three-month-old Emily—but now it's a thing to be tolerated, endured.

She stops well above the water line, afraid if the sea comes in contact with her skin she'll follow it in, screaming for Emily as she did that night a long year ago. Only this time she won't get knocked back to shore. This time, the waves will pull her in, and she'll let them.

After a time, she lifts the teddy bear to her nose, breathes in, but it no longer smells of Emily, merely terrycloth and fiberfill. "I'm sorry, punkin. I'm so sorry," she says, her voice hitching. "I love you." She hurls the teddy bear as far as she can. It bobs on the surface for several long moments, and then the tide sucks it down.

Clouds scuttle across the moon, turning the ocean black. The weight of the air changes, a pressure Tess senses in her ears. The thunder of the waves striking the shore amplifies, and a stabbing cramp sends Tess doubling over. Her vision blurs, the salt tang of the ocean floods her nose and mouth, and a sensation of swelling fills her abdomen.

She staggers back. Presses both hands to her belly, feels the expected flatness there. The clouds shift again. Something dark and impossibly large moves deep in the water, and she flees from the beach without a backward glance.

It's all in your head, she tells herself. *All in your head.*

When she gets close to the apartment, the bright end of a lit cigarette glows from the shadows of the front porch. Tess waves a still-shaking hand and the orange glow makes a responding arc, but neither she nor her neighbor say a word.

∾

Mid-afternoon, Tess slides a box into the trunk of her car, wipes sweat from her brow, and heads back to the house. Her neighbor is sitting in her usual spot—the battered lawn chair in the corner of the porch—with a lit cigarette in her hand and a glass by her side. Gauging by the bright sheen in Vicky's eyes, the liquid in the glass isn't water.

"What are you up to, lady?" Vicky asks, her smile turning her face into a tissue paper crumple.

"Getting ready to go to the thrift store to drop off some stuff." Tess cups her elbows in her palms, hunches her shoulders. "I finally boxed up some of Em's things."

Vicky nods. Exhales a plume of smoke. "Good on you. It might help, you know?"

"I hope so. I kept putting it off, kept thinking I should leave everything the way it was, just in case, but I guess I'm ready to try and let her go. That's why I went to the beach the other night, to—

(*see the shape in the water*)

—say goodbye." She touches her stomach. Swallows the unease.

"Grief is a bitch of a monster." Vicky stubs out her cigarette in the overflowing ashtray. "You think it'll kill you, but it's a hell of a lot more clever than that because it lets you live. Only thing you can do is give it the finger and move on as best you can. Only thing anyone can do." She shakes her glass, rattling the slivers of ice inside. "I need a refill. Want one?"

"How about a rain check for later?"

"Absolutely," she says, surprised by the conviction in her voice.

In front of the full-length mirror hanging on the back of her bedroom door, she strips off her dusty, sweat-damp clothes. She's all arms and legs and narrow hips and small breasts and her belly has no loose skin, no pooch that says a child once sheltered there. Morning sickness lingering well into her second trimester and a waitressing job kept her from gaining too much weight, but now she wishes she'd gorged on ice cream and chocolate and gained fifty pounds, slashing her skin with stretch marks in the process and turning her breasts to sagging teardrops.

Move on as best you can ...

She pushes out her stomach, runs her hand over the curve, remembering the fluttering of butterfly wings and later, the heel of a tiny foot, the point of an elbow.

The air goes heavy and thick with the smell of the ocean. Beneath her palms, her skin ripples, and she yanks her hands away. She feels the tremor again, from the inside, and makes a sound low in her throat, then both the smell and the sensation vanish. Frowning, she pokes her abdomen with her fingertips and doesn't stop until her skin is patterned with tiny red marks like overlapping scales.

~

When Tess stands, the world swims around her, and she grabs the porch railing with both hands, swaying on her feet.

Vicky laughs in commiseration, not mockery. "Need some help?"

"No," Tess says, cupping one hand to her forehead, although it doesn't stop anything from moving. "I got it."

She takes each step to her apartment with careful measure,

ascending one tread at a time the way Emily did as a toddler. Tess can't remember the last time she drank this much. Long before she got pregnant, of that much she's sure. Thankfully, she left her door unlocked because sliding a key right-side up in the lock would require a bit more dexterity than she's currently capable of.

Not bothering to remove her clothes, she drops on her bed, leaving one foot on the floor—she can't remember if that truly prevents a hangover or if it's an old wives' tale—and squeezes her eyes shut. The grey lure of sleep begins to tug.

"Mommy?"

The word cuts blade-sharp through the haze of alcohol, and Tess struggles to sit, her eyelids at war with her intention. Her arms and legs tingle. Her limbs elongate, her fingers and toes deform, her abdomen expands, and a slimy, brackish taste slicks her tongue. She gags, staggers from the bedroom into the bathroom, her body a peculiar, heavy weight to bear, and makes it—barely.

The alcohol and the two slices of pizza she had for dinner come up with a burning rush. She retches again and again until nothing's left but bile, and then again until even that's gone. She runs frantic hands over her arms and legs and torso to find everything the way it's supposed to be and rests her head on the edge of the bathtub, breathing hard.

She flushes the toilet and hears, "Mommy," this time from the chaos of the Coriolis swirl.

"Emily?"

An unintelligible voice—too deep, too *big*, to be Emily's—mumbles something Tess can't grasp, black clouds of octopus ink coalesce in her eyes, and she slips to the floor into darkness.

～

"Hair of the dog?" Vicky says with a smile.

Tess shudders. "Oh, god, no." She half-sits, half-collapses into a lawn chair and holds her water bottle against her forehead. "How much did we drink?"

Vicky shrugs. "Enough to make you laugh. Hell, you even flirted with the pizza boy."

Tess's cheeks warm. "Ugh, there's a reason I don't drink like that."

"Plenty of reasons why I do," Vicky says, her lips set into a grape-fruit twist. "I lost a daughter, too, a long time ago. I was going to bring it up last night, but what's the point? We were having a good time and you seemed happy for once."

"What happened, if you don't mind my asking?"

"Course I don't mind. I wouldn't have brought it up otherwise. So, what happened to my daughter?" She lights a cigarette, exhales sharply. "Her boyfriend."

Tess gnaws on a cuticle.

"She hid the bruises from me, but I knew something was wrong, and when she finally got the gumption up to leave him, he came after her. And I wasn't there to protect her." Vicky takes a long swallow from her glass. "The bastard got his a couple years later. Got jumped in prison after he mouthed off to the wrong guy." A smile dances on her lips and dances off just as fast. "Still didn't bring Crystal back, though."

"I'm sorry."

"Me too. For both of us. And for the record, I don't think you were lying about what you saw that night. Depression, my ass. Anyone who met Emily even once would know that child didn't have a depressed bone in her body. Damn fool doctors don't know what they're talking about most of the time."

"Thank you." Tess touches her water bottle to her forehead again, thinks about what she saw—

(*the shape in the water*)

—and didn't—

(*the shape*)

—see.

"Hell, at least your story doesn't make you a cliché or a stereotype. Never sure which one is the right word, but either way, had to be some truth before the word made sense, right?"

Tess can only nod in reply. She closes her eyes. In the shadows there, the waves recede and Emily walks into the space they left behind, and Tess almost remembers what her daughter said.

∾

Tess wakes and she's cold, wet, standing in the shower. Although the faucet is set to hot, the water pouring down is ice, her skin is bright pink, and there's a thickness in her head as though she's been listening to someone speak for hours or for days. Her nightgown is plastered against a protruding belly. She blinks, and it's gone. Her fingers distort, turning too long with jagged fingernails that resemble lobster claws, but the image proves no more real than her stomach; when she reaches for the faucet, her hands are fine.

"Mommy?"

With a grimace, she shuts off the water. Leaves the nightgown dripping on the edge of the tub and curls up in bed, shivering. Disoriented. Scared. She hasn't walked in her sleep since she was a child.

Is this some sort of involuntary penance for thinking Emily was sleepwalking that night, even though she'd never done it before? Tess followed her, remembering how her mother always said waking a sleepwalker was a bad thing, curious to see where she'd go, and she was only a few paces behind her. More than close enough to keep her safe.

When Emily approached the beach, Tess took her arm, intending to turn her back around, but Emily pulled free with surprising strength and kept walking, heading across the sand toward the water. And then the world changed, became a rubber band stretching Tess into one place and Emily into another with a huge distance between them.

As before a tsunami, the waves pulled back and they kept receding, the sea folding back on itself to reveal an endless stretch of wet sand littered with driftwood, tangled clumps of seaweed, and fish trapped in the throes of death. Tess screamed her throat raw, but Emily kept walking, and no matter how fast Tess ran, Emily remained out of reach. Between her screams, Tess heard Emily say a word (and why the hell can't she remember what Emily said?), and then the waves curled into their rightful place again and Emily was gone. In the space between, did Tess see a shape, an unknowable being, deep inside the water? Her mouth yearns to say no; her mind says an emphatic yes.

Even if the police didn't believe her, she saw *something*. It wasn't an optical illusion, as one police officer suggested, not unkindly. The media shitstorm and the blame from the legions of armchair detectives seems a distant dream now. The press was all too willing to give up when they realized Tess didn't make a good subject. She wouldn't answer their questions, wouldn't get mad and curse them out, wouldn't tear her hair and break down in hysterics. Not in front of them anyway.

~

T wo steaming coffee mugs in hand, Tess pads downstairs, knocks on Vicky's door with her elbow. After she refills their cups a second time, Tess scrubs her face with her hands, clears her throat, and says, "I keep hearing Emily. Every time I turn on the water, I hear her saying *Mommy*." She fiddles with the drawstring on her pants, hating the quiet desperation of her words and wishing she could take them back, inhale them like cigarette smoke.

Vicky takes several sips of her coffee before she answers in a soft voice. "Well ... You're trying to move on and you're feeling guilty about it. Emily disappeared in the water so it makes sense you'd hear her like that."

"But it sounds so much like her."

Vicky leans forward. Fixes Tess's gaze with her own. "For a couple years, I used to see Crystal all the time. Once, I even followed a girl nearly a mile because I was convinced it was my baby. And I identified Crystal's body. I *buried* her. I knew she was dead, but I knew it up here." She taps her forehead. "I didn't know it here." A second tap, to her chest. "Once my heart caught up, it stopped. You'll get through this part of it too."

"Right now, I don't feel like I will. Not today or tomorrow or ever."

"But you will. One day you won't hear her, and then a little while later you'll realize you haven't heard her, and then a little while after that, you'll realize you don't need to hear here anywhere but in here." She touches her chest again.

Tess wants to believe her, but her fingers curl in and her fingernails leave half-moon bruises in her palms.

～

"**M**ommy?"

Tess's head snaps around, the washcloth falls from her hand. She places her palms on the porcelain, bends over the bathroom sink. Takes a shuddering breath. No one there, no one there, she thinks, but another sound emerges from the water, an evocative yet inhuman voice, one she knows she's heard before— *No.* She had too much to drink that night. She heard nothing then and hears nothing now.

Her belly curves, her breasts swell, her limbs are taffy caught in the pull, her mouth is salt tang and bitter.

"No," she snaps. "Do you hear me? No."

Her ears pop, and a dull throb spreads through her abdomen, radiates in a slow spiral to her back. Moaning through clenched teeth, she fumbles for the faucet.

The pain ebbs. Her stomach, her limbs, are perfectly normal, perfectly fine. She rinses away the taste of the ocean with mouthwash, hears only the normal rush of water when she turns the faucet back on.

～

Tess wakes in the middle of the night with her pulse racing. In her dream, she was on the beach, running toward Emily, and she stopped her before her feet met the water but when Emily turned around, she wasn't Emily but *other*, her skin the white of a deep-sea creature and cold as the Atlantic Ocean in January.

Tess turns on her bedside light and scrubs the sleep from her eyes. The sheets are gritty against her feet, and she throws back the covers—sand coats both cotton and skin. Hands clamped tight over her mouth can't keep in the shout.

∼

W ithout curtains hanging at the windows, sunlight floods Emily's bedroom. Tess lugs in paint, brushes, and a canvas tarp, and pulls the bed toward the center of the room. From behind the headboard, something thumps to the floor, and she retrieves the fallen sketchbook with tears shimmering in her eyes.

From the time she could hold a crayon in a chubby fist, Emily loved to draw and while not a prodigy, her passion made up for it in spades. Tess holds the sketchbook to her chest, waiting for this bout of sorrow to pass before she opens the cover.

The first picture is a pencil sketch of Emily's favorite dinosaur, stegosaurus, the spines on its back carefully shaded. The pages that follow show more dinosaurs, a picture of Tess wearing a superhero cape, the beach at night, a second sketch of the beach with a scattering of shells, and then the beach with the waves high and arcing and a dark outline in the raised water.

Tess sinks down on the edge of the bed. The shape in the water, done in crude graphite strokes, is not a whale or a prehistoric shark. It's alien and wrong with too many limbs, too many curves. Tess flips the page. Yet another sketch of the same, the lines more defined, darker, the likeness slightly different, but still improbable. In the next sketch, the shape has altered even more, as if Emily couldn't quite capture on paper what she wanted. Tess's fingers leave indentations in the paper. This can't be real. It can't be right.

"Who are you?" Tess says. "*What* are you?"

What she can't bring herself to say aloud: why did you take my daughter?

~

T ess stands on the beach, wind tossing sand into her face and twisting her nightgown around her hips. Her mouth opens but nothing escapes. Is she dreaming? Dreaming awake? She turns in a slow circle, spies the steady tracks her feet left behind.

The waves begin to recede, and she freezes in place. A dark silhouette twists beneath the changing water, pain threads through her body, the darkness moves closer, and she sees—

No. It's too much. She closes her eyes, can't bear to look. The agony seizes her tight. When it loosens its hold, Tess runs, kicking sand in wide arcs. Behind her, the waves crash upon the shore, and she hears something else beneath—a moan, a whisper.

(Emily said *Mother*. That's what she said, and Tess knew she wasn't calling out to her, wasn't referring to her in any way.)

By the time she gets to the porch, she's sobbing hard enough that her chest aches, and when Vicky grabs her arm, she shrieks.

"Tess? What's wrong? What's wrong? Talk to me. Are you okay? Are you hurt?"

Words spill from Tess's lips, and she knows they don't make sense, but she can't make them stop.

Vicky shoves a glass in her hand. "Drink."

Tess does, grateful to wash the salt from her tongue.

"Now take a deep breath and talk to me. What happened?"

"I woke up on the beach, and I saw something in the water. I saw, I don't know, I couldn't look, but I know it was there. I felt it. It was there the night Emily went into the water, too. I know it was. I didn't want to believe it, but it was there. I think it wants something from me, but I don't know what it wants. I don't know what to—"

"Shhh, take another drink."

"You don't understand. Emily saw it too. She drew it in her sketchbook—"

Vicky presses the glass gently to her mouth. Tess drinks, this time wincing at the liquor burn.

"Okay," Vicky says. "I don't know what you thought you saw, or whether you just had a bad dream or what, but maybe you need to get away from here for a while. I know things have been rough, maybe being close to where it happened isn't good for you right now."

Tess pushes the glass back in Vicky's hand. Vicky continues to talk, and Tess responds in the right places with the right phrases while her thoughts drift elsewhere.

∾

She sleeps on the bathroom floor with the water running. Spends the day in the kitchen with the faucet on full blast and the sketchbook in her lap. Ignores Vicky's knocks at the door.

"Why did you want my daughter?" she says over and over, the tone of her voice as foreign as the thing in Emily's sketches. "What more do you want from me?"

After the sunlight bleeds from the sky, she waits until Vicky goes back into her apartment and creeps down the stairs as quickly and quietly as possible. Her hands are shaking when she walks onto the beach, and she steps as close to the water as she dares.

"I'm here," she calls out into the wind.

The waves break and crash, break and crash. Tess steps closer.

"I'm here," she shouts. "Isn't this what you want? Goddammit, isn't this what you fucking want from me?"

The wind tears her words to ribbons. She steps into the waves, hissing at the sudden sting of cold. Like fabric gathered in a hand, the waves recede, and Tess links her fingers together, wills herself to keep still. The water withdraws even more, and a leviathan, the shape from Emily's sketchbook, undulates beneath the darkness. Goosebumps rise on her arms; her nipples go hard and painful; a shiver makes a circuit on the racetrack of her spine. The air thrums with an electric undercurrent.

A distant gaze bores into hers. A distant mind delves, tastes. An image of Emily's face flickers in her peripheral vision, flickers and breaks apart into nothing at all.

"I'll do whatever you want," Tess shrieks. "Just give me back my daughter."

Her mouth is salt and seaweed. Crab claws dig into her stomach, and she falls to her hands and knees. Her abdomen swells. Something unfolds inside her, shoving razored points and spiked edges against the confines of her womb. She grips fistfuls of sand and arches her back, lets loose a keening wail.

Muffled by the water, another wail echoes her own, but Tess isn't sure if she's hearing it in her ears or only her mind. She rolls onto her back, supports herself with her elbows, and draws up her knees. The grotesque curve of her belly ripples, and as the claws dig in again, the other cries out as well, a great and terrible groaning cry.

Tess arches her back as an urge to push fills her body. She strains with all her might again and again. The world melts into shadow and stardust, leaving only the torment inside her and the exertion of her muscles. She screams as something breaks free and falls flat on her back, panting.

Reaching under her nightgown, she expects to find ribbons of torn flesh, and although the contact makes her wince, her vulva is intact, albeit swollen, and there's nothing beneath her but sand. Her stomach is flat, but the skin is loose, elastic.

Emily emerges from the water, walking as though she's forgotten how legs work. Tess climbs to her feet, staggers forward, and then halts, her mouth in a wide O. Beneath a mottled covering of viscous liquid and traces of sand—a nightmarish mockery of lanugo—Emily's skin is sea-pale. Where once she had a navel, she now has a fleshy protuberance resembling an ornate skeleton key emerging from a lock. She blinks once, twice, and nictitating membranes roll back, revealing black eyes—shark eyes—and Tess swallows a scream. This isn't Emily, it can't be.

"Mommy?"

Tess's entire body jolts. The eyes and skin might be wrong, but the voice and smile are all Emily, yet when Tess holds out her arms, Emily steps back, not closer, and lifts her chin. Moonlight reflects in the black of her eyes, and an image comes in view: a still-swollen

abdomen, pendulous breasts, vulva concealed by a thick thatch of
curls, long tentacular limbs, eel-like fingers ending in claws, a dark eye
emerging from tendrils of coiling hair.

Tess backs away, her hands held palm out. Emily stands, face
impassive. Her lips don't move, but a deep, mellifluous voice says, "I
see you, first mother of my firstborn."

Tess bites back a sob. "What, who, are you?"

"I am the mother of all, she who birthed the world and made it
whole. I am all that was, and all that will be."

Emily takes her hand, and Tess hisses in a breath—Emily's skin is
cold, so cold—and the world melts away. Tess sees the shape, the
mother, sitting atop a throne. Another being emerges from beneath the
ocean floor and wrenches the mother from her place. Sand obscures a
great battle, then settles to reveal black blood and lifeless limbs, and
the mother, battered and bruised, crawling back to her throne. A
second beast rears, rends; the mother's mouth opens in a silent scream;
battle begins anew. More blood and sand and fury. Endless creatures,
endless battles.

Tess covers her eyes. No more. She can't bear this.

Emily pulls her hand away. Tess sees her daughter walking on the
beach and into the waves, into the mother's embrace; sees inhuman
hands guiding her between two great thighs, pushing her into a
cavernous womb; sees Emily floating, sleeping with her hands clasped
together beneath her cheek; sees small creatures crawling from her
navel to drift and grow beside her in the amniotic fluid.

Emily withdraws her hand. "Now you see," the voice, not Emily's,
says. "The usurper gods are finally dead, and it is time for my children
to put the world right. The birthing is over, but your work is not done.
You must open the door."

"But why me? Why my daughter?"

"Because you are her first mother and she alone had the strength
to answer my call."

Tess swallows hard, pushes defiance in her words. "And what will
happen if I don't?"

There is a silence, a profound absence of everything, and stars glitter in the sky. Tess's fingers tremble. In the black pits of Emily's eyes, the mother quivers.

A peal of inhuman laughter slices through the quiet. "Then I will take my children back into my womb, and I will unmake the world."

In Emily's eyes, a face begins to rise to the surface, and every instinct tells Tess to avert her attention, to run, then the face slips into the depths again with more laughter.

Emily steps forward and touches Tess's cheek. "Everything will be okay." She takes Tess's hand and places it on her belly.

The pulsing warmth of the umbilicus is unexpected, and Tess sobs, fighting the urge to pull away. It changes, softens, wraps around her fingers. The narrow strands dance across her skin, and in the center of it all, Tess's fingertips meet a hardness. Emily's gaze, with its strange, black un-Emily eyes, locks on hers.

Panic courses through her veins. What is she going to set in motion? What if this is the end of everything?

"I love you, Mommy. I've missed you so much."

Tess sobs harder. The panic shatters. "I love you, too, punkin, with all my heart. I've missed you every single day."

Emily smiles. "But now I'm back and everything will be okay, I promise."

Tess sucks in a breath and turns the key. The umbilicus shrivels, turns the shade of an oyster shell, and falls to the sand. The weighted silence returns, hangs, and then comes the creak of a great doorway opening. From the water emerges a thousand, no, a hundred thousand Emilys, all black eyes and pale skin, but there is something inhuman in their faces, something painful to look upon, as though their Emily skin is nothing more than mimicry and a closer inspection will reveal the truth and send her screaming into madness.

They move with odd, liquid strides and when they pass, each pauses to pat Emily's shoulder and whisper, "Sister." Tess catches sight of jagged teeth, too many teeth, and where navels should be, they have a circular patch of translucent skin that reveals not organs, but a darkness hiding in a shifting sea. As they leave the beach, disappearing into the shadows, Tess whimpers. What are they going to do? What has she unleashed? And how can such wrongs set anything right?

"Don't worry," Emily says. "They won't hurt you." She blinks and familiar green eyes replace the black, wraps her arms around Tess and the cold is gone, too.

Tears turn Tess's vision to a blur, and she can't speak, can only hold Emily tight, breathing her in, terrified to look too close, to see beneath the camouflage. But she has her daughter back, and that's worth everything and anything at all. No matter what, it has to be.

A LIE YOU GIVE, AND THUS I TAKE

*D*on't be fooled by the breadcrumbs in the forest. This is not a fairy tale.

The first lie is pretty and spirals from your mouth like candyfloss; sweet, so sweet, and I'm melting under your tongue. Baby, baby, baby, you say, and I gobble it up, unaware that every word you say comes with a candy thermometer and you've made me your latest caramel bonbon.

(We'll get to that later.)

It isn't your fault that I'm starving. It *is* your fault that your recipe is gourmet bullshit, and you want to know what I look like with the apron strings tied around my neck and how best you can fit me into your oven.

(This is where I admit I'm caught by the sugar rush, but you already know that, don't you?)

You'll be safe here, you say. You'll be safe with me.

How perfectly charming. Obviously you're not a witch, and my brother is nowhere in sight. Things get lost in translation. Things get changed. And there's no reason for me to doubt your royal peerage— you have the epaulettes and posture to prove it. I think you expect me to curtsy, but the moment passes and I wipe icing from my lips instead.

Your house, in the middle of the woods in the middle of a town in the middle of a muddle, is small, but it's bright and cheery and my feet sink into marshmallow fluff. It's the sort of floor on which a girl could dance a pirouette and a woman, a waltz. I do neither, afraid I might trip over my own aspirations. I suspect even a queen in heated shoes could find comfort. Marshmallow root is good for burns, or so I've read.

Do you invite all the lost girls here, I ask.

You smile and say of course not. You're special.

The words are strawberry shortcake, a little cloying, the portion too large, but I swallow it all.

Okay, I say, and I want to smack myself because it's late and I should be heading back, but the only thing waiting is a woodcutter's axe with my name on it, so I say okay again. The light changes and for an instant, your teeth are canine sharp, your jaw a little too long, but that's the wrong story, isn't it?

(You might think the axe is from the wrong story, too, but there's always a woodcutter and always a blade waiting around the corner.)

Anyway, your teeth are fine and if you bite a little when we're in your king-sized bed, it's okay. I may have a sweet tooth but I'm not delicate.

≈

In the morning, you're already up when I wake and I hear you in the kitchen: wire whisk against glass bowl, mortar and pestle crunch, metal teeth tearing wax paper. I whisper good morning and look for the coffee, but you've got a piece of marzipan at the ready.

I've been waiting for you my whole life, you say, and the sweet sticks to my teeth and there's a cyanide burn when I swallow it down, but I don't pay attention because you're already pushing another piece between my lips.

Then you hand me a bucket and a scrub brush and I'm confused; that's definitely the wrong story, no tricks of light required, and you flick one hand.

All the stories are the same story, you say.

No, you're wrong, I say.

Your mask slips again and what big teeth and what the hell? A blink of an eye and you're back.

Good trick, isn't it, you say, but there's something hiding in your eyes and later, when I'm scrubbing meringue from the linoleum, I realize you quite neatly sidestepped the whole story explanation bit. Clever.

When I finish the floor, you kiss my pruned fingers and I swear I see those teeth again, but maybe it's the fumes from the cleaning solution.

I'll keep you forever, you say.

You're so sweet I can feel the cavities take root in my teeth, and what am I, a toy, I want to say, but I can't talk around the chocolate-covered cherry and you're laughing when you wipe the sticky syrup from my chin.

You pat my hips, my thighs, my stomach, but I haven't been here nearly long enough yet, have I? Later, I touch the oven to make sure, but the burners are off.

～

You leave me alone most days and I pluck gingerbread from the roof to tide me over. I take naps in the afternoon or try to anyway, but I can't ever fall asleep. And yes, I've checked beneath the mattress for a pea. No such luck, not that I was counting on it. Still, a girl can dream.

At night, *babylove* tastes like peppermint and dark chocolate; *always* is orange marmalade; *forever* leaves a dusting of confectioners' sugar on my lips.

But I'm still hungry.

I feel your eyes watching my ass; when you're not looking, I check it in the mirror but it still looks the same to me.

~

I'm searching the cabinets for a package of chicken soup or even a cube of beef bouillon to rid the sugar residue from my throat when you storm in, your epaulettes crooked.

You were with the dwarves, weren't you?

I laugh because I'm certain you're joking but you whip out a handful of Polaroids and shove them in my face.

How is that even possible, I say, looking at the tangle of limbs and the woman in the center. The photos all seem to be variations on the same theme. I'd say they're from a staged photo shoot, but some things can't be faked.

That isn't me, I say. I don't know any dwarves. They're not part of this story.

This isn't a story, you say.

I nod toward the pictures. Those *are* a story, I say, and definitely not mine. Look, she has a birthmark, you can see it on her leg. I offer my thigh as proof, the skin as pale and unblemished as freshly fallen snow. (No, I'm not *that* girl. She's yet another story. In spite of what you may have heard, fair skin isn't unique.)

You move my leg this way and that and then drag me over to the window so you can examine me in the bright sunlight. I hold as still as possible because you have thorns in your eyes. You keep muttering under your breath and I wonder if it's a spell and you're trying to magic the birthmark into existence.

Fine, you say as you let go of my leg and stomp off, crumpling the photos in your hand.

But that night you bite a little too hard, a little too many times, leaving me with a set of oddly-shaped, half-moon bruises.

I stare at the ceiling, so exhausted I can't sleep, and listen to the rumbling of my stomach.

∾

Y ou never apologize. Not for the bruises or the false accusation.
Love, oh, love, I'll never leave you, you whisper instead.

Tiramisu, my greatest weakness. Funny how you figured that out
so quickly. Then again, maybe not. Maybe before the lies, you read
everything you needed in the spaces between the grains of my
own sugar.

You measure the width of my hips with your hands, frowning all
the while. Love, oh, love, right?

I toss and turn beneath the sheets, drum my fingers along the xylophone of my ribs, and wish I had an enchanted spindle to help me
to sleep.

∾

I love you, you say, and then a name, but it doesn't feel like my
name. The syllables are wrong, all soft and slippery instead of
hard and clipped. I have the sensation of falling, falling through layer
after layer of whisper-thin vellum, and I'm not certain how I got here
at all. Then you touch my arm and the sensation ebbs.

And I can't remember ever being this hungry before.

∾

I stop eating bits of the house when you're not here. My vision gets
swimmy, my hands shake, and my stomach feels as if it's caught in
a battle between a tin soldier and a goblin, but my thoughts are
sharper at the edges. I find a sheet-covered mirror, but the distorted
face inside the glass belongs only to me and there's nothing magical
about that.

When you get home, I'm caught in the taffy pull of your hands
again. Every morning, I stick my finger down my throat, but it's always
too late, and nothing comes up but bile.

∼

I'm scrubbing the floor again when I hear a tiny squeak. I follow the noise until I get to a closet door I've never noticed. The door isn't locked, and surely if you didn't want me to look you would have locked it and given me the key with strict instructions never to use it.

I reach for the doorknob, but hesitate. What if the door is booby-trapped so you'll know I've opened it? What if there are severed heads inside, runnels of red dripping down ornate pedestals? I scoff and open the door—I've never been afraid of a little blood and I'm fairly certain Bluebeard's last wife escaped in the end—and there's a tray of chocolates on the top shelf. All the sweets are marked with the impression of your teeth and before I can wrap my head around that little fact, the air shimmers and there's an old woman standing with a wand in her hand.

Who are you, I ask.

No one to concern yourself with, she says and waves the wand.

The chocolates drop to the floor and change shape and color. Grey fur, tiny feet, whiskers, and long tails emerge and a swarm of mice run between my feet and head toward the front door, the little old woman following close behind.

You're a fairy godmother, aren't you, I ask.

She rolls her eyes. What, she says, did the wand give it away?

Do you think you could give me a hand?

Sorry, she says. I'm not *your* fairy godmother, so step aside and let us out.

On the front lawn, she waves her wand again, and the tails and whiskers and fur fall off. Another wave of the wand and women stand in place of the rodents. They huddle in a circle, squinting in the sun and covering their nakedness with their hands.

They're lovely, that goes without saying. I wonder how long they've been here and who's writing this story after all. I wonder if the women walk on mermaid feet of broken glass pain, but the air shimmers again and I hear a ruffle of paper as they slip back into their own stories and it's too late to ask.

Probably for the best. Some tales shouldn't overlap.

~

E very morning, you disappear into the forest. I've thought of following you but it takes all my energy to keep a smile on my face. Are you pining by a glass casket? Waiting for a gullible girl who'll believe she can spin straw into gold? Or searching for elves so you can start a new career in shoemaking?

I'd like to think clearly. I'd like for something to make sense. Maybe it's the hunger pangs. I'd give my kingdom for a slice of roasted chicken right now, but that's never on your menu.

When you return, you poke my side, and tell me I'm too skinny, I need to eat. I point to the raspberry preserves you've shoved in my mouth to remind you of the folly of your statement. You scrape the spoon against the side of the jar and tell me to open up.

~

T he ceiling in the bedroom has a crack in the center I've never noticed before, or maybe the crack wasn't there before at all. I ignore the noises from my gut (in truth, they sound a little like Berlioz's *Symphonie Fantastique*) and dig through the kitchen drawers until I find a pastry knife.

I stand on the bed and wield the blade until the ceiling starts to break off in chunks. And here then, is your story, hidden behind the sickeningly sweet fondant. I'd recognize your handwriting anywhere.

This story doesn't have a proper narrative arc or a clear-cut plot. It rambles like lost children in a dark forest and here and there, things are scratched out and rewritten and scratched out and rewritten again where you've altered things to suit your fancy.

It's nothing more than a vignette made up of all the leftover bits of other stories, but the pieces don't quite fit together, no matter how many once upon a times you've scribbled in the corners. I chip away more fondant to reveal that I'm neither princess nor captive nor anything at all. I'm a character with no face, no self. Quite inter-changeable with almost anyone really.

In the kitchen, I take a good look at your recipes, running a fingertip down the list of ingredients. Sure enough, your creations are as wrong as your story. You've been feeding me saccharine and geneti-cally modified flour. This is why my ribs are showing, why my skin looks like the inside of a well-used cast iron pan.

And I'm not surprised. Not at all.

∾

Y ou walk in all smiles and lollipops, and I hold out a recipe card. How was I supposed to exist on this, I say. What were you thinking?

It's nothing, you say. You are my everything.

Your hands are on me before I can blink, and I taste licorice in my mouth. Black licorice. I can't stomach the stuff. It isn't candy at all, merely some vile substance cooked up in a kitchen full of grim. I spit it out onto the floor and wipe my lips with the back of my hand.

That isn't the way this works, you say. I don't like girls who won't eat.

The skin of your face splits in the middle and the two halves fall apart to reveal another face as much unlike your face as it is the same. Yet these eyes hold no expression, this mouth no mirth or kindness. You're a blank slate and for the first time I'm afraid. I can't tell if you're a wolf in sheep's clothing or a rabid sheep dressed in wolf skin, a bear in a man-suit or a man caught in a bear-suit in desperate need of a good fitting.

I know one thing, though. This isn't what I was expecting. I take several steps back as your skin splits again.

I ate all the breadcrumbs, the you-thing says with a sneer and a flash of teeth. You'll never find your way out. The woods are too dark.

Do you expect me to stay here after all this? I'll need a huntsman to cut me out of your belly when you're done, I say and I'm not sure if that's an exaggeration or not.

Wrong story, you say.

I thought you said all the stories were the same story?

I never said that, you say.

I want to laugh but the ersatz sugar has drained the humor from my veins and for a long moment, I can't remember what my own laughter even sounds like or if I've laughed since I've been here or if I've ever laughed at all.

How many stories will you tell before you realize they're all the same story? I say.

Claws emerge from the tips of your fingers. My chest tightens, but I can't move, as if my legs are fused together. I open my mouth to speak, to cry, but nothing emerges. My hands are shaking and inside I'm empty, a woman of bone and pain and little else, and there's a hole inside me where the words should go.

Please, I finally whisper, hating the weakness of the word, hating the implication, hating myself most of all, for turning into the sort of person who says such a thing.

You say nothing, merely split again from wolf to you-thing to bear and back again. The oven kicks on with a whoosh of orange-blue flame. This can't be the way this story ends, not with this cruelty.

A sharp pain wrenches my breath away, as if I've a thousand tiny chefs carving slices of carpaccio from my heart. The oven might be a kindness after all.

No, I say. No. This isn't right.

You roar and the sound eclipses the ache inside me, but I don't care if I get lost in the woods anymore. I'm tired and I'm hungry and I've had enough. I'm not a princess in need of rescue, nor a maiden without a voice, no matter how many times you've written me thus.

The End, I say, my voice sandpaper and stone.

Your eyes go wide. You can't do that, you say.

You look like you want to say something else, but your shoulders hitch and your mouth opens, unhinging like a broken nutcracker. Out pours a kaleidoscope of spearmint rounds, caramels with cream centers, butterscotch bits, chocolate chips, candied orange slices, peanut butter cups, and lemon drops. The air fills with a cloying reek, a strange mix of sweetness and decay.

Then you change yet again, but instead of splitting into new, the pieces of you fold *in*. Each origami fold reveals a flicker of man, of beast, of man, as if you've told a hundred stories, crafted a hundred masks, and can't find the truth inside your fiction.

The truth is that you can tell a lie a thousand times, but it still won't make it true.

The air rushes around you, swirling in to claim the space you're leaving behind. You roar again but it chokes off into a wheeze, you growl but it fades into a strange mewling, and you keep folding in, reducing.

There's a sound of tearing, of something ripping free, and I feel it inside my chest. You fold in one last time and then there's no you at all, only a scatter of blank pages seesawing to the floor. Cracks appear in the walls, in the floor, and all around me, the smell of burnt sugar and scorched pans.

I've no hidden wings and my hair isn't long enough to braid into a rope, so I crawl out of your story and back into mine, tearing my hands and knees bloody. Even though I know my skin will heal in time, I'm afraid I'll never wipe away the bitter taste of anise from my mouth.

There are no happy ever afters, not truly. Someone always has to pay a price.

LITTLE GIRL BLUE, COME CRY YOUR WAY HOME

J ackson hears Brianna crying before he even opens the front door of their townhouse. The baby might only be three weeks old, but the cry isn't anything he's heard before and he doesn't understand why Abby's letting her sob like that. Panic oil-slicking his tongue, it takes him three tries to fit the key in the lock and two hard yanks to get it back out again once the door opens. He drops the packages of diapers and wipes, takes the stairs two at a time, and runs into the nursery, heart thumping a painful tattoo. Abby is holding Brianna close, whispering, "I'm sorry, baby. I'm so sorry."

"What is it? What's wrong?" he says.

Abby turns toward him, eyes as wide and wild as a snake-startled horse. "I don't know. She started crying and now she won't stop. I fed her, I changed her diaper, and I don't know what's wrong." Her voice is thready, tremulous.

"Want me to try?"

Abby nods. He puts Brianna against his chest, rubbing her back as he gently bounces her up and down. Funny how eight pounds can feel as light as hope and as heavy as rage. "Hey, sweet face. It's okay. Everything is okay now."

Abby picks up something from the floor—the baby monitor, the small device that usually sits on her nightstand. Her face creases into a strange expression. "I brought it in with me and dropped it," she says, the words flat.

The minutes tick by and Brianna's cries don't let up. He catches himself when his bounces get less gentle and he tries rocking her side to side. Tears continue to spill from her eyes, each one a silent accusation. "Why don't you call the doctor?" he asks.

"Do you think we should? What if it's just gas?"

"Better to call and find out it's nothing, right? She's never cried like this before, has she?"

Abby shakes her head. "Okay. Okay then."

Several hours later, they're home with a diagnosis of colic and assurances it will go away on its own by the time Brianna is three or four months old. Jackson watches Abby rock their still-crying baby, his chest tightening. Is this their fault? Did their genetic blending gift Brianna with this? He scrubs his face with his hands. Dumb-ass. The doctor said there was no known cause. Lots of babies had it. It wasn't their fault, just bad luck.

Brianna's cries begin to hitch and soften. He and Abby exchange a hopeful look. Slowly the baby's eyelids flutter shut and the tension in Jackson's shoulders bleeds away. Abby carries her upstairs, and when she doesn't come back down, he heads up to find Brianna in her crib and Abby in their bed, fully clothed and sound asleep, the baby monitor gripped in one hand.

He tries to fall asleep, but instead, stares wide-awake at the shadows on the ceiling while the minutes drag by. The monitor crackles with static and he jumps. Brianna's cries fill the room and Abby is out of bed and near the door before he can kick off the sheets.

~

"Do her eyes look different to you?" Jackson asks.

"What?"

From his end of the sofa, where he's sitting with Brianna on her back, stretched out along his upper thighs, he fixes Abby with a look.

She's busy fiddling with the baby monitor, turning it over and over, her face pensive. Thankfully, she has the volume turned low. This time of night, Brianna is wearing out, her cries not quite as ear-splitting, but he doesn't need to hear her in stereo.

"Her eyes. Do they look different to you?"

"What? No, of course not."

"You didn't even look."

"Trust me, I see them all day long."

"Right, but you can see them here in the light and they look different." They look lighter, but that isn't all. There's something else, something he can't put his finger on, no matter how close he looks.

Abby scoots over, peeks at Brianna, and says, "They look the same to me," before moving back to her end of the sofa.

"You know you can put that thing upstairs." He nods toward the monitor. "She's right here with us."

"I know that. I can hear her." She gets up, clips the monitor to her waistband, and extends her arms. "I want to feed her, then put her to bed."

"It's a little early, isn't it? And didn't she just eat?"

Abby barks a laugh. "My boobs say it's time."

He hands over the baby with a wry grin. "Who am I to argue with your boobs. Feed away."

~

At the end of the day, Jackson's boss stops by his cubicle, leaning against the half-wall with the air of a man unable to stand on his own. An act, Jackson knows, never mind the deep grooves in Charles's face and the sagging skin beneath shrewd eyes. The man ran several miles each day with a near-religious fervor. "How's fatherhood treating you?"

"Colic is another word for hell."

"You look like hell yourself." Charles laughs to soften the words. "With kids, it's always something. Just wait until she's a teenager. These days will seem like cake."

Jackson groans and after Charles leaves, he inputs numbers into a spreadsheet until they blur into nonsense. His co-workers file out, and he texts Abby to say he has to work late, but he closes the spreadsheet and rests his head on folded forearms. Brianna was up most of the night and although Abby did her best, he didn't get much sleep.

He jolts upright to a stiff neck, a small puddle of drool, and the sound of a vacuum cleaner. "Shit, shit, shit," he mutters. It's just shy of eight o'clock and the half-dozen messages from Abby range from *Coming home soon?* to *Your dinner's in the fridge* to *Hello???* He texts a hasty *Sorry. Charles pulled us into an emergency mtg. Left my phone at my desk* to which she responds *Fine.* The lie mixes with guilt on his tongue, but Charles *is* known for spur of the moment, end of the day meetings and sometimes, they run for several hours.

Still, he drives well over the speed limit, giving cursory checks for cops, and races through yellow lights that turn red before he's through the intersections. Abby's in the living room, the shadows beneath her eyes a dusky purple and her eyes filled with recrimination. Through the baby monitor, Brianna's cries are low and plaintive.

An hour later, Jackson turns in for the night, but the nap works against him. From the way she's breathing, he can tell Abby isn't asleep either, but she's on her side, facing away. Definitely still angry. The monitor crackles, the sound stretching out longer than it seems it should, long enough for him to wonder if it's broken, then Brianna cries, and Abby stumbles from the room like an extra in a zombie movie.

He wakes in the middle of the night in an empty bed, the sheets on Abby's side cool to the touch. He hears a low, rhythmic creak coming from the baby monitor, and it takes a few seconds for him to identify the sound: the rocking chair in Brianna's room. Abby is whispering, soft and low.

"I'm sorry, sweetheart. Everything will be okay. I won't do it again."

He frowns in the dark, unable to make sense of her words and too foggy headed to try.

"I feel so helpless," Jackson says, standing in the hallway outside Brianna's room. Her arpeggio cries are sometimes softer, sometimes louder, but always insistent, the moments of silence and contentment few and far between. While taking out the trash, he mentioned to his elderly neighbor that the baby had colic—better that she know over hearing her cry and thinking they were abusing or neglecting her —and she suggested a bit of whiskey.

"For the baby or for us?"

She grinned. "Both."

"I tried to balance the checkbook today," Abby says. "And it was impossible, I couldn't concentrate, so I put her in the stroller and took her around the block." She cups her elbows in her palms.

"And?"

"What do *you* think?"

"In a few months, it'll be better."

Abby half-laughs, half-sobs. Runs her fingers over the baby monitor clipped to the waistband of her pants.

"You don't have to carry that around all the time," he says, gentling his words.

She shrugs. Doesn't meet his eyes. Finally, she says, "I know."

"Do you think the static's normal?"

"What?"

"The static from the monitor. Right before it picks up her cries, there's static and it sounds weird."

She blinks rapidly, her fingers drifting to the monitor again. "No, it works fine. That's just interference or something."

"All right, if you think so. Hey, what did you mean last night, you wouldn't do it again?"

"What are you talking about?"

"I heard you through the monitor when you were feeding Brianna. You told her you were sorry and you wouldn't do it again."

She waves one hand. "Oh, that. It was nothing. I moved and my nipple popped out of her mouth." She smiles, but it doesn't reach her eyes and the shape is off. It's too small and too tight. He lets it go, not wanting to provoke an argument. They're both way too tired for that.

∽

While Abby's in the shower, he scoops a crying Brianna from her crib and holds her at arm's length, angling her so the light strikes her face. Her tiny fists and feet flail; her cries rise and fall and rise again.

But he's right about her eyes. They *are* different, no doubt about it. The blue isn't nearly as deep, but it's not just that. She looks ... afraid. His cheeks burn and even though the water's still running, he glances over both shoulders. Of course the baby's scared with the way he's holding her. In a few years, she'll probably love it, especially if he lifts her overhead, but babies like to be wrapped up tight and held close. That's what the nurses said at the hospital.

He tucks her into the crook of his arm, wipes her tear-streaked cheeks, and whispers, "It's okay, Daddy's got you. It's okay."

He manages to elicit a few smiles and a funny little pursed lip expression that reminds him of a British comedian he saw a couple years back. He kisses her tiny fingers and her tiny nose, his chest tight. How can he possibly love someone this much?

"To the moon and all the way back home again," he says.

He's just beginning to relax when she starts crying again.

∽

When he gets home from work, Abby, dressed in jeans and tennis shoes, is waiting in the kitchen, jingling her keys in one hand, and after a quick peck on the check, she grabs her purse. "We need diapers."

"I would've picked them up on my way home."

"I know, but I need to get out of the house. I won't be gone long, and I just fed her so she'll be fine for a little while."

"Was today a bad one?"

"You can hear her, can't you? And she isn't nearly as loud now as she was earlier." Her face creases and she blinks away the glitter of tears.

He nods. He's pretty sure the neighbors two blocks away can hear her, too. Whiskey might not be such a terrible idea. For all three of them.

Another peck on the cheek and she's out the door. It's only when the car pulls away that he realizes he can't hear the telltale echo of Brianna's cries and the baby monitor is nowhere in sight. As ridiculous as it seems, he suspects Abby took it with her. Truth be told, he's glad. He'd just turn it off anyway. It's not like they need it.

Upstairs, he lifts Brianna to his shoulder. "Come on. sweet face, give Daddy a little break. There's no reason to cry. Everything is okay. Daddy had a long day and he's tired, so maybe his girl can smile instead? Just for a little bit? I know you can."

He tries singing to her, rocking back and forth the way Abby does, dancing around, making silly faces, blowing raspberries, all with the same result. Finally, an ache firmly nestled in his temple, he places her back in her crib, shutting her bedroom door behind him. It helps, a little.

∾

Charles calls him into the office for an after-hours meeting, and he sends Abby a message, but she doesn't respond. Fortunately, the meeting doesn't run very long.

Abby's asleep on the sofa and Brianna must be as well because the house is quiet. He breathes a sigh of relief. Maybe it's only a momentary peace—unless the colic is over, a thought too precarious to grasp too long—but he'll take it.

He brushes a stray lock of hair away from Abby's cheek and her eyelids twitch. "Hi, honey. I'm going to change, but I promise, I'll be quiet."

She murmurs something indistinct.

He slips off his shoes before ascending the stairs and tiptoes down the hallway. At this rate, he could moonlight as a cat burglar. Even in their bedroom with the door shut, he keeps as quiet as possible. Abby says it's better to be as noisy as normal so Brianna will get used to it, but he'd rather not run the risk.

Once changed into jeans and a t-shirt, he peeks in Brianna's room, but he can't see the baby. His fingers tighten on the doorframe. Brianna's too small to wriggle around much and—

"Jackson," Abby calls out from behind, her voice thin and bird-chirp high, and as he turns to look, Brianna lets loose with a sudden, keening wail.

He rushes over to the crib, hoists Brianna to his chest. "It's okay, it's all okay," he whispers into her hair.

Abby runs into the room, the monitor in hand.

"Is she—"

"She's fine. A wet diaper, that's all. Can you shut that thing off? Hearing her cry is bad enough. We don't need to hear her through that, too."

～

Abby comes down in her pajamas, her freshly washed hair wrapped in a towel, Brianna's cries echoing from the monitor in her hand.

"Tell me you didn't take that in the bathroom with you," Jackson says.

Her cheeks pinken but she doesn't deny it.

"But I was with her. I told you I was putting her down. Don't you trust me?"

"I know, and of course I trust you. I just like having it near. It makes me feel better, hearing her. And *I* told *you* that before."

He lets loose with a bitter laugh. "We can hear her fine without it, all the neighbors can hear her, and hell, *she* can probably hear it, too."

"So I'll turn it down. Will *that* suffice?"

"Just turn it off. Jesus, Abby, you carry it everywhere. You don't need it."

He goes to grab the monitor and she whirls away with a snarl. "I said I'd turn it down," she snaps.

"What the hell, Abby?"

She fixes him with a blank stare and doesn't answer.

"Fine. Leave the fucking thing on if you want." He stomps into the kitchen, the echo of Brianna's wails following him in, and grabs a beer from the refrigerator. Maybe if he drinks a few, he'll care a little less.

～

At a small café halfway between his office and his sister's, Jackson slides into a booth and waits for her to arrive. She's a few minutes late, as always, and the first thing she says is, "You look like hell."

"I love you too."

"I assume the screaming mimi is still screaming?"

"Like nobody's business."

"It'll pass, I promise. Just like a kidney stone."

He groans. "That's not even funny. You have no idea what a mess it is."

After they've ordered, she traces her finger in the condensation from her water glass. "Everything else okay?"

He shrugs.

"Come on. 'Fess up. I can tell something's bothering you, something else anyway."

"It's Abby."

"And? You have to give me a little more than that to work with here. I'm not a mind reader."

He rakes his fingers through his hair. "This is going to sound stupid or weird, but she carries the baby monitor around all the time. I mean all the time, even when Brianna's in the same room."

"Uh-huh. And?"

"And that's it. Don't you think it's weird?"

She flicks her hair over her shoulder. "Did you ask her why?"

He drops his chin and peers up through his lashes. "Of course I did. She said she likes keeping it close."

"Don't you believe her?"

"No. Yes. Hell, I don't know. It's just ... It bugs me. It's like a kid with a security blanket. And every time it turns on, right before it picks up Brianna's cries, this weird static thing goes on. It's making me crazy."

"Well, there you go."

"What? The static?"

"Okay, we'll blame this on a serious lack of sleep, but never mind the static, you just explained the whole monitor thing to yourself. Brianna cries all the time, right?"

"Pretty much."

"So instead of a precious newborn to cuddle, you have a little crymonster. I mean, it can't be easy to hold her when she's crying, right?"

"No, but ..."

"So, maybe Abby is transferring that wish to the monitor."

He sits back in his chair. "That has to be the dumbest thing I've ever heard."

"Really? It makes perfect sense to me. I bet once the colic is gone, Abby'll be fine. I bet you both will, or, at the very least, you'll manage to get more sleep. Let her carry the damn thing if she wants. In a few months, it'll all be over."

"Yeah, yeah, I guess you're right. It's a ridiculous thing to even worry about."

"I agree, it is, but you're a first time parent. Everything is something to worry about."

～

The pediatrician, a middle-aged woman with a kind face, frowns as she measures Brianna and it deepens after she puts the baby on the scale. "She's eating well?"

"Yes, very much so," Abby says. "From the breast and when I pump it in a bottle so Jackson can feed her. Either way."

The doctor nods and re-measures Brianna's head. "Yes, yes, we can hear you, little one. Just a few minutes longer." She bends close to the baby's face and shines a light in her eyes.

Jackson's gut clenches, but when the doctor finishes, the frown is gone. "Okay, she's a little smaller than I'd like, but she's healthy," she adds. "Let's try supplementing her daily feedings with eight ounces of formula. Four sometime in the morning, and four again at night."

"Okay," Jackson says.

Abby is chewing her lower lip.

"Not to worry, Mom," the doctor says. "You're not doing anything wrong and I'm not overly concerned. She might just be a slow grower, but we'll see what happens with the formula. And you—" she turns back to Brianna "—I'll see you back in a month. Maybe we'll get lucky and your colic will be gone. That will make everyone happier, won't it?"

∾

He wakes in the middle of the night alone. The house is quiet, the monitor missing from the nightstand. He sneaks down the hall and sees Abby standing beside the crib, her head bowed, rocking slowly from side to side even though Brianna's not in her arms. She's whispering, but whatever she's saying, it's too low for him to hear, and, feeling like an eavesdropper, he creeps back into their room before she notices him.

∾

On Saturday afternoon, with Brianna's cries reaching every corner of every room, Jackson takes Abby gently by the shoulders. "Why don't you go out for a little while? Go to the coffee shop or the bookstore. Just get out of the house and give yourself a break? You just fed her so she'll be okay for a while, and if she isn't I'll just give her some formula."

Her face shifts with indecision, but finally, she says, "I haven't been to the bookstore in ages."

"I know you haven't."

"If you're sure?"

"I'm positive."

"Okay, maybe I will. It'll be nice to get out of the house and be a grownup for a change instead of just a mom."

He watches as she gathers her keys and purse, saying nothing as she slips the monitor into the latter, but when she goes into the powder room, he pulls it out, rearranging her things so its absence won't be immediately noticeable. Her face wreathed in relief, she heads out the door, and once the car is out of sight, he sinks down on the sofa, surprised his plan worked at all.

The monitor is about the size of a walkie-talkie. Plastic, with two switches on top. One to turn it off and on, the other to adjust the volume. He exhales through his nose. His hands are shaking and he doesn't know why. A hunk of plastic is nothing to be afraid of, but still, unease settles into his chest as he turns it off. The house falls silent instantly, as though Brianna's cries were severed with a knife.

He turns it back on. There's the too-long crackle of static before Brianna begins to cry again, but it doesn't sound like a fresh cry. It sounds as though she paused to take a breath and the monitor picked it up right in the middle. If that were the case, he still should've heard her; the door to her bedroom is open.

He flips the switch again. Silence. Is it possible something in the monitor itself is making her cry? There are people who can feel electric wires hum in the amalgam fillings of their teeth. Maybe it's using a frequency that hurts her ears. He puts his ear near the monitor and turns it back on. Listens to the hiss of static and hears something else faintly in the background, something he can't define, can't explain, but then Brianna cries and the static is gone. His arms go all over goosebumps.

He turns the monitor off again and takes the steps two at a time.

Something's not right. That cry, that cut-off cry. He's heard it before. And what he heard behind the static ... He walks into Brianna's room and his mouth goes dry. Her crib is empty.

~

A bby comes home with a bag full of new books, her smile wide and easy. Jackson has Brianna in his arms and the monitor, with the volume turned down, in the middle of the coffee table.

"How long have you known?" he says, his voice velvet soft.

The bag drops from her hands. Her mouth works. Guilt brings red to her cheeks and a tightness around her eyes.

"But the more important question is, how many times have you done it?" He presses a kiss to Brianna's forehead and places her gently on the sofa. Stares at Abby while he closes the distance between them with long, lazy steps. He curls his hands into fists, but what he really wants to do is grab her by the shoulders and shake her. The only thing that keeps him from doing so is the fear that if he starts, he won't stop. Won't *want* to stop.

She drops her gaze. "I only did it a few times, I swear," she says in a rush. "You have no idea what it's like to be with her all day, every day. You have no idea how awful I felt that I couldn't fix her, that I could make her feel better, and then I—"

"You shut her off. You sent her away."

Abby wrings her hands. "Jackson, I swear, I didn't mean to—"

"How could you? How the hell could you do that to our daughter? You have no idea what it's doing to her, let alone where she goes when she's not here. Maybe this is why she's crying all the time. Maybe she's terrified we'll send her back. Did you even think about that? Did you even fucking think?"

"No, I didn't. I didn't think. You get to go to the office all day so you don't hear it. I can't think, I can't sleep, I can't read, I can't even take her for a goddamn walk!"

Brianna's wails grow even louder.

"And she's fine. She isn't hurt. She comes back perfectly fine."

"She's fine? Do you remember what the doctor said about her being too small? And her eyes? Do they really look fine to you? Because let me tell you, they don't look fine to me. They look scared. Wherever she goes, wherever it sends her, it isn't a nice place. And tell me this, were you ever going to tell me, or was it going to stay your little secret?"

"I don't know, okay? I don't know."

"Well, no matter. It's over now. Do you hear me? I'm going to put an end to it."

With Brianna back in his arms, he races up the stairs, Abby at his heels. "What are you going to do, Jackson? What are you going to do? Please, don't do anything. Please. We can figure something out, okay? We can ..."

He shuts the door to Brianna's room in her face and locks it.

"Jackson, no, please. Let me in. Let's talk about this some more. Please."

The monitor's nursery unit is plugged in the outlet behind Brianna's bureau. Ignoring Abby, Jackson slides the furniture away from the wall. "Don't worry, sweet face, everything is going to be okay now." With one quick move, he pulls the cord free, and Brianna stops crying. Abby falls silent as well.

He wipes Brianna's cheeks dry, and her rosebud lips quirk into a smile. "See? You're all better now. Daddy fixed it. Daddy fixed everything."

He unlocks the door. Steps out into the hallway. Abby's face is streaked with tears and her mouth opens, but all that emerges is a steady hiss of static.

SUGAR AND SPICE AND EVERYTHING NICE

First of all, the whole thing was Madison's idea. All of it. She saw that movie, the one with the prom and the pig blood. And no, before you ask, we weren't going to hurt any pigs. We're not psychos. Where would we find one in Edgewater anyway? A pig, I mean, not a psycho. It was just the idea of doing something like that. Something big.

She wanted to cut off Tara's hand, that's what, and that's all she wanted to do, nothing else.

Why? Because she wanted to know if she was right about what Tara really was. See, after the first week of school, we—me, Ellie, and Madison—knew something was wrong. In ninth grade, Tara was normal—we hardly even paid any attention to her. She wasn't in any of our classes or anything, but we saw her so we knew what she looked like and stuff—but when tenth grade started? We didn't know what was wrong at first, but we knew *something* was. For one thing, she smelled.

Yeah. Obviously you never met her or you'd know what I was talking about. She kind of smelled like a hospital. It was barely there, the way perfume is when it's mostly worn off. You almost didn't notice it, but when you did, you couldn't not smell it. Except Ellie couldn't smell her at all, so maybe some people couldn't, you know? Then Tara started wearing perfume, so I guess someone said something, probably her mom since she was the one who did everything to her. Oh, and also, she had a weird walk. It's hard to describe. Kind of a limp, but not really. I guess weird is the only way I can describe it. Ellie asked her about it—her locker was next to Tara's this year, that's how come we knew everything, I guess I should've said that before—and she told her she twisted her ankle over the summer.

Well, yeah, Ellie believed her. Me too, mostly. It was Madison who said it was bullshit because when she twisted her ankle it didn't leave *her* with a limp. So she said we should keep an eye on Tara. No big production about it, just sort of watch the way she walked and talked and stuff.

No, we didn't talk to anyone else about it. We kept it to ourselves. Anyway, since we were watching her, that's how Ellie saw the stitches, but we already knew from what happened with Tyler—

Okay, sorry, I'll try not to confuse you. It's hard to tell it right. Forget about the stitches for now, then. I'll tell you what happened with Tyler.

Yeah, Tyler Braxton. He has a thing for grabbing girls' asses. Total middle school stuff, but he's always been creepy-ass weird, like live in his mom's basement for the rest of his life weird. Anyway, a bunch of us were in the hallway by the computer lab, right? And Tyler grabbed Tara's ass. There weren't any teachers around. Tyler might be creepy but he's smart creepy. So he was laughing and the rest of us there were trying to ignore it. It's the only thing you can do. But Tara's face got all weird. I don't know how to describe it. Like angry, but calm, too. And she pushed him, not even that hard, and he went all the way across the hallway and hit the wall on the other side.

No, no one did anything or said anything either. We were all too surprised and I was trying to figure out how she was so strong because she was kind of skinny, maybe not model skinny but still small. I think it seriously freaked Tyler out, and I thought he might hit her, but he didn't and then Miss DeMeester showed up and we all split.

Sure, people talked about it, but everyone said she got lucky and caught him off balance, you know? Ask him about it, I bet he'll tell you, but it probably isn't that important anyway. He left her alone after that. A couple weeks after that, that's when Ellie saw the stitches. See, Tara dressed almost Amish, wearing stuff that went all the way up to here and down to the floor. Not Amish dresses, they were normal clothes—jeans and shirts—but the kind that cover everything up. And she never pushed or rolled up her sleeves. Ellie said Tara was getting something from her locker, and her sleeve caught on the edge and pulled back a little bit. Ellie said the stitches were blue and they were pretty small. She thought Tara had on a bracelet or something, but by the time she realized what they were, Tara'd already unhooked her shirt and closed her locker and was gone. So Ellie told Madison and me and we thought at first maybe she tried to kill herself and didn't want anyone to know, but the stitches were in the wrong spot. They were on top of her wrist, not underneath where all the veins are. So Madison asked Alex, who lives on the same street as Tara, if he noticed anything weird over the summer at Tara's house, and he told her that Tara and her mom—Tara didn't have any brothers or sisters and her dad died in a car accident when we were in fifth grade—were gone until the week before school started. He said they told one of the other neighbors that they were spending the summer with Tara's grandparents. Madison asked him if they ever did that before and he said no, not that he could remember.

No, she didn't tell Alex about the stitches. Maybe everything would've been different if we knew right away what Tara was and what happened to her. The accident, I mean.

No, I'm not saying what we did was her mom's fault, but maybe things would've been different, that's all. What did her mom think would happen? For a super smart scientist, she isn't very smart, and my mom always says just because you *can* do something doesn't mean you should. Why did her mom even send her to school? She should've homeschooled her or something if she wanted to keep it all a secret. Think about it, the only reason anybody knows the truth is because of what we did so people should be happy, not pissed off.

Well, whatever. After that, Madison wanted to try and see the stitches herself, so she started hanging out with Ellie at her locker, trying to bump into Tara and stuff. But nothing ever happened. I'm the one who saw them, but I swear the whole thing was an accident. A real accident. For my birthday last year, my dad gave me a charm bracelet, the one you found. I love it but it catches on everything. I even yanked out a bunch of my hair with it one time. So I was leaving school late—I was out sick the day before and had to take a make-up test—and Tara was leaving, too. We bumped into each other on the way out the door and our wrists hit each other. You know, like this, back to back? One of the charms caught on something and I pulled it the way I always do, not thinking about it. I heard this noise, a wiry *boing*, but my bracelet was still caught so I pulled it again. There was the *boing* again and then I was unstuck. She took a deep breath and that's when I figured one of the charms had caught on her shirt or something and I said "I'm sorry" but she didn't say anything. She was looking at her wrist so I looked too. The stitches were all the way around her wrist, and my bracelet had yanked a couple open. It was like two puzzle pieces but instead of clicking together, the stitches were holding them, and inside, there were other things connected. I didn't want to know, not really—I can't even watch gross stuff on TV, it makes me want to puke—so I looked away super fast. There wasn't any blood, though. There was that weird hospital smell, but it was different, like it was mixed with a funeral home—my grandma died last year so I know how they smell—and I was all lightheaded and sweaty. I thought for sure I was going to puke. Tara's eyes got all huge, and she took off, practically running. I almost didn't tell Madison and Ellie about it, it freaked me out so bad.

What did I do? Nothing. I stayed there for a few minutes until I felt okay again and then I went home. *Then* I called Madison. I probably shouldn't have because she loves horror movies and has a crazy overactive imagination. One time in fourth grade she was convinced that Mr. Barron was a zombie because his skin got all pale and he started walking slow. Know why? He had the flu. Normal flu, not brain-eating walking dead flu. After I told Madison what I saw, she told me not to tell anyone else, not even Ellie, and to act like nothing happened and to be nice to Tara.

No, I don't think she had anything planned then, but she was probably thinking about it. So I started being nice.

What do you mean? I said hi to her when I saw in in the hall, asked her how things were going, stuff like that. Haven't you ever been nice to anyone before? We weren't hanging out together after school or anything.

By that time, though, me and Ellie weren't the only ones who knew about the stitches. Bastian saw them in Geometry, but *he* saw them on Tara's ankle when she bent down to tie her shoe. The difference was, he asked her about them, and she said she cut herself on a broken glass. Then Leila saw some on the back of her neck one day when it was windy, and Van said he saw some on her shoulder except we figured he was lying since she didn't wear tank tops. Plus, it was starting to get chilly. A couple other people said they saw them, too, but I think they just wanted people to think that. I don't think they really did, but they didn't want to be someone who *didn't*. No one else saw what I did, though, or at least if anyone else did, they didn't say anything and I think they would've. So after that, there were a bunch of rumors. She tried to kill herself, she had a bunch of warts removed, she was in an accident and didn't want anyone to know—which is pretty funny when you think about it—they were tattoos, she was fucking with us, you know, by drawing them on. It was pretty much only a joke at that point, even when Alex gave her the nickname. He was the one who called her Frankenstein.

Wait. That *isn't* the monster's name? Then how come everyone calls it that?

No, I haven't read it, but it's really old, isn't it? I don't like to read. It's a big waste of time. But whatever. When Alex called her that, he wasn't trying to be mean. He was being, I don't know, stupid-funny I guess. He said something like what's with all the stitches, Frankenstein? I wasn't there so I only heard it from Ellie, and she said Tara said people were pretty stupid if they believed that and hadn't he ever cut himself before?

Sure, people believed her—wouldn't you?—because thinking she was really Frankenstein was crazy. If we were still in middle school, maybe, but now? The world isn't like that. At least that's what we thought.

The nickname stuck, though, and she acted like it didn't bother her, but you could tell it did. Alex is the one who made the picture, too, the one with her face Photoshopped on a Frankenstein body. The green one with bolts in the neck and stitches all over. He stuck it to her locker. She took it down as soon as she saw it, but he did it a couple more times, on her locker and then in it, you know, folded up and put through one of the slots at the top. Nowhere else, though.

The teachers? No. They probably didn't see it or if they did, they probably thought it was for Halloween or whatever. You should ask them if you really want to know. And I know Tara didn't tell them. They definitely would've done something if she did.

No, I still didn't say anything about what I saw. *Ellie* still didn't even know. Honestly, I didn't even really believe it, even with what I saw, and I started to think that maybe I just thought I saw it. I don't think Madison believed it either, but she knew something was up and she wanted to find out *what*. She wanted to be the one who found out.

I don't know why. I guess because she's Madison, that's why. While everything was going on, I was still being nice to her, to Tara, I mean. Ellie and Madison started to, too. We told her to ignore them. I even took down one of the pictures and told Alex to knock it off. That's when he called me Igor. I told him to fuck off, and Tara was there, too, and she said, "He thinks he's funny, they all do, but they're all idiots." She said I wasn't Igor anyway, but more of a Justine. I didn't know who she was talking about, but she was smiling, so I smiled back.

She's in the book? Really? What, is she like someone's sort of friend?

So Frankenstein—

Oh, okay, got it, the monster, not the doctor, kills someone and she gets blamed? They find out the truth though, don't they?

They *kill* her? But she didn't do anything.

That's so not funny. Not funny at all. You don't think Tara knew

... No, never mind. So what happened next was that Madison told me to try and bump into her again, but only when she was around so she could try and get it on her phone.

Why wouldn't we?

No, I mean, I understand what you're asking, but—

Mean? I don't know. We just wanted to see it again.

Okay, okay, yes, I'd already seen it, but *Madison* still wanted to see it.

I didn't ask her what she wanted to do with the picture or the video, but yeah, I guess I kind of knew she wanted one so she could put it online. But we weren't going to hurt her, and it doesn't matter anyway because we never got the chance. I tried but I guess Tara knew she had to be really careful now that she had that nickname—maybe her mom yelled at her or something—and I didn't want to bump into her and have her know I was doing it on purpose. It was a pretty stupid idea anyway, so after a couple of weeks—and by then people were hardly talking about Tara anymore because everyone thought Anna was pregnant so they were talking about her instead—Madison said we needed to come up with something else. That's when she told me to invite her to the Faraday house. That's the one on Beach Road that's been boarded up forever but there's a way to get in. You have to be careful, the house is on a corner and there are lots of neighbors around, but we sneak in it all the time, no big deal.

No, I still thought Madison wanted to do the stupid break a stitch thing. I knew she didn't want to be Tara's BFF, not for real, and I guess maybe I should've known she was planning something bigger but I didn't. Not right away anyway. Not until the night before. And even when she told me she wanted to cut off Tara's hand, I didn't believe her. She didn't even tell Ellie what I saw or what she wanted to do until they were on their way. I mean, we didn't even know if the stitches were still there. I thought that if they were, Madison would tell Tara what she wanted to do and scare her or make her cry or maybe both, maybe even pretend that she was going to rip open a stitch or two, but I knew she'd chicken out before anything really bad happened.

What do you mean, how? I just knew. I've known Madison since we were like four years old.

I don't know. I guess I thought it would be funny. And I figured we could pick on Madison for chickening out, the way she gave us a hard time when we wouldn't do something she wanted us to.

Well, yeah, the whole thing was kind of stupid and mean, but I told you, I didn't really think anything would happen. I didn't even think Tara would show up. I was surprised she even said yes when I asked her to come with us. I told her how to get in and she said she'd meet us there. Me and Madison and Ellie were there for a while, and Madison said Tara wasn't coming, but she did, and when she showed up at the house, she scared the crap out of us. We didn't even hear her come in and the floors are all creaky. We were up in the back bedroom —you can turn on flashlights there or light candles and you don't have to worry about anyone seeing, not that they probably could with the windows boarded up. Madison had one of her parents' bottles of rum and we were sitting around and talking about the teachers and stuff. Nothing major.

Yeah, Tara took a couple drinks too. Finally, Madison looked at Tara and said, "So what's the deal with the stitches?" Tara smiled and said, "I figured that's why you wanted me to come. You sure you want to know?" And Madison said yes, so Tara pushed up her sleeve and we all saw that the stitches were still there. Then she pushed up her other sleeve and there were stitches there, too, but not on the wrist, they were near the elbow. The whole way around.

We didn't say *anything*. We were way too surprised. It's one thing to think something's true, but it's another thing to know it so ... So, Tara kept smiling and then took off her sweater. She had on a tank top underneath and we could see stitches on the top of her left arm and they wrapped around and went up to the back of her neck. She pulled up the tank part of the way and there were more stitches across her stomach, and you could see that the skin didn't quite match. Parts of it were darker and other parts lighter. "My mom thought everything would be healed by now, but I guess she was wrong," she said and Ellie said, "Your mom did this?" Tara nodded. "I told her people would find out," she said. "She said they'd find out if I didn't go back to school. Act normal, she told me." "What happened?" I asked. "There are more," Tara said. "Want to see them all?" Ellie and I both said no at the same time. Then Tara said, "It was an accident. My mom and I had a fight and I took her car. I hit a tree and boom. The next thing I remember is waking up and my mom telling me that everything was going to be okay because she fixed me. And I was like this." "Fixed you?" Madison said. "She made you a freak." Tara didn't say anything, and I could see that Madison was pissed off.

Why? Yes, she wanted to find out, but she didn't want to just hear about it. She wanted to be like one of those Anonymous guys, the ones that wear the masks and figure out a story before everybody else knows the truth. "Is that why you smell?" Madison said. "You *stink,* like something that's been dead and then brought back to life, like Frankenstein. You wear that perfume to hide it but it doesn't."

No, Tara still didn't say anything. "Where did your mom get all the parts?" Madison said. "Cause you can see they don't match. Did she dig them up?" Tara shrugged and said, "She didn't tell me." Then Madison said, "Are you even you anymore?"

No, she didn't answer, but she had this funny expression on her face. "Do you think those people whose parts you took would want that?" Madison asked and then Tara said, "My mom said she got permission from their families." "Right," Madison said. "Their families, but not them. Because they were probably dead." Tara said something about organ donors, I don't remember exactly what, and Madison laughed. Her cheeks were all pink and her eyes were bright. Tara still had that weird look on her face, but she was kind of smiling, too, and I thought she was going to hit Madison or something, but she didn't. Madison said, "What do you think would happen if we undid the stitches? Would you fall apart?"

No, I kept my mouth shut. So did Ellie. It was Madison's thing. Tara shrugged and held out her hand for the bottle, acting like nothing was wrong at all, and that pissed Madison off even more. "Fucking freak," she said and she hit her with the bottle on the side of her head, here.

Yeah, the temple. She must not have hit her that hard because Tara didn't pass out or shout or anything. It didn't even break the skin. There was a red mark, but it didn't even look like it hurt her at all. Then Madison took a pair of scissors out of her purse and said, "Maybe we should find out."

Yeah, those are the ones. I can tell by the blue handle things. And Tara didn't even look scared, that was the weird part. She grabbed Madison's wrist, and said, "Go ahead." Madison tried to yank her arm back and couldn't and her eyes got really wide. Then Tara let go and we could see the marks on Madison's skin. "Maybe I will," Madison said. Ellie said, come on M, let's just hang out, okay, and Madison told her to shut the fuck up and if she wanted to leave, she knew how to get out. I could see that *Madison* was scared, but she was more pissed off and that's why she wasn't going to back down.

I could tell by her face. And the thing was, neither was Tara. I didn't even know her that well, but it was obvious. I don't think she thought Madison would do it, but Madison did. I think she had to, otherwise Tara would've won, you know? First she held up her phone though and gave it to Ellie and told her to record it. Ellie didn't want to, but she did, and even that didn't bother Tara, even though she had to know that it would probably go viral and then everyone would know. Madison held the scissors for a long time and then she cut one stitch, and then, super fast, almost like she wanted to do it before thinking about it too much, she cut another. The whole room smelled bad, like really bad, rotten bad. I swear, I didn't know Madison was really going to do it. She wanted to make Tara cry. If Tara had, it would've stopped right then and there.

Believe what you want, but I'm serious.

No, I'm not saying it was Tara's fault. Not really. But she could've stopped it.

Ellie and I were just sitting there. What were we supposed to do? Tara wasn't fighting or anything. She kept holding out her arm and she *still* didn't look scared. So Madison kept cutting the stitches, even when the smell was so bad Ellie and I were practically gagging. There wasn't any blood, though. Not then. Ellie was crying and I knew she was trying to figure out what would be worse—staying or going. And the look on Tara's face the whole time, it was fucking creepy. Her hand was hanging off and the inside, it was awful. I knew I was going to puke so I ran out of the house—I didn't even say goodbye—and threw up outside in the bushes.

Because I didn't want to see anymore. I told you I can't watch gross stuff.

I don't know. I wasn't thinking about Tara, I wasn't thinking about any of them. I didn't even care if Madison never talked to me again. I was halfway home when I realized my bracelet was missing, and that's why I went back.

No, I didn't call anybody. I wanted to go in, find my bracelet, and leave. The house was quiet—I thought maybe everyone left already—and my bracelet wasn't anywhere downstairs, so I went up to the room. Tara was still there, but she was alone. Madison chickened out after all, like I thought she would.

No, Tara wasn't doing anything. I didn't even see the blood right away because she had her arm kind of off to the side. She asked me if I knew. "Knew what?" I said. "What Madison was going to do," she said. I lied and told her no. Did it matter anyway? If her mom could do all the rest, she could fix that easy. "She's going to put it online, isn't she, so everyone can see it." I shrugged, but I think she already knew the answer just by the way she said it.

Yeah, by that time I saw it was completely off, the whole way. The scissors were on the floor beside her, next to the blood and the hand. I didn't really look at it, though—I couldn't—but she saw me not looking and said, "It didn't even hurt that much." She said she thought there'd be more blood and she was going to undo the rest. I told her she should go home, that the video wouldn't be that big of a deal, that her mom could fix her. She laughed, gave me that weird look again, and said she hit that tree on purpose. "I left a note and everything," she said.

No, I didn't say anything, but she asked if I wanted to stay. She said I could even record her if I wanted to, said it would be better for me if I did.

Are you kidding? Uh-uh, no way was I going to stay there. I mean, what would you have done? And I didn't think she was serious. I thought she was trying to scare me or gross me out. Payback, you know?

No, I didn't call anybody that time either. I went home and didn't even text Madison or Ellie.

No, not until later and then all I did was text Madison that she was a bitch. She texted back *fuck you* and that was it. I didn't even know Madison put the video online until the next day.

I'm telling the truth. I felt sick from puking so I went to bed early. When I got up, my mom told me Ellie's mom had called her because Ellie told her what happened.

What do you think? She was pissed off. She told me we were stupid, what were we thinking, she raised me better than that, all the normal stuff moms say. But how were we supposed to know what Tara was going to do?

No, uh-uh, you're wrong. We didn't just stop recording. I told you, I left first and when I went back, Ellie and Madison were gone but Tara was still there and she was fine. Her hand was off, but she was okay. Her arm wasn't even bleeding, not that I could tell. That's the truth. And when I left, she was *still* okay. If you watch the video, you can see everything that happened.

I don't know why she had my bracelet in her hand. I told you I lost it. I guess she found it.

No, that's not what happened. You have to believe me.

Because I'm telling the truth, that's why.

I know she left a note. She told me so.

A different note? What did it say?

Bullies? Us? That's such bullshit.

Well, maybe her mom's lying.

I don't know why. I never met her.

No, *Alex* came up with the nickname and made the pictures, not Madison. I don't care what her mom says the stupid note said. We were *nice* to her.

I *am* telling you the truth.

She didn't tell me why she was going to do it. Maybe she was unhappy. Maybe she wanted to see what would happen. Maybe she figured her mom would just put her back together.

No, I don't know how she did it all. I told you, I wasn't there. Nobody was except her.

Then maybe someone else came in after we left and helped her. I don't know.

I don't care how stupid it sounds. I'm telling you the truth. Maybe she wanted you to think we did it, but we didn't. I swear we didn't. She did it to herself. That's the truth. Ask Madison and Ellie, they'll tell you the same thing. She did it to herself.

IN THE SPACES WHERE YOU ONCE LIVED

A doe picks her way from between two trees at the edge of their back yard, keeping to the narrow path, her legs moving with a dancer's grace. Helena holds her breath, even though she and the deer are separated by a wide expanse of lawn, a deck, and locked French doors. Somehow, it seems the right thing to do. Her hand instinctively reaches for Jack's, touches empty air instead. They say it takes twenty-one days to break a habit; the heart knows nothing of such things.

The doe lifts her head, tips it in Helena's direction. Its eyes seem wrong, pale where they should be dark—blind, perhaps? Or ill?—and several patches appear to be missing from its fur. Helena squints and leans closer to the glass, but before she can take a good look, the animal's ears twitch and it turns tail and disappears back into the woods, moving too surefooted to be blind. A few orange leaves spiral down from the trees, as if marking the doe's passage, but as yet, the branches hold more than they've shed. The temperature is still mild, and Helena longs to follow the doe into the deeper woods. Maybe if she were younger, maybe if circumstances were different.

Their house sits on the southern edge of the woods surrounding Loch Raven Reservoir, the largest body of water entirely within Baltimore County. The woods contain nearly seventy miles of hiking trails.

Over the course of their forty-eight years in the house, most of the trails have worn their footprints, their daughter's, and more recently, those of their grandsons.

Autumn was always Jack's favorite time of the year for hiking. "For a little while, Lena," he'd say, "everything is different, like the world is opening up to show us its secret side."

"Then winter comes to hide it away again," Helena whispers. Tears prick her eyes, and she blinks them away. Too many of those these days, far too many.

From behind her Jack says, "I can't find my keys."

He's wearing a wool scarf, a windbreaker, pajamas, and slippers. His hair resembles the quills of a porcupine; it's too long but when she tried to trim it three weeks back, he pushed her hand away as soon as he saw the scissors. She hasn't had the heart to try again, and, frankly, the length of his hair is the least of her worries.

"You moved my keys again," he says, his voice heavy with accusation. "I need to pick up my wife, and I can't find my damn keys. Where did you put them?"

She recoils from the force of his words. *Her* Jack rarely cursed. "I got a ride home from Naomi today because your car is in the shop. Remember?"

A necessary lie—his car was sold months ago—but guilt clings bitter to her tongue nonetheless.

"Oh," he says, his face softening. "Oh. I guess I forgot again."

She twists the wedding band on her finger. It doesn't move nearly as easily as it did a year ago. Jack has lost both the weight she's gained and his wedding band. The former is easily explained, the latter still a mystery as to how and where.

"Did you finish reading the newspaper?" she asks, her voice holding a tone similar to the one she used when Cathy was small.

"It came already?"

She nods. "It did."

"Today's paper?"

"Yes."

"Oh."

His gaze flicks from her face to the window. The sun is only beginning to set, but the room holds the suggestion of shadows. Helena bites back a curse at her own forgetfulness, not his, twists the kitchen window blinds closed, and pulls the French door's drapes tight.

"Did the newspaper come today?" he asks.

"Yes, it did. It should be on the coffee table."

His brow creases. "Okay."

She moves toward him. "Do you need any help—"

He yanks his arm away before she makes contact. "Help? To read the newspaper?"

"No, how silly of me. Of course you don't need help, but would you like to help *me* shut the rest of the curtains?"

He glances at the window again, shakes his head.

"Okay, well why don't you go ahead and read the paper while I take care of the curtains, and then we can have some dessert." She thinks of mentioning his scarf and jacket, but decides against it. It takes so little to upset him these days. He'll take them off if and when he wants.

"Before dinner?"

She catches her lower lip briefly between her teeth. "Well, we had dinner already, but if you're still hungry, there's some chicken left."

His brow creases again, deeper this time, but instead of responding, he retreats back to the living room. Once she hears the crinkle of the newspaper, she takes a deep breath. Then she starts the nightly routine of shutting the rest of the curtains and turning on all the lights, hating the way it makes the house feel closed-in, hating the way it will affect him if she doesn't.

∿

When Jack gets up in the middle of the night, Helena snaps awake. The wandering is a recent development and odd, too, given his newfound fear of the dark, but after the first time, when he stubbed his toe hard enough to tear half the nail away from the bed and left a small crime scene in the dining room, she's started to leave a handful of lights on. He uses the toilet—luckily, he's only had a few minor accidents thus far—and then his feet take to the stairs. She debates whether or not to stop him, to try and guide him back to bed, but her forearm still wears the ghosts of finger-shaped bruises from her last attempt, so she follows him instead.

He skirts the living room furniture with ease, pausing in front of their wedding portrait hanging on the wall. They were both so achingly young, so vibrantly smiling, and she can't bear the thought of the hole in his memory where that day should live. In the kitchen, he opens the curtains to the French doors and stands with his hands behind his back. His posture reminds her so much of the days before the disease, before he started forgetting, a lump takes hold in her throat.

"This is the wrong door," he says, and she startles. "This isn't my house."

"Jack, honey, it's late. Come back to bed. It's still dark outside, that's why it looks different, but it's the same house we've lived in for a long time."

He shakes his head. "No. This is the wrong door. The right one is out there." He reaches for the doorknob. Before she can move toward him, he takes his hand away. "Okay," he says softly. "Not yet."

She steps close. "Let's go back to bed, okay? Everything will look right in the morning."

His eyes narrow and his lips tighten, then he moves past her and heads back upstairs. She stares out the window, elbows cupped in her palms. The sky is just beginning to lighten at the edges, a lessening of dark as opposed to real light, and wind rustles through the trees, turning the leaves to a rippling fan of orange, red, and yellow. Autumn, like Alzheimer's, turns everything strange and unfamiliar, and when you look for the shape of the real hidden within, you find only a promise of the winter to come.

There's another stir of movement in the woods, back where the path curves into the trees, and Helena catches a quick glimpse of ears, legs, and tail. She waits, but whatever was there, if not a trick of the shadows, has moved on.

When she returns to their bed, Jack is already asleep. She clasps her hands beneath her breasts and stares at the ceiling, knowing she won't fall back to sleep.

~

"How is everything, Mom?" Cathy asks.

Helena looks up from the dinner plate she's scraping into the sink. In the back yard, her grandsons are playing catch while Tim, her son-in-law, watches from the deck. Jack stands nearby, and Helena wants to think he's watching the boys, too, but his gaze is trained on the woods.

"Much the same. He has good days and bad, and luckily, today is a good one."

Cathy takes the plate from Helena's hand and slides it into the dishwasher. "Not with Dad. I mean how is everything with you?"

"Everything's fine, sweetheart." Helena smiles, and even though it feels too tight, she does her best to make it convincing.

"Is that the real answer or just the one you want me to hear?"

Helena waves one hand, grabs another plate.

Cathy makes a sound low in her throat. "I see dark circles under your eyes, and you only get that way when you're really tired. Are you sure you don't want me to arrange for someone to come in and sit with Dad so you can get some rest?"

"I'm fine. Your father woke up in the middle of the night a couple times, that's all, but he slept through last night. It'll take me a little while to catch up on my beauty sleep." Another small lie, another false smile, both more palatable than the truth.

"Seriously, you don't have to do it all."

"I know, but I'm afraid a stranger coming here will only make things worse for him, especially on the not-so-good days."

"I can talk to my boss, take some time—"

"Hush. You have your hands full with your job and Tim and the boys as it is. I'm perfectly capable of taking care of your father right now, and if things get too bad, I'll call someone in."

"Do you promise?"

Cathy's youngest son barrels into the kitchen. "Mom? Nana? We're gonna go for a walk, okay? Pop-Pop wants to go, and Dad said to ask you guys."

"Are you okay with that?" Cathy asks.

A nervous twinge stirs in Helena's belly. Jack is still steady enough on his feet and she trusts Tim, but Jack's good day can change in an instant without provocation.

"How about if I go, too?" Cathy says, catching Helena's eye.

"Please, Nana?"

Helena nods, although the twinge bites again.

Cathy smiles. "Good. Leave the rest of this until we get back, okay? Go sit down and read the paper or watch TV or even take a nap."

Helena watches them take the path, Cathy gently holding her father's arm. When they disappear into the woods, she leaves the dishes on the counter, knowing Cathy will be upset with her if she doesn't, and sinks into her corner of the sofa. She'll rest her eyes for a moment, then she'll finish cleaning up. It's been ages since she had the opportunity to take a catnap. She probably won't even be able to fall asleep.

When the back door bangs open, Helena, still on the sofa, blinks awake.

"Nana, Nana! We're back."

Once jackets have been shrugged off and set aside, Helena touches Cathy's shoulder. "Was everything okay?"

"Yes, pretty much. Dad got a little upset at one point because he said he couldn't find the right place, but then we started to come back and he seemed better. He did say that you don't let him walk in the woods anymore." She says this last with a small smile, but there's a kiss of sadness on her face, too.

∽

A fter breakfast, Jack starts pacing from room to room, now and again pausing to cock his head. Helena lets him make three full circuits on the first floor, including the half-bath, but when he shows no signs of stopping, she says, "Jack, what's wrong?"

He brushes past her, keeps silent. In the foyer, he pauses again, his mouth moving in silent conversation.

"Jack?"

According to his doctor, he isn't truly hearing voices or seeing things. His brain is misinterpreting reflections in windows, house noises, or sounds from outside. Still, it's unnerving. He comes to a stop in the living room and whirls around to face her.

"This isn't my house," he says, his voice razor-sharp. "I know it isn't."

"Would you like to watch a movie?" She keeps her voice bright, cheerful.

"Stop talking to me. I know what you're doing, but it won't work. This isn't the right house."

She takes a deep breath. Redirection doesn't always work, but it's the best technique to use to keep his irritation from becoming true anger.

He cocks his head again. "But I'm tired of waiting."

"What?"

"I'm not talking to you. I'm talking to *them*. Leave me alone."

Another deep breath. "What if we take a walk into the woods, like you did with Cathy and the boys?"

He smiles then, and all she sees is *her* Jack, and she fights against the sting of tears. He allows her to help him with his boots and coat, waits while she dons hers, but when she tries to take his arm, he shrugs her off. She lets it go but keeps close to his side as they cross the yard to the path, not speaking. Focusing on the pleasant chill in the air, the smell of pine and earth, the vibrant oranges and reds and yellows of the leaves around them, some of her tension abates. No holding hands, true, but it could be a normal day, a normal walk with her husband. Even Jack's posture changes: his strides grow longer and easier, his

arms swing, his eyes gleam with purpose instead of confusion or ire.
Fallen leaves crunch and whisper beneath their soles.

His fingers brush hers, and then again; the third time, he entwines
them with hers and she bites the inside of her cheek to hold in a sob.
The path becomes a wider trail littered with small twigs that crack
with each step. Sun glimmers through the trees, speckling the ground
with bits of bright like crushed glass. Day stars. He always called them
day stars. The words linger on her tongue, but she's afraid to say them
aloud and break the fragile spell, for this, his hand around hers, his
easy walk, is a kind of magic. The best possible kind.

A thick branch lies across the trail, and Helena pauses, wondering
if they should go back, but Jack tugs her hand, helps her over. Their
gazes lock, and once more her throat tightens. Warmth radiates in his
eyes; more than that, recognition, familiarity. This is the Jack that
stood beside her and said "I do," the man who cried with her when she
had her first miscarriage and her second and her third, the man who
cried even more when she gave birth to Cathy, healthy and whole.
This is the husband whose weight she felt atop hers more times than
she could count, whose hand she held at funerals, at weddings, at
birthday parties. In this moment, she is companion, not caregiver.

*Please let him stay Jack for a little while longer. Just for today, let
him remember, let him stay.*

Around them, the shadows grow, but they continue to walk. Her
boot begins to rub against the baby toe on her right foot, and although
she knows there will be a blister to pay, she says nothing, tries only to
shift her foot as she places it down.

Jack pauses. His fingers tighten around hers; his head turns this
way and that. His mouth moves, forming silent words, then his hand
relaxes and he starts walking again. She bites her tongue. A small
misstep, not worth the mention, not worth the worry. For all she
knows, he did hear something she missed.

They come to a slow incline. Halfway up, he freezes in place, and
she does the same. At the top, half-hidden by the brush, stands a doe.
No, not *a* doe, but the doe with white eyes and missing fur. The
animal is so thin its ribs resemble a xylophone, its remaining fur is dull,

and threads of frothy spittle dangle from its jaws. Her mouth turns to desert, her fingers to ice. Her body jolts, and beneath her heel, a twig breaks, the sound loud and sharp. The doe doesn't run as expected, but slowly turns and disappears down the other side of the incline. Helena shudders.

Jack pulls his hand free, shakes it as if removing the memory of her touch. "We have to go back. It isn't time yet," he says.

"Time for what?"

The Jack mask falls; in its place, an angry old man with narrowed, suspicious eyes. "We have to go back. Now."

"Okay, Jack, okay. We'll go back." She shoves her hand in her pocket, the warmth of fabric a pale substitute for the warmth of skin.

Several times on their way home, she feels the weight of unseen eyes, but when she casts a glance over her shoulder, she sees nothing unexpected, nothing save trees and falling leaves.

～

She wakes to find the bed empty and panic sours her mouth. Upstairs, Jack is nowhere to be found. As she takes the stairs as quickly as possible, the blister on her toe bursts wet and warm against the adhesive bandage. Her breath comes fast and harsh, easing when she finds Jack in the kitchen, once more standing at the French doors with the curtains partially opened.

He mumbles something and frowns. He speaks again, his words tangled and indistinct. The tone of his voice is strange, thick and yet somehow liquid, as though he's speaking around a mouthful of half-set gelatin. A cold chill dances the length of Helena's spine.

He frowns yet again, followed by another slur of words, and turns toward her.

"Soon," he says, his voice perfectly measured, perfectly *normal*, and leaves her alone in the kitchen.

She waits until the upstairs floorboards creak before she moves to shut the curtains. There, at the end of the yard, the white-eyed doe. More patches of fur have fallen out; the bare skin beneath holds a strange grey cast. Her arms go all over goosebumps, and the icy waltz makes a second spin on her back.

She doesn't know if diseases can pass from deer to human, doesn't understand why it keeps showing up or how it can even find its way, but most of all, doesn't want to believe that Jack was holding an imaginary conversation with the animal.

"Go away," she whispers.

As if on command, the doe turns and slips back into the woods. Her goosebumps remain.

~

Jack refuses to get dressed in the morning, and after tempting him with several shirts that were once favorites, she gives up. What's the real harm in letting him keep to his pajamas and slippers? He sits at the kitchen table without argument, though. A small victory.

While the coffee is brewing, she asks, "Jack, last night, when you woke up and came down here, you said, 'soon.' Do you remember? What does that mean? Is something going to happen?"

He smiles. "I'm waiting for the door, the real one, to my real house, and it's almost time. They can fix everything, they can fix *me*. They said so."

"Who said so?"

He looks down at his hands. "I can't tell you."

"Can't or won't?"

"Are we having eggs today? I think I want eggs."

She puts away the box of pancake mix. "Yes, of course we can have eggs."

Midday, while Jack's napping, Helena dials Cathy's number but hangs up the phone before it can ring. What's she going to say? Your father is talking crazy, and there's a doe that keeps coming to the house, a doe with white eyes and missing fur? Oh, and I think your father is talking to it, too?

She shakes her head. It's the disease. She knows it is. The disease and the toll it's taking on her, his paranoia bleeding into her, and the deer is obviously ill. Sick animals usually remain close to familiar areas until they find a place to die. And Jack isn't talking *to* the deer, but *at* it, as if it were a newspaper or a television show. Soon enough, he'll be fixated on something else. Soon enough, the animal will be fodder for the flies and beetles.

The truth is, she can't handle this, can't handle Jack on her own anymore. She needs to put aside her own pride and bring someone in to help because it isn't going to get any easier and she knows what's coming: more anger, more confusion. The disease will continue to strip every bit of Jack away, and when it's done, it will destroy his body. Like an autumn tree, he's shedding his leaves, leaving bare branches behind, but for him, the new growth of spring will never come.

She wishes for a stroke or a heart attack, something quick to end his suffering—and hers—but as soon as the thought takes shape in her mind, guilt drapes itself across her shoulders, and she scrubs her face with her hands. This is the way the world breaks you. It takes everything you know and love and turns it inside out. It leaches the color from your hair, yellows your teeth, and curves your spine, and even though you wish you were the same person you've always been on the inside, you go grey and stained and frail there, too.

Stop. Get hold of yourself. You need a good night's sleep, that's all.

Tears burn and she lets them fall, unsure if she's weeping for Jack or for herself or maybe for them both.

❧

He's pacing again. Living room to dining room to kitchen and back again, pausing at each window to peer outside, muttering incoherencies all the while. She does her best to ignore it, but when he shows no signs of stopping, she asks if he wants to go for a walk.

"No," he says.

"Would you like to watch a movie with me?"

He tips his head to the side, then nods. "Okay."

Once settled on the sofa, he pats the back of her hand. "Lena, I'm sorry I'm so forgetful sometimes."

Her name. He used her name. A knot tightens in her chest, and she has to untangle her voice. "It's okay, Jack. I love you."

"I love you, too."

She cups the side of his face in her palm, and although he doesn't lean into her touch the way he used to, he doesn't pull away.

~

Arms around an empty laundry basket, Helena walks past the bathroom and grimaces. Jack's toothbrush, still holding a bright blue swoop of toothpaste, is on the edge of the sink, but there's no sign of Jack. Leaving the basket in the hall, she checks their room, but it's empty as well. She was only in the guest bedroom long enough to put the freshly washed sheets back on the bed. How did he get past her without her hearing a thing?

Once again, she finds him downstairs by the French doors.

"Jack, what are you doing? It's time to get ready for bed."

"No," he says, reaching for the lock. "It's time for me to go. They said so."

"Let's go back upstairs now. You need to brush your teeth."

He whirls around, his face a snarl. "You can't stop me. This has nothing to do with you. It's only for me."

She takes his arm. His mouth twists again; he puts his hands on her shoulders and growls. "No," he shouts, shoving her away.

Her arms flail, but she grabs only air and lands hard on her tail-bone with a sharp cry. The door thumps shut, and she struggles to her feet, breathing through her mouth, ignoring the starburst of pain in her lower spine. Her fault, this is her fault. She should've replaced the locks with keyed dead bolts. What if he falls, what if he gets lost and hurts himself? Or worse?

The night air is chill, full dark with no hint of sunrise, and clouds veil an almost-full moon. Too dark to see much of anything but shadows and the pale blur of his pajamas.

"Jack, please stop. Come back. It's too dark outside."

But he doesn't stop, doesn't look back, simply keeps moving across the lawn faster than she's seen him move in years, moving as steady and sure as if it were a sunny day. He reaches the path and, with a flash of striping, disappears into the trees.

She scrambles across the kitchen to the junk drawer, pawing frantically through the contents. At the very back she finds what she's looking for: a small flashlight. "Small, but bright," Jack said when he bought it at the hardware store, long before his diagnosis. She pauses by the phone. She should call Cathy or even 911, but no one will arrive in time and if he wanders off the path ... She checks to make certain the flashlight works and shakes her head. No, Jack won't go far. He *won't*. Not in the dark.

Beneath her feet, the ground is cold and her nightgown isn't nearly warm enough, but she's wasted enough time already. She sweeps the light across the lawn; the last thing she needs is to trip and fall. Pressing her lips together tight, she takes to the path. A few steps in and the shadows hang even heavier. She scans the trees with the light. No Jack.

Impossible. He has no light. He can't have gotten that far. She trains her light on the path and keeps moving, her back awash in a cold sweat, her mouth pinched and acidic. She calls out his name, gets no response. The path turns to trail, and still she sees nothing but darkness and shadows. No sign of her husband. The woods are silent, unnaturally so. Shouldn't there be small animals scurrying about or insects or something? This quiet is absolute and terrifying.

She nearly stumbles over his discarded slippers, but they alleviate some of her panic, for even in the dark he's managing to stick to the path. On the other side of the branch Jack previously helped her with, she sees both foot and handprints. The shake of her hands makes the light bounce, but there's no blood on the ground, so if he fell, maybe he didn't fall hard.

"Jack?"

When she reaches the bottom of the incline, she calls his name again. She needs to go back and call for help. She was a fool to try to find him on her own. *Stupid woman. Stupid, prideful woman.*

Then she hears Jack's voice, low and unintelligible, but distinctly his, and a wave of relief crashes over her.

"I'm coming, Jack. Stay there. Please stay there."

"I'm here," he says.

On the incline, her thighs start to burn, and her feet slip on twigs and scree. Halfway up, she hears Jack say, "Will it take me to the right house? Is it the right door?"

"It is all doorways," another voice says, a guttural, inhuman voice, one she doesn't hear with her ears but with her bones, each syllable pressing its indelible shape into her marrow. Every instinct says run, but she can't. She *can't.*

"You will carry it until it's time," the inhuman voice says. "The animal wasn't strong enough."

A pale, sickly light spills over the top of the incline.

"Oh," Jack says.

Ignoring the ache in her legs, Helena scrambles the rest of the way up. Jack stands at the bottom, his arms slack at his sides, and in front of him, the doe. The light is seeping from the corners of its white eyes, the way sun finds the edge of a window blind. There's no sign of the speaker, no sign of anyone or anything else.

The doe's body ripples, its eyes expand, and more light spills out, a greenish-yellow light that hangs heavy in the air. The sound of tearing fabric—no, worse than that, tearing flesh—breaks the quiet, and the doe's body topples, landing with a soft thump. In its place hovers a fist-sized ovoid of the blackest black haloed within the strange light. It begins to slowly rotate, absorbing the light and expanding to the size of a basketball. When the light is gone, the sphere resembles an oil slick dotted with flickering lights. Starlight comes to mind, but it isn't that exactly. It's something more, something bigger than she can put a name to. A truth, a nightmare, a *doorway.*

Yet for what?

Jack holds out his arms.

"No," she cries, but the word shivers into the air and is silenced.

The sphere collapses, draping over his skin like a blanket of space. It seeps into his flesh one galaxy at a time, leaving strange whirls and spheres in between, patterned as if they, too, are galaxies, but those her eyes are not able—or not allowed—to discern. A scream tears its way from her lips, but if it holds a sound, it lives only in her mind. Pressure thuds behind her temples, sharp jabs blade through her head, and she falls to her knees, dropping the flashlight and covering her eyes. She hears: a slow thrum, a symphony of voices speaking in a language she wasn't meant to hear and can't understand, the sound of strange and ponderous bodies moving closer then away.

Her ears pop and silence falls once more. She scrabbles in the dirt for the flashlight and rises on rubbery legs, her breath a rasp of sandpaper laced with sobs. The air is thick with the stench of a rotting carcass; underneath that, a peculiar metallic heat.

"Jack?"

He turns toward her voice, his shoulders slumped. As far as she can see, no trace of the black remains.

"They couldn't fix me," he says. "I'm too broken."

A lump in her throat steals her voice away.

You will carry it until it's time.

Looking down into his eyes, all she sees is Jack, lost and afraid, but she feels the presence of something else, something *other*.

What is he carrying inside him, and what will happen when it's time? How is she supposed to pretend everything is fine? This isn't fair. It isn't right. He's too old for this, whatever this is. They both are. Haven't they suffered enough?

She swallows hard, her thumb tracing a circle around the flashlight's on-off switch. She could turn around right now and leave him here. No one would know. She could call the police in the morning and tell them he wandered out sometime in the night without her hearing. He wouldn't be the first, or the last, to do such a thing.

But how can she do that to him? Even if he isn't wholly Jack, he hasn't been Jack for a long time. Still, she remains where she is, staring into the shadows.

"I'm cold," Jack says, his voice trembling. "And I don't feel well. I want to go home now. Please, Lena, can we go home?"

PUBLICATION HISTORY

"Tooth, Tongue, and Claw" — originally published in November 2015 in *Nightscript I*

"Deep Within the Marrow, Hidden in My Smile" — originally published in May 2016 in *Black Static*

"On the Other Side of the Door, Everything Changes" — originally published in June 2016 in *Gutted: Beautiful Horror Stories*

"This Is the Way I Die" — originally published in May 2014 in *Nightmare Magazine*

"The Hands That Hold, the Lies That Bind" — originally published in January 2016 in *Cemetery Dance Online*

"Not My Circus, Not My Monkeys: The Elephant's Tale" — originally published in August 2015 in *Apex Magazine*

"The Judas Child" — originally published in December 2015 in *Nightmare Magazine*

"S Is for Soliloquy" — originally published in May 2015 in *B Is for Broken*

"The Floating Girls: A Documentary" — originally published in September 2014 in *Jamais Vu*

"Take a Walk in the Night, My Love" — originally published in November 2016 in *The Madness of Dr. Caligari*

"Falling Under, Through the Dark" — originally published in May 2015 in *Black Static*

"The Serial Killer's Astronaut Daughter" — originally published in January 2014 in *Strange Horizons*

"Umbilicus" — originally published in April 2016 in *The Mammoth Book of Cthulhu*

"A Lie You Give, and Thus I Take" — originally published in December 2014 in *Lightspeed Magazine*

"Little Girl Blue, Come Cry Your Way Home" — originally published in July 2016 in *Lost Signals*

"Sugar and Spice and Everything Nice" — originally published in October 2016 in *Eternal Frankenstein*

"In the Spaces Where You Once Lived" — originally published in May 2016 in *Autumn Cthulhu*

ACKNOWLEDGMENTS

I've been here before, staring at a blank Word doc, terrified I'm going to forget to thank someone. Terrified they might then read this and wonder why I didn't include them. It's more frightening than imagining someone reading the stories and hating them. Then again, that's dreadful, too.

Thank you to Jason Sizemore for being willing to do this again. I hope this collection does well enough to make you not regret that decision.

Thank you to Lesley Conner for helping me sort through all the maybe stories in addition to everything else you did. I'm still sorry a few of the stories made you cry.

I might not be telling the truth about being sorry.

Thank you to the editors who first published these stories: C.M. Muller; Andy Cox; Doug Murano and D. Alexander Ward; John Joseph Adams and Wendy Wagner; Blu Gilliand, Brian Freeman, and Richard Chizmar; Jason Sizemore and Lesley Conner; Rhonda Parrish; Paul Michael Anderson; Joe Pulver; Julia Rios; Paula Guran; Max Booth and Lori Michelle; Ross Lockhart; and Mike Davis. It was an honor and pleasure to work with each one of you, and I hope I have the chance to do so again.

Thank you to Kristi DeMeester and Paul Michael Anderson for being honest and tough when you beta read my stories. Your comments and critiques are more helpful than you know. Always.

Thank you to my family for their love and support.

And finally, thank *you* for buying this book. Without you, none of this would be possible. I hope you enjoyed the stories. I hope the time you spent reading them was worth it. Most of all, I hope they made you feel.

DAW
August 2017